Behind the Red Mist

FICTION BY
HO ANH THAI

Edited by Wayne Karlin

Chief Translator: Nguyen Qui Duc
with translations by Regina Abrami,
Bac Hoai Tran, Phan Thanh Hao
and Dana Sachs

CURBSTONE PRESS

Printed in Canada on acid-free paper by Transcontinental Printing, Best
    Book Division

Cover illustration: Ho Huu Thu, lacquer, 1987.

This book was published with the support of the
Connecticut Commission on the Arts and the National
Endowment for the Arts, and donations from many
individuals. We are very grateful for this support.

Library of Congress Cataloging-in-Publication Data

    Ho, Anh Thai.
        [Phía sau vòm tròi. English]
        Behind the red mist : short fiction by Ho Anh Thai / edited by
    Wayne Karlin; chief translator, Nguyen Qui Duc.
            p.   cm. — (Voices from Vietnam; 2)
        ISBN 1-880684-54-3
        I. Karlin, Wayne. II. Nguyen Qui Duc. III. Title. IV. Series.
    PL4378.9.H47P513   1998
    895.9'22334—dc21   98-20562

published by
CURBSTONE PRESS   321 Jackson Street   Willimantic, CT 06226
        phone: (860) 423-5110   e-mail: curbston@connix.com
                    www.connix.com/~curbston/

ACKNOWLEDGEMENTS

All material reprinted with the permission of the author.

Trong suong hong hien ra, N.x.b. Tac Pham Moi, Hanoi, 1990. (*Behind the Red Mist: a Novel*, New Works Publishing House, Hanoi, 1990.)

"The Barter," ("Cuoc Doi Chac"), first published in October, 1994, in *Tuoi Tre Thanh Pho Ho Chi Minh* (*Youth of Ho Chi Minh City*).

"The Chase," ("Cuoc San Duoi"), first published in December, 1995, in *Van Nghe Ho Chi Minh* (*Literature and Art of Ho Chi Minh City*).

"Fragment of a Man," ("Manh Vo Cua Danong"), first published in January, 1991, in *Tac Pham Moi* (*New Works Magazine*).

"The Goat Meat Special," ("Mon Tai De"), first published in December, 1988, in *Van Nghe* (*Literature and Art*).

"The Indian," ("Nguoi An"), first published in August, 1993, in *Van Nghe* (*Literature and Art*).

"Leaving the Valley," ("Di Khoi Thung Lung Moi Den Nha"), first published in May, 1985, in *Nguoi Ha Noi* (*The Hanoian*).

"The Man Who Still Believed in Fairy Tales," ("Von Tin Vao Chuyen Than Tien"), first published in January, 1998 in *Truyen ngan Ho Anh Thai* (*Short Stories by Ho Anh Thai*), N.x.b.. Van Hoc, Hanoi (Literature Publishing House, Hanoi).

"The Man Who Stood on One Leg," ("Nguoi Dung Mot Chan"), first published in October, 1992 in *Van Nghe* (*Literature and Art*).

"A Sigh Through the Laburnums," ("Tieng Tho Dai Qua Rung Kim Tuoc"), first published in May, 1994, in *Van Nghe* (*Literature and Art*).

TABLE OF CONTENTS

Introduction

"So we beat on, boats against the current, borne back
ceaselessly into the past."

The Great Gatsby,
F. Scott Fitzgerald

In Ho Anh Thai's novella, *Behind the Red Mist*, the protagonist,
seventeen year old Tan, drifts back and forth in time between
1987 and 1967, in the process witnessing his own parents'
courtship as well as life in his home town of Hanoi under the
American bombing raids. Yet the author at one point takes us
even further back, and tells a seemingly discursive tale of a
passenger boat sunk in the Red River during the French
colonization of Vietnam. Later in the narrative, in a resonant
passage that ties the novella together thematically, he writes this:

> *But the past, like the sunken boat, did not have the
> right to sleep quietly in the river bed. One day, it
> would be dug up, some of its parts replaced, and it
> would be repaired and refurbished. Then that boat
> would sound its foghorn and glide again on the Red
> River, reminding everyone of its presence in the
> future.*

The struggle of the postwar generation in Vietnam that Ho
Anh Thai examines in this gentle yet sharp fantasy is the struggle
of every new generation: how to sustain and incorporate the
strengths of the past into their lives while examining, and either
discarding or repairing, its mistakes. The generation that
preceded Thai's in Vietnam was the generation of revolution and
struggle. Thai and his contemporaries, on both sides of the war,
had for the most part been too young to participate as fighters—
though not too young to be caught up in the fighting, to suffer

under the bombings and to lose loved ones. They came of age in a country their parents and the generation just before theirs had fought and died over, a country reunified after centuries of struggle, yet suffering from the social and economic problems endemic to a developing country and excerbated by the great damages caused by the war and by the subsequent American economic embargo, as well as by an entrenched resistance to internal criticism and change. During war time, any critique of policy or leadership was proscribed in the name of solidarity and discipline, a direction that continued after victory, when criticism might be also be seen as being disrespectful of the dead and their sacrifices. The past was sacrosanct, and more so to writers who had not been combatants. For Thai's generation, the war years had become a kind of revered and severe parent, sanctified within a shell of myth that excluded the parent's flaws as well as his/her tender humanity. When Tan's father, who of course doesn't realize Tan will be his son, calls him "brother," Tan feels elated: "Who ever gets to address a father as brother, to talk to a father as though to a brother....his dad was showing himself to be an open-minded and funny guy, but he was used to a serious person who always spoke in measured tones...could it be simply that his father had labored to give that impression to his son so that he might have the authority with which to raise him?" *Behind the Red Mist*, a best seller in Vietnam, seems to express a yearning by the Postwar generation to look through the mist of heroic myth and authority that shrouds the generation of the war, not to debunk, but to examine its own origins clearly.

Tan is thrown back from 1987 to 1967 when his apartment building collapses and he receives an electric shock and is struck on the head. The building had been constructed under the supervision of a Mr. Tuu, who, in trying to build up his portfolio so he could be recognized as an official "Hero of Labor," allowed it to be inadquately constructed on marshy land. When he awakes, what Tan finds is the war, and the people of the war, he has grown up hearing stories about. Some, such as Mr. Tuu, are hypocritical and petty, while others demonstrate a generosity, courage and self-sacrifice, while going on with their lives under the daily rain of American bombs, that he finds lacking in the postwar world. That dichotomy between the simple altruistic purity of the past and also its hidden corruptions thread the novel in images as startling and vivid as the dead butterfly, "fragile and still as if it had been pressed into a book," its colors still delicate and bright, blown by the blast of an American bomb into the face of a man in a shelter. The solidarity of the war years, the spirit of altruism and easy fraternity, and the unifying vision of a new and idealistic society that would be built in the years after the war, the novel seems to say, need to be remembered and incorporated into the more self-centered present, remembered not as utopian, but as real and human and filled with triumph and sadness and huge losses, with bravery...and with errors—badly built, rotten foundations that needed to be examined carefully, to prevent their collapse and the damage they would cause. The past can be a time-delayed five thousand pound bomb that lands in a museum in Hanoi and explodes years later, killing fifty people "Just because...people were not alert enough or were irresponsible, they had allowed [the bomb] to sleep, only to explode...years later, during a time without bombing..." But the past can also be an old man rescuing relics from the ruins who tells Tan, when admonished about the risk, "Man will turn to ash and dust tomorrow, but we cannot afford to lose these objects. They are the proof of our ancient civilization," and Tan, looking at him, thinks: "In the world of twenty years from now, I have met no one with a face like yours." The past can be Tan's maternal grandmother, who he gets to know for the first time in his life: she is both a selfless revolutionary, and a scheming, opportunistic careerist who blocks her daughter's courtship with someone she considers socially inferior, and separates from her husband for his lack of ambition, even though she allows him occasional visits to her bed when she feels the need. But it can also be the brave young woman Trinh, who, with her father away in the fighting, tends her sick mother in a bomb shelter, and wants to join the Young Volunteers defusing and clearing bombs on the Ho Chi Minh Trails after her mother's death, a decision that horrifies Tan, whose reaction, begging her not to go, in turn horrifies Trinh, who "stared at him dumbfounded, unable to believe he had said such words":

> *Tan sobered. He realized that if she indeed thought that was his advice, then its cowardly nature would not be forgiven. His reaction had come from the time of twenty years from now. His generation had come to understand the price of war through the memories and stories of older people; they knew how may had died and they had come to hate war in general, did not want to think about it or be connected to it. Never would they spontaneously decide to enlist and join the fighting the way Trinh had. And now he had expressed that attitude in front of her.*

* * *

In *Behind the Red Mist* and in other novels and stories, whose humor, whimsy and Kafkaesque twists challenge Western expectations of Vietnamese literature, Ho Anh Thai's unique imagination illuminates the mores, attitudes and preconceptions of contemporary Vietnamese society. His work is popular, and often controversial, in Vietnam for those reasons, as well as for the lyrical and versatile styles he adapts in his fiction. "I believe in creating beautiful and unique language that makes readers come back to read the story again, even though they already know the plot. I think a real writer should have many styles," he says, "and he should change his style according to the theme and plot of the story."

The work of many contemporary Vietnamese writers didn't flourish until the period of *Doi Moi* (Renovation), which began in 1986. However, two of Thai's books, *The Women on the Island* and *Two Men and a Vehicle in the Moonlight*, both considered bold and very liberal even today, were published before that time, and Ho Anh Thai states that Renovation didn't affect the way he wrote: "I write only for myself and my friends and an invisible reader...I don't write with the sole goal of publication."

What *Doi Moi* in fact allowed was the publication of works previously impossible to bring out through the state-owned publishing houses. The policy lifted centralized control and encouraged a market economy in Vietnam; one of its side effects was the permission given to writers to create literature that broke away in form and content from "socialist realism" and that was allowed to criticize the incompetence and corruption of high officials, to depict the losses of war as well as its heroism and sacrifice, to create characters who were complex mixtures of good and bad (*cai xau*), even if they were communist party members; to write of the personal as well as the social. At one point in *Behind the Red Mist*, characters that once would have been depicted as single-minded heroes of the people instead are seen as not only brave but also human: when Tan comes across men in a Hanoi anti-aircraft unit listening to waltz music and dancing, they think he is a cadre who would punish them for doing a "degenerate dance," and immediately assume their positions around the rocket launcher, and break into a patriotic song. It is only after they see he is just a visitor that they stop singing, laugh, and invite him to help them learn the waltz steps, and we're given the touchingly strange image of men breaking the tension by waltzing with each other until the bombers come. "Tomorrow, teach us the tango," they tell Tan. It is a scene one would think difficult to publish before *Doi Moi*.

Although the open market economy has been in effect in Vietnam since 1986, since 1991 there has been a considerable rollback from the openness permitted to writers— Thai has said that even though a second edition of *Behind the Red Mist* was published in 1997, the novella probably would not have been published now if he was submitting it for the first time. Yet *Doi Moi* has left an indelible mark on writing in Vietnam in many ways: both the inefficiencies and corruption of the orthodox communist system and the disruptive and corruptive effects of the market economy on Vietnamese society and culture have become the subject of some of Vietnam's most perceptive and imaginative writers. These concerns thread many of Ho Anh Thai's short stories, including the four set in Vietnam in this collection.

"Fragment of a Man" is a tender and realistic love story that is thematically close to *Behind the Red Mist*; as in that novella, the protagonist, again a member of the postwar generation, looks back with tenderness and respect—and a kind of protectiveness—at his parents' lives: his father was a pilot, killed in the war, his mother, who has never recovered from her grief, tries to reconstruct their life from the fragments, the scraps, she hunts for in their backyard. The narrator's own prefunctory and obligatory military service, his sexual initiation by an older woman who is a saavy hustler in the new free market society, his loveless marriage, all stand in contrast to the purity of his parents' relationship, and the depth of his mother's grief. He is wiser and less innocent than his parents, and his life is somehow grayer and more superficial.

In "The Goat Meat Special," the corruption, incompetence and laziness of older careerists are encapsulated in an official who turns into a goat while watching porno movies. His wife has no trouble recognizing him; to her he was always "a bearded goat insensitive to human beings." Besides, the narrator's wife tells him: "all I see around me is a society of goats. The houses and streets are swarming with goats. Goats riding bicycles and Honda motorbikes. Goats sitting in Toyotas."

"The Chase" also limns a conservative society trying to force its youth, no longer defined by the war, to fit its preconceptions. Set in a small rural town just after the war, the story depicts a conformity campaign during which young men who have taken to wearing their hair long, "prawn-tail shirts" and tight, bell bottomed trousers are rounded up by local police and "Red Banner" militia, who shred the youths' trousers with scissors. After hiding in a tower which commemorates liberation fighters, the narrator and his friend are caught, and the former, a privileged youth from a powerful family in Hanoi, watches infuriated as the other youths are humiliated: "Why did all these young men have to bow down silently as if all their tongues had been shortened?"

The protagonist in "The Man Who Still Believed in Fairy Tales," is a Vietnamese who after living in the United States for six months, wakes up one morning to find he has turned into a (white) American. After he returns to Vietnam, where he is seen as an American who speaks Vietnamese fluently, he becomes a man in demand, his approval sought to legitimize projects and behavior, his sexual favors sought by the wife and daughters of the architect whose project he gets approved by declaring solemnly that it is "genuine French achitecture...influenced by the architecture of Greece, plus Rome, plus Western Europe, plus Turkey, as would be seen by Mr. Eiffel." Set in present day Vietnam, the story gently satirizes the faddish tendency towards adapting some of the worst aspects of Western culture, and using them as measures of legitimacy: i.e., if its Western, it's good. It is a story that will resonate to anyone who has visited Hanoi in the last few years and seen the concretizing of that graceful, tree-filled city, the grotesque architecture of the new condos, hotels and villas springing up everywhere to accomodate the Hanoian noveaux riche and the employees and executives of foreign corporations.

During Ho Anh Thai's career as a diplomat, he studied in Australia and India, (where he was First Secretary to the Ambassador), and earned an M.Ph in Oriental Culture from the Central Institute of Hindi, in New Delhi, in 1991. His background has made him something of a rarity in contemporary Vietnamese literature, and this collection marks one of the few works in which a writer from Vietnam focuses his imagination on another South Asian country: five of the stories in this book are set in India. As "The Man Who Still Believed in Fairy Tales" satirizes Vietnamese who idolize Western ways, both "The Indian," and "The Barter," are wry commentaries on the type of Westerner who romanticizes Asian culture. In the former, Kitty, the young wife of an aging British archaeologist in India becomes driven by the desire to enter forbidden temples and other territories, including finally an affair with her Indian guide, a man carrying his own burden of secrets, and of the past, literally on his back. In "The Barter," the narrator tells of Heinrich, a young German studying Hinduism in India, who is so taken by Indian culture that he refuses to speak his own language, torments his Vietnamese roommate with early morning prayers, and eventually marries a temple prostitute from a small village, who is in turn enthralled by the non-Indian cultures, and men, with whom she comes into contact. The other Indian stories focus on aspects of India itself—though they can also be looked at, in theme and style, as fables about Vietnam—and the human condition. One, "The Man Who Stood on One Leg" is the funny and sad tale of a simple, determined and pious man who vows to stand on one leg in front of a condom factory until the owner of the factory donates a million rupees to a fund to build a temple to Shiva. The second, "The Wind Through the Laburnums" is a deeply felt and horrifying look at the effects of the dowry system, which requires poor families in rural communities to save for years in order to have a dowry so that their daughters can be married—a situation that leads to the killing of female children, and bride burning by husbands and their families as a way of earning money and ensuring male heirs. Both stories are marked by Thai's love for India, which, like his love for Vietnam, is deep but never blind.

The final piece in the collection is a fable the author describes this way: "'Leaving the Valley' is my vision of the world: full of brothels and revolutions and gods and icons, and no one who can look up and see the horizon." It is a statement that might encompass all of Ho Anh Thai's fiction. His work disturbs people—and is popular—because it refuses to be categorized by anything but its own honesty. Although it can rightly be called postwar fiction, it might also be seen as post-Cold War. Thai and his contemporaries in Vietnam are on the edge of a literature from the developing countries that is no longer defined by the either/or parameters of the Capitalist/ Communist struggle. It is a Pan-Asian, and indeed Pan-global literature that concerns itself with the tension between repression and the desire for freedom, and between the desire for economic security and the erosion of human relationships and culture, when life becomes driven solely by the desire for possessions and money: tensions that mark the defining struggle of much of the world as it moves into the twenty-first century.

—Wayne Karlin

My thanks to Nguyen Qui Duc, who has taken on the thankless task of healing the wound that rifts his people, to the author, Ho Anh Thai, sleepless in Hanoi, and to Le Minh Khue, for her friendship and encouragement.

Behind the
Red Mist

Fragment of a Man

I heard that my mother was the most beautiful girl in the village of Yen. Every time she combed her hair, she stood on a chair and the ends of her hair would still touch the floor. Everywhere she went, the scent of grapefruit and lemon lingered discreetly in the air.

Near the village there was a military airstrip, and because it was a target for destruction by the American planes, the village of Yen was also in danger of being obliterated at any time. All the villagers understood this, but many still hesitated to evacuate the place. The responsibility of persuading them to go fell on the village beauty—Miss Tinh—the vice-chairperson of the village and commander of the militia's short-range artillery squad. In order to increase the force of their argument, the village leaders decided to send Miss Tinh to contact the air force unit and invite a youth representative to come speak about the latest news and persuade the villagers to leave.

When Tinh arrived, she saw three or four young pilots surround a young man and drag him by the collar to the mess hall bulletin board so that he could see clearly whether that day the mess hall would serve *thit trau* (water buffalo meat) or *thit chau* (the meat of a young man named Chau). When Tinh raised her voice to inquire, they all walked away, leaving behind the young man, whose hair and clothes were now a mess from the scuffle. He rearranged his uniform, then said shyly, "I am Chau."

They got to know each other very quickly, communicating easily because Chau was only 25, five years younger than Tinh.

Getting permission from his commanding officer, Chau accompanied Tinh back to the village. The road ran for more than three kilometers across an empty plain and was dotted by A-shaped tunnels and manholes. Suddenly, a cluster of American planes swooped down, diving and climbing and bombing for half an hour. Chau and Tinh jumped into an A-shaped tunnel and held each other tightly throughout the convulsions of the tunnel and the earth. Tinh's heavy bun fell out, covering everything with a cascade of hair. Suddenly, they didn't hear the bombs anymore, but only the soft sounds of the cascade, carrying with it the fragrance of the wild plants and flowers of the forest. The young man's throat went dry and he felt that he was drowning in hair, like a person who has never been at sea taking his first dive into the ocean.

The two had to do this several more times on the road that crossed the empty plain, taking refuge in the tunnel of destiny, abandoning themselves in the Yen village beauty's cascade of hair.

Ultimately, Tinh had to admit all this to the village leaders. They discussed ways to punish her. Tinh found Chau just before takeoff. "Big Sister Tinh, why are you so worried?" he asked. When she was finished telling him, Chau smiled happily, sprinted into the hallway, grabbed a passing pilot, and danced in a circle. "I'm about to get married." "Marry who?" "Big Sister Tinh. She's over there." He hadn't had a chance to change the way he addressed her yet.

Tinh and Chau returned to meet the village leaders, announcing their decision to get married. However, even a wedding couldn't get her out of trouble. Discipline was discipline, and the code of conduct for a cadre did not permit a girl to get pregnant before she was married. Suddenly, Tinh lost her political status: she was expelled from the Party and removed from her position as vice-chairperson and commander of the squad.

She had to leave the village and Chau took her to Hanoi to live with his widowed mother. His mother looked dazed, as if she'd just been robbed. During the meal, Tinh used her chopsticks to place a morsel of chicken into her mother-in-law's bowl. The mother-in-law returned it to the platter and spoke through her tears: "I beg you to let my son go." The family had a cottage with a big garden in the suburbs, and so Chau had no choice but to take his pregnant wife there. A few months later, a boy was born.

Still, the young mother was secretly tortured because in an instant she had lost everything; she'd been forced to abandon her home and, like an uprooted tree, had no place to which she could cling. Unloved by her mother-in-law, she still consoled herself that the most precious things in life for a woman were her husband and children, and therefore she couldn't regard herself as having lost everything. In the end, her husband and child were all my mother had.

After 1973, because the pirates would no longer be counterattacking from the air, my mother thought that she could relax about my father, but then suddenly the news hit: the airplane carrying my father and a few army officers was lost in the border region. They searched for a month without any results. But one day when my mother had just lit three sticks of incense and put her hands together in front of the altar to my father, a middle-aged neighbor woman stepped through the door: "Stop. Snuff out the incense and stop praying. The airplane flew to Thailand. They're having fun over there. Get ready for him to send some packages home." This rumor spread everywhere and for months the relatives of the missing half-believed and half-doubted it. A few dismantled their altars. But my father never came back.

I became the only possession my mother had left.

*   *   *

Every time there was the sound of an airplane in the sky, my mother would shiver, not even daring to look up. But I was different. To a small boy, that tiny speck in the blue sky embodied all my boundless desire. Whirring like a plane, I would run after it with my face upturned until I tripped and fell, diving into a shrub in the garden.

My mother lifted me up. "When people want to run far,

they don't look up at the sky. Instead, they look down at the ground, son."

That was an instruction only suitable for great people in their youth. But I was an ordinary boy with what was probably a very ordinary destiny. If from my childhood I only knew to look at the ground, then when I grew up my soul would be like a balloon filled with helium but tied to the ground, able to do nothing except wait until I exploded, never able to fly to the sky. It's only now that I'm able to think like that. But at that time I was a very obedient child, and therefore I listened to my mother, carefully watching my steps wherever I went. Also at that time, I could perceive the pain that grass felt when our feet tread upon it, and would cry inconsolably if I inadvertently stepped on a cricket in the road.

My mother didn't want me to look at the sky and dream about flying things, repeating the unhappy destiny of my father. She wanted to keep me by her side, not lose me to some lofty ideal or to some other person.

But an active boy cannot stay forever by his mother's side within the family garden. Eventually, I crept into the neighbors' houses and into the house of a woman named Thach. "That's a venomous snake," one of the female neighbors said to my mother about Thach. I remembered one time my mother sent me to buy some cold medicine. Thach was selling medicine in front of a glass case that had a chart of poisons on it and a drawing of a snake dropping its poison into a glass. Probably that was the reason that the woman called her a venomous snake. One night we heard the sound of Thach's voice wailing. The neighbors hurried over but her husband was dead already. People said that it was a deadly cold. The neighbor lady whispered to my mother, "That was no cold. He died when he was sleeping. In the old days, when a girl went to live at her husband's house she would carry with her a sharp hairpin, not just to keep her hair in place."* In her opinion, Thach was a slut who would be the death of any husband. But with me Thach was exceedingly gentle. Twenty-

*Refers to folklore about a type of acupuncture performed on the husband's spine to stimulate flagging virility.

nine years old, widowed while still childless, she left the pharmacy to trade in ration coupons and after that became a traveling merchant. Every time she came back from a trip, she would invite me into her house and let me eat until I'd finished everything she'd saved especially for me. Sometimes there were plums, sometimes oranges from Vinh, sometimes Gold Dragon green bean cake. In return, I read to her from various torn books saved from some unknown time.

That year I turned sixteen, still so naive that I wore shorts and sat with my legs spread wide apart when I read to her from *Two Graves on a Pine-Covered Hill*. She leaned toward me, looked at my hairy legs, and said, "You should choose your friends carefully." I stopped reading and looked at her, puzzled. "Don't make friends with boys who don't have hairy legs." I was more puzzled. "That type, every one of them are cowards." She sighed, her eyes staring off into the distance: "With all due respect to my husband, he was that type."

At that moment, my mother ran in breathlessly and saw me sitting next to Thach in my revealingly loose shorts.

"Bao, come home immediately."

"Let me finish reading first, Mother."

"No. No. Come home." She grabbed the torn book, threw it at Thach and dragged me home. If she had not come at that exact moment, my mother would have been cheated out of her last remaining possession.

Thach's torn book became extremely boring. But I still slipped out without my mother's knowledge, sometimes going to her house to watch TV. Thach had just bought a black and white TV and the tears would stream down her face whenever she watched a *cai luong* opera. Whenever she watched a concert and saw the face of Thach Lan with its enormous mole or Le Duyen who tried so hard to charm people that her mouth became permanently distorted, Thach would say, "If I were rich I would smash this TV into pieces."

I asked, "You aren't rich?"

"How could I be rich? I'm more miserable than you could ever know."

One time on the TV there was a play critical of illegal activities and one character loudly scolded, "You lousy merchants..." Thach went crazy: "What? Lousy merchants? They should say Mr. Merchant, Ms. Merchant. Do they think being a merchant is so easy?"

My mother put the money together to buy a TV that was used but still pretty good. I sensed that my mother wanted to entice me to stay home and avoid that *venomous snake*. But not long after that, Thach brought home a color TV with a remote control. When it reached that stage, my mother gave up, unable to compete any longer. She had to resort to radical measures and flat out forbid me, giving the explanation: You have to study for your exam.

I graduated high school but failed the university entrance exam and wanted to go work. An acquaintance tried to get me a job in a textile factory. The factory accepted me, but on one condition: I had to complete my military service first. They didn't want their operations thrown into disarray when an employee was drafted. My mother feared nothing more than this profession of guns and planes. Our acquaintance reminded her that the division commander had been a friend of my father's and in his hands I would be very safe, wouldn't have to work hard, and could come home at the end of three years. So I enlisted as an employee of the factory during that drafting period, but, by special arrangement, I joined the division of Commander Dac and worked as a clerk, safely away from the border.

Commander Dac was a strict person, but he was very fond of me because he saw in me the image of his young friend from the old days. Thanks to his occasional visits and his memories, I learned about the love between my parents. He told me that in 1972, when I was six years old, my mother brought me to the base to visit my father, hopeful that she could get pregnant. We waited in the guest house for several days but my father hadn't yet come back from an assignment and so we packed up to go back to Hanoi. The division car carrying us back to the train station had only gone a little way when we met my father's truck on the way back to the base. Commander Dac sat with me in the cabin of the truck and waved the reunited couple away: "You two get in the back to confide in each other, and we'll stay here."

I protested: "Let me go with Mother and Father."

He gave me a spank and said, "Behave yourself and I'll let you go in an airplane." The remainder of the distance to the station, Dac told the driver to drive slowly in order to give the couple more time for lovemaking. "If your mother had not had a miscarriage, your little sister or brother would be twelve years old by now," the commander said.

Three years in the military were about to pass uneventfully. I would return to work in the factory, an ordinary occupation with no time for me to look in the sky and dream of flying. That was my mother's wish, and she was reassured because my period of service was almost completed. But then something happened that turned everything upside down. It was the fault of my parents, who gave birth to such a soft-hearted son.

*   *   *

Than was a soldier belonging to the reconnaissance unit. Many times he had gone AWOL in order to go home, or, by his own decision, prolonged his leave, and so there were also many times that the military police had to send someone to bring him back and throw him into the military jail. Finally, he was granted a seven-day leave, and when he drew it out to ten days they were waiting for him to turn up at the base so they could immediately strip him of his military credentials and send him home. Only on the twelfth day did he return to the base, and the first person he looked for was me. On his leave papers, he had erased the dates of his leave, changing the return date from March 14 to March 19. I was the person who filled out these papers for my boss to sign. Than begged me to bail him out, to say that I had made a mistake on the papers so that he could avoid being discharged and sent home, where he would face reeducation. His village was suffering from famine and when his younger siblings went to school, they would lean against the wall and fall down from hunger. He had stayed at home longer in order to search for extra rice for his family.

Although I knew that Than was not a truthful person, I was still moved by his story. I accepted the blame and prepared myself to go to jail, telling myself I was only taking a week-long rest in the mountains before returning in time to prepare my discharge papers. People asked the opinion of Commander Dac. "We have to uphold military discipline," he said firmly, simply thinking that seven days in detention would pass by peacefully.

And so I sat there in the late afternoon, almost completely worn out after a day using a pick and shovel to widen a road through a mountain village. I sank down at the foot of a kapok tree, breathing heavily and turning my face up to look at the ever-lonely evening star. Looking at stars and counting them was something that the children do, and something that my mother never wanted me to do. But put yourself in my position, finally unsupervised, my limbs exhausted, not smoking a cigarette or taking part in the dirty jokes of all the other convicts sitting nearby. What was there for me to do but sit looking at the stars?

At dusk on the second day, when the whistle screamed for the end of labor, I flung aside the shovel and dropped down next to the kapok tree. But before I had a chance to even look up at the sky, someone shoved some plums into my hand. The silhouette of a girl limped by, joined a group of women, then rapidly disappeared into the mist. Perhaps this is the image I will remember forever of that crippled village in the mountains, with only 30 or 40 houses and several small drink shops: faceless forms in the mist.

Every day the miscreants with their shaved heads maintained a gentle and harmless appearance, standing neatly in two straight lines. They didn't dare to go into a shop if they didn't have money. When they craved a cigarette, all they could do was stand in front of the shops and pick up the littered stubs, which they called "fried fat," then light them up and suck deeply. They all wanted to appear obedient so they could return to their units as soon as possible, only to break the law again later on, and then come back here again as a convict.

That morning, pausing in front of a few of the shops, one of them had the bright idea that one person should collect all the fried fat, open them up for the tobacco, and then use some paper to roll real cigarettes. I don't even smoke, but I was pulled into the drawing of lots and had the misfortune to draw the short one. Reluctantly, I took my hat in my hand and ran into the drink shop in front of us, then stuck my head down to look between people's feet under the benches.

Looking through the pairs of legs, my hand deftly felt its way through all the cracked feet in order to collect all the stubs of cigarettes.

Suddenly, between all those calloused feet, those feet marked by the sorrow of daily struggle that is within every man and every woman, my eyes fell upon a girl's pretty foot. But what I saw immediately after that made me jump. That foot was matched by another that was shrivelled. Those feet would limp like a seven with a ten. One was like a young branch bursting with the sap of life. The other was dried out. One was the foot of an 18- or 20-year-old girl, while the other was that of a worn-out 60-year-old woman.

My eyes were mesmerized by the pair of feet facing me. In this position, the feet had to belong to the shop girl. I slowly stood up, my glance traveling across the backs and shoulders of the customers sipping their drinks. Everything became blurry when I looked into the face of that girl. In all the far corners of the countryside, I had never seen a face that was so beautiful and so demure. That face and that foot, a mythical flower that would blossom once in a hundred years, but blossom on a dry branch.

"Please come in and have a drink," she softly invited me, a convict, as if recognizing an acquaintance. I was petrified, momentarily rooted to that spot. Then, hugging the hat full of fried fat, I turned and ran. It was at exactly that moment that I realized that she was the girl who had shoved the plums into my hand the day before.

After dinner that night, Vinh, a guy who was awaiting trial for molesting a woman, proceeded with the presentation of his story for his friends. "I didn't rape that bitch. We'd known each for a while already, so obviously she wanted it. After it was over, she sat in the bushes crying so loud. Some people came by and they jumped on me and brought me in."

I asked the jailer if I could go outside to do something. The discipline in the camp was very strict, but everyone had a lot of respect for me, a military bureaucrat for the division who was rumored to be the nephew of the division commander. I sprinted for two kilometers through the misty night, occasionally catching the glimmers of stars over my head. The shop was closed. A weak light came through the cracks in the walls. "I came to buy cigarettes," I replied to the girl when she called from inside. The door opened a crack and the girl's face appeared rosy from the light of the hurricane lamp in her hand. "Is that you? What a shame. If it was daytime I could invite you into the house." It seemed like she had picked up some of my nervousness.

"Why can't I come in now?"

"No, my mother lives at the end of the road. I'm only here by myself." She was foolish enough to say it, but with a person like me, such foolishness wasn't likely to cause her any harm. "But standing here talking like this isn't convenient. Okay, please come in." I spent all the little money I had buying cigarettes, and it was only too bad I didn't have more, even though later I might throw them all away anyway. In order to appear natural, I lit a cigarette, but after only one puff I coughed and coughed. She was concerned and so she gave me something to drink. "Smoking cigarettes isn't good for you," she said.

"Then I'll give it up once and for all, immediately."

"Then let me take all these cigarettes back, okay?"

"No, let me take them back for my friends."

At that moment a child's voice called through the door: "Hey, Duyen!" In a panic, she lowered her voice: "That's my little sister. Go. Go. Whenever you're free, come back to visit me." She opened the back door, whispering the way for me to sneak out. Inside the house, in order to mask her deformity, she would either hold on to the back of a chair, the edge of a door, or a wall. But if she had to run an errand, then what could she lean on?

Every night I went to visit her, and retreated before the appearance of her spying little sister, who came from the same mother but a different father. The mother sent her to stay the night in order to chaperone Duyen. But it had to happen that one night I carried her to the bed. The happier my hands were to touch her normal foot, the more frightened and bitter they were to touch the deformed one. She told me that the foot became shrivelled after a bout of illness when she was eight years old. I took it upon myself to compensate for all her suffering. "You're not going to cry, are you?" I asked. I couldn't help being a little concerned, remembering Vinh's story. She answered, "With you by my side, I'll never cry."

We lay there for a long time, dozing off, until we heard the familiar sound of her little sister. This night was all our own. No one had a right to share a part of a sacred night like that. She called out: "Go home. I already turned out the lights and I've gone to sleep."

"No, no. I'm scared." She had used up all her courage in carrying the lamp one block down the street, believing that she'd be let inside immediately.

"If you don't go quickly, then the ghosts will come out and jump on you." Complete silence. Perhaps she was both running and crying. The destiny of spies is usually much more tragic.

Duyen's mother was lucky to have married the most resourceful and handsome man in the area, but was unlucky to have acquired as a mother-in-law an old woman who had developed at the end of her life the habit of cruelty. Every day Duyen's mother had to put up with a fit of curses, and she wasn't the only one who had to listen. The old woman would stand at the front of the house so that the neighbors could know that she was cursing her daughter-in-law. Duyen's father went with people to trade fragrant wood in Quang Binh and was attacked by a tiger. The anniversary of his death became the day that the mother-in-law would curse "the woman who was the death of her husband." When Duyen was ten years old, her mother took the next step, and was cursed: "The time of mourning isn't even over yet and she's already taking up with another man."

Duyen's mother believed that her mother-in-law was so cruel and disagreeable partly because her younger son told lies and always criticized her. Finding herself so unhappy, Duyen's mother vented her rage in revenge against that brother-in-law. After her grandmother's death, Duyen lived by herself in the house with the family altar. Her mother found out about the brother-in-law's plot to marry Duyen off early, give her a little money as dowry, then take over the house. The mother was outraged: "She's only twenty years old. Why be so crazy as to hurry up and put the yoke around her neck? Look how ugly I am, and I had no trouble finding a husband." The uncle had a decent place near Duyen's house but he never bothered to look after his niece. On the contrary, he felt that the more men she had courting her the better, so that when one of them got her pregnant, she'd have to marry him. Duyen's mother complained: "An uncle is like a father, but this one is completely irresponsible. When I first came to live with this family, if he had to pee at night he was so afraid of ghosts that he asked me to go out there with him and I had to smell his awful pee. He's really a parasite." Determined to destroy her brother-in-law's selfish plan, she had her younger daughter keep close tabs on Duyen every day so that the mother would know who came to visit often and who stayed a long time at the drink shop. Better that her daughter never marry anyone and keep the house because that would kill the uncle.

Inadvertently, the mother became the biggest hurdle in my efforts to marry Duyen and take her back to Hanoi. "I'm prepared to go anywhere with you. Wherever you go, I'll go as well," Duyen said.

My time in military prison was over. In Vinh's rape case, the victim and her family had submitted an appeal to release him because, in fact, they loved each other. He and I traveled together for a short distance. Vinh said: "She made me go to jail, and now it turns out that she loves me? Well, despite everything, at least I've found a wife." I was jealous that things were so easy for him.

Back at the base, I met Commander Dac. "I'm about to get married," I said. "Will you please certify this document for me?"

"Are you kidding? You're only 21 years old. Has your mother agreed yet?"

"It would be hard for her to agree immediately. That's why I have to seek your help," I said. He could see that I wasn't being impulsive or joking.

Commander Dac frowned. "Let me think about it."

On the night of the second day, he summoned me: "I've sent people to secretly investigate. It's an ordinary family, not landowners or reactionaries." He returned the document, already certified, and held my hand tightly, lowering his voice: "I pity you two. How can you make it with a foot like that? Your mother will curse me all her life."

I went back to find Duyen. The local committee official had a lot of affection for Duyen, so he agreed to do as we wished, taking steps to register our marriage and giving us the certificate. He also promised to keep it a secret until the wedding. Duyen and I decided to get a contract before the wedding because we were worried that something might thwart our plans in the time it took to convince our parents. Now we were reassured. That night, like every night, there wasn't a soul on the street. When we left the committee headquarters, I didn't have the heart to let Duyen limp by my side, so I lifted her up and carried her all the way through the mountain village.

*   *   *

When I got to my mother's house, I went straight to the point: "Mother, I'm about to take a wife."

She smiled: "Who would object? You can take as many wives as you want."

I solemnly handed her a photograph of Duyen, a face so gentle and beautiful it would break anyone's heart. "No!" She screamed as if she had just recognized that it was a picture of a hunted criminal. "No!" She held her head, collapsing onto the bed, completely unprepared for such news. Before that, her only joy was in my return, returning to become again the small child of the old days, a child with its mother, a mother with her child. Suddenly, that child was no longer completely her own. Cracks were beginning to appear that could shatter her treasure.

That was the first time I realized that people could fall ill simply because of shock and misery. She lay feverish for several days. Not a single question about the girl in that photograph, neither her name nor age nor even her family background. Bad or good, she wanted to take away a mother's only child and that was unacceptable. When my mother began to recover she stood in front of my father's altar and lit incense to pray, holding in her hand a small comb made from a piece of an American warplane. With his own hands, my father had made two combs that were exactly the same, engraved with the words: Tinh-Chau. He gave one to my mother and kept the other in his inside jacket pocket, always carrying it with him. That comb was the only remaining fragment of the life of her lost husband. She had put it on the altar and a day never passed that she forgot to dust it.

I was as restless as someone sitting on hot coals. In that remote mountain village, Duyen was waiting for me as each minute passed. I wondered if she ever doubted for a moment, if she ever thought I'd deserted her. As for me, I couldn't mope around the house forever without achieving any results.

I wandered like a lost soul, my feet taking me to Thach's house without my even being aware of it. Since the day of my return, I had noticed a handsome guy going into and out of her house. One time he was washing his feet at the public spigot in front of the gate. His legs were hairy.

Thach sat by herself silently drinking rice wine and eating roasted dried squid. That silence was rare for a person like her. Tears streamed down. She pulled and tore at the squid with the hands of a person who wanted revenge. In one gulp, I finished a bowl of wine that she gave me and saw that inside her house she already had a VCR. Finding it handy, I switched on the tape that was already in the machine. A shocking film. The porn stars were giving lessons in love. I turned it off immediately, not because I didn't want to watch it, but because it wasn't proper to watch it in front of Thach. "You're still too young. Watching this film isn't good for you," she said.

"Not so young. I'm about to get married." I recounted my circumstances in detail.

"Why didn't you tell me immediately?"

"What's the point of telling you?"

"Oh, that means you still don't understand me. When are you going to go get her? Is tomorrow morning too late?"

The next morning, we carried two heavy sacks to the station and caught the train going back up toward the mountain village. The hairy-legged guy went with us. I had to lie to my mother, telling her that I was returning to the base in order to have someone correct a mistake on my military release papers. The merchants' car was full of goods and people lying and sitting all over the place. I felt a sharp pain when one woman tried to step over me. She recognized Thach: "Who are you traveling with?"

"Well, with two younger men."

"Really? I've also got a younger man, but only one." She gave an easy smile demonstrating that she understood. Then she took the hand of her younger man, who was only about eighteen years old, led him to a corner of the car, and spread out a nylon sheet for them to sit on. Night slowly fell. I could see that woman and her man discreetly rolling under the blanket. Perhaps a lot of people noticed, but everyone pretended to be dozing off.

Following Thach's plan, we first went to meet Commander Dac. "On such an important matter as this, why didn't your mother come?"

Thach cut in, "His mother was unwell, and we also needed someone at home to prepare for when we brought the new daughter home. I'm his aunt, so I'm taking care of this."

Commander Dac was surprised. "Then what do you need me for?" he asked.

"Why do you say that? You're like a father to Bao. Please participate as a sign of authority. You won't have to do a thing. I'll take care of everything."

Our registration for marriage had already been discovered by Duyen's family. A few days earlier, Duyen's uncle had proposed a family meeting, inviting everyone, including his now-remarried former sister-in-law, to announce that he had found a match for Duyen. According to him, Duyen was twenty years old already and admittedly good and beautiful, but because of her deformity she should know enough to limit her expectations and marry as soon as possible, before it was too late. "I don't want to get married yet," Duyen replied immediately.

Her mother joined in, "That's fine. Each pot will find its own lid. Why worry?"

The uncle countered, "Do you want your daughter to die old and alone in some corner of the house?"

The mother smiled sarcastically, "It's better to stay single and take care of yourself. I've been foolish enough to get married twice, so I know."

The squabble was fierce and the mother was in danger of being cornered. Therefore, Duyen reluctantly admitted, "I'm married already." She showed everyone the marriage certificate. Who's Van Ngoc Bao? What does he look like? "He's a very good person. He was a prisoner being reformed through manual labor here."

The mother held her face in her hands, screaming. After a pensive moment, the uncle said, "A prisoner but a good person. That's okay." He announced that he would give Duyen two gold leaves for her dowry. That much money proved that he wasn't an unreasonable man. But Duyen's mother continued stomping her feet.

"Your greed has made you blind," she said.

Several days went by with no movement or sign from me, and Duyen's mother began to think that I had disappeared, as slippery as an eel. Perhaps it was good that way, or would be even better if Duyen had become pregnant because then she would be content to stay home, without ever thinking of any other husband.

Duyen's mother completely lost control when a jeep pulled

up in front of the house and a military official stepped majestically down. The uncle was called over and, along with Duyen's stepfather, met with Commander Dac. Thach didn't waste any time before giving out candy, cookies, and toys for the children in the family and around the neighborhood. In terms of gifts there was silk for the women, flashlights and cigarettes for the men. Having carried with her a Sony cassette recorder, she now put in a cassette of *cai luong* opera and played it loudly.

While Thach was engaged in a lively conversation, she happened to hear the sound of voices haggling in the back of the house. She turned her head and saw the hairy-legged guy pulling things out of a burlap sack and showing them to a few of the neighbors. She waved him to the side, "As the saying goes: even a whore leaves herself a way to find a husband. So don't sell those worthless things here, okay?" She told him to put the sack away and distribute the gifts to the neighbors: a pack of cigarettes for this one, a scarf for another. Everyone was satisfied, and turned to heap praise on the groom.

There was no need to send out invitations. It was only necessary to put the word out and not a soul in the whole village was absent. Plates of cookies and candy were passed around, turning this into a modern-day wedding. In the evening, after everyone had gone, I found Thach and Duyen's mother sitting behind a closed door in the bedroom, drinking. Duyen said that whenever her mother sat by herself drinking, she had the habit of calling their yellow dog over, putting her feet on its back, and gently pushing the dog back and forth. But now she stomped her feet on the dog as if she wanted to trample it, as if she wanted to trample everything that had made her so unhappy. The two women were covered in tears. The mother took Thach's hand and sobbed, "No one understands me but you."

The next morning, with mixed feelings, the whole family saw us off. Duyen's mother called after Thach, "I'll prepare to come and visit you and the children."

I lifted Duyen into the jeep and repeated the question of that night, "You're not going to cry, are you?"

She answered, "With you by my side, I'll never cry."

When we passed by the division, Commander Dac got out and let us continue with the car to Hanoi. I went home and had to put up with a number of tension-filled days. Duyen had to remain temporarily at Thach's house, waiting until I had a proper chance to speak with my mother. But it seemed that both of us were on the defensive. My mother was afraid of the moment when I would declare again that I was going to marry that girl in the photo. As for me, I was afraid to tell my mother that I was already married and have her continue to reject it. I always found an excuse to go out and secretly visit Thach's house, staying there until late at night. Because Thach was so busy with her business, she was almost never home. It was only when we returned to Hanoi that Duyen found out that Thach and I were not actually aunt and nephew. She still showed that she was grateful to Thach, but she became somewhat suspicious. She also sensed that there was still some obstacle keeping me from taking her straight home. I understood this because she always asked about "our house" and about my mother.

Eventually the moment came when my mother asked very seriously, "You still often go to Thach's house, don't you?" I shook my head vigorously.

My mother said sharply, "Don't lie to me. She's not even home, so why do you dare to go in and out so naturally like that?" I sat quietly, trembling with fear.

"This morning I saw a girl over there. She seemed well-mannered, but she has a deformed leg. Who is that?"

I didn't dare to lie and, furthermore, my mother's question was meant to test if I was telling the truth or not. My mother already knew Duyen's face from the photograph. "Dear mother, that's my wife."

She fell silent and it was only after a long time that she was able to find her voice. "So you've become husband and wife already?"

"Dear mother, it's been a week already. She's been living at Thach's house."

The mention of Thach's name made my mother jump,

bringing out the anger once again, overpowering even her sorrow. "No. No. Not over there. Bring her back here immediately."

Within half a day things changed with the speed of a whirlwind. I brought Duyen home and introduced her to my mother. Then the three of us organized the house, pulling out a bed that had for so long been pushed into a corner. My mother had compassion for a young girl who had the same disadvantages of fate that she herself had known, and that compassion proved to be stronger than her anger. She led Duyen around the house and into the kitchen, where she showed her in detail where all the saucepans, woks, fish sauce, salt, and spices were. When they were finished with all that, my mother immediately fell ill with a light but persistent fever. The neighborhood doctor came over and examined my mother very carefully then said that she hadn't come down with any particular illness, but was suffering from a physical breakdown.

In my heart I understood that this physical breakdown was caused by sorrow.

*   *   *

It is only now that I understand that once she accepted her daughter-in-law into the house and throughout the time that we all lived together, my mother felt that she had lost everything. Our son was born, weighing four-and-a-half kilos, and so whoever saw him had to admire him. My mother was happy, but it was the happiness of looking at someone else's treasure, not her own. After some time, I bought a sewing machine and took Duyen to some sewing classes. My mother looked after the baby. One day, people ran up and told her to take her grandson to the district's "healthy baby" contest, convinced that he would win first prize. She agreed that the child would be at the top of the chart, but she couldn't take him. Her reason was that she had not yet asked our opinion and did not know if we would agree or not. That afternoon, when Duyen and I returned, the contest was over and the prize had been presented to a boy who could not compare with our son. Hearing about it, some people couldn't understand, but I vaguely sensed something terrifying. My mother had found that she no longer had any power in this house. I once was her last remaining possession, and now I wasn't even that anymore, so the baby was only someone else's treasure that she was supposed to care for and that was that.

We were completely naive, not yet having had enough experience in life, so we didn't know what to do to change her way of thinking. In those days, she began to spend a lot of time in the garden, staring at the trees and bushes as if she were searching for something. One day, I spied on her, watching her sneak into the garden and carefully search everywhere. Her hand turned over every pile of leaves, every rock, every clod of earth around the bases of the trees, until she finally found what she was searching for. It was the metal comb made from a piece of a warplane and engraved with the names of my parents. Her eyes brightened. A look of infinite happiness infused her sad face, as if she had found the comb that my father had carried on his own body. With the happiness of a sleepwalker and walking like a sleepwalker, she cradled the comb in her hand, groped her way toward the house and reached the altar. She laid the comb on the altar, hoping to find there another comb exactly like it, her own comb lying on the altar.

The fairy tale didn't happen. The comb in her hand was the comb I had seen on the altar the day before. She had probably left it in the garden so that she could go and find it again. When she realized this, her sleepwalk ended and she slid again into a long delirium.

In the months that followed, her mind was no longer as sharp as before. She got into the habit of collecting trivial things. She wandered in the wide garden, bringing inside reels of copper wire, screws, and pieces of scrap metal. Then she would clumsily take them out and count them, looking for a way to put them together. Deep inside, I felt miserable. Only when they realize they've lost everything do people try to look again for the things they've lost and put them back together. This meant that my mother considered herself to have lost me and that she felt she was now only left with the hope of finding that missing airplane. No one said that my father had died. He was only missing with his airplane.

We lost all hope when we saw my mother's energy gradually draining, although her health had been strengthened by vitamins. One day, she said, "Last night I dreamed I saw the village chairman. He invited me to go back to the village for a meeting, and he restored everything to me." The village chairman had been dead for a long time. I assumed it was only the dream of a sick person, but two days later she passed away.

Now I knew that it was possible to die not from a real illness but from debilitating misery, from torment over lost possessions.

A widowed woman is a fragment of the man who died. Some women bear the fate of a fragment, living silently in seclusion, all the while clinging to the dream of finding and putting all those fragments back together again. Others are fragments lying here and there on the road, piercing and cutting the feet of luckier souls as a way of wreaking revenge for their own sad fates.

My mother never wanted me to look up into the sky, and counting stars was really for children, but that night, all alone in a corner of the garden, I lifted my eyes to a sky that was filled with stars. A shooting star cut open a wound in the sky. I understood then that on the face of the earth there was one more fragment.

*   *   *

After my mother died, there were some evenings after work when I stopped by a drink shop planning to have only a glass of tea and ended up drinking. Before, there had been times when the atmosphere in the family was gloomy, when I didn't dare show my affection for Duyen in front of my mother, and I thought to myself that without my mother perhaps my love for Duyen would have been stronger. Thinking back, I realized that I hadn't been fulfilling my duty as a son. And then, after my mother died, my love for my wife didn't become stronger. Instead, it diminished. As for my love for my mother, she had taken it with her forever.

I don't know if something was leading me there or not, but somehow I found myself going into Thach's house. "Drink up," she said. She poured me another glass, and stood up to light some incense, whispering her prayers. Then she came back and drank with me. "Your mother died too soon. I prepared her for burial and saw that her face was still young and fresh, like someone sleeping." She began to cry. "In those days, she was right. I was a worthless woman." Even in my fuzzy state, I had been rather afraid that things would turn out like this. A moment later, she dried her tears and said, "Do you want to watch a film?" I shuddered and shook my head. "No, not that kind of film," she said. "This is a love story, very happy. The ability to love always means happiness." A love that is so ideal would be true happiness. On the TV screen, the actors only loved each other in the clouds with a kind of platonic love….But Thach and I carried out the earthly aspect that was missing from the film.

As time passed, it wasn't any easier to forget the pain caused by the loss of my mother. Then one day I suddenly heard that they had found the missing airplane buried deep in a gorge within an untouched forest. The news came too late and my mother had gone too soon. I received the comb that my father had always carried with him. Both combs were finally reunited, but it was a reunion on the altar.

For many months, Thach's house was boarded up. I didn't know where she went.

One day, I happened to see the good-looking guy who had once dated Thach. He was sitting with one foot up on the seat of a crimson Honda Cub 70, perhaps waiting for someone by the side of the road. I went up to him, said hello, and asked, "Do you know where Thach went?"

He brushed the question aside. "Which Thach? I don't know her. What a weird question."

I was bewildered and walked away, then turned around immediately and said firmly, "You have to tell me. If you don't, then I won't leave."

He considered it for a moment, glancing left and right, then lowered his voice, "She went to jail. Now get lost. There's nothing between you and me anymore, you understand?"

I didn't go away immediately. I stood looking at the thick thighs showing beneath his shorts. His legs were hairy.

I bought some canned food and fruit, then went to visit Thach. We sat looking at each other across a wide table. She had never thought that anyone would come to visit her, especially me. She wept softly. "Now I really am a worthless woman." When I was about to stand up, she said, "Now I don't believe that there are good people in this world." I fell silent, not knowing how to console her. "God is like that, too. If he was good, then he would have brought you and me together."

I went home. Duyen was busy in front of the house. She tripped over something and fell, but wasn't badly hurt. I lifted her up and carried her into the house. I realized now more strongly than ever that I had been right to approach her first out of pity. If it had been only love, then eventually it would have dried up. Only through pity and the bond of marriage was I able to live with her forever. Although I wasn't always faithful to her, I would never think of leaving her. Able to reach that conclusion, I only wanted to sell the house and take my wife and son away, to go to a faraway place without revealing our new address, in order to protect the happiness of our small family. Vacillating for a long time without being able to reach a decision, I asked Duyen's opinion. She said, "There's no place better than here. Why should we move?"

After that, I was constantly troubled, worrying about the day that Thach would return.

1993
Translated by Bac Hoai Tran and Dana Sachs

The Indian

After so many years living among the Indians, I can recognize them immediately at any airport terminal, even if the waiting area is seething with a mix of colors and nationalities. Here they are, a whole family, husband and wife, father and children, their complexions blending from nearly black to wheat brown to a shade of white strained through the generations from some irrepressible Aryan gene. They create their own world, talking and laughing boisterously and familiarly with each other as if nothing existed around them but a barren desert.

But if the Indian is travelling alone, then he is a solitary planet, a world intent on self-exploration, with no time or energy to waste on the other beings whirling around him in the chaos of the terminal.

I have discovered one such lonely world. A young man, definitely alone; he has buffered himself by occupying not only his own seat but also by claiming the last one in the row with his backpack. I approach him and speak a few friendly words in his mother tongue, to let him know I've been to his country, to put him at ease. He hesitates, then reluctantly lifts the black and white stripped backpack in order to give me a place to sit— though instead of putting the pack down on the clean, shining floor, as I'd expect, he puts it on his lap, as if it is a child who needs a comfortable seat. With the pack wrapped snugly in his arms, he seems to totally forget that the foreigner sitting next to him can speak his language. And suddenly the backpack has become an object of mystery and fascination for me. I begin to wonder if it contains something whose discovery might make the customs officers of any country deliriously happy.

It takes a six hour delay of the Bangkok-Delhi flight due to technical difficulties—six hour after we've waited four hours already!—to break down his policy of isolation. But finally, thanks to that delay, I get his story—and my suspicions about the contents of his backpack are put to rest.

*   *   *

The first time I saw her she was standing in front of a Hindu temple, dressed in a sari like any Indian woman. But she seemed small and fragile and somewhat overwhelmed by the heavyset women surrounding her, and even at a distance, as she ascended the stone *ghats* (steps) by the Ganges river, I immediately recognized her for what she was. I'd been working as a tourist guide for nearly five years by then and I could spot a foreigner with the certainty of a predator scenting his prey. I approached quickly, wanting to lay claim to her before any of my prowling colleagues pounced. She headed straight for the temple entrance and, without hesitation, began to remove her shoes, as if to demonstrate that she knew our ways and had no need of a guide. I knew this was exactly my chance. I stepped in front of her, shielding her from the rude reception she'd surely receive from the temple guard standing just beyond the shoeminder. Excuse me, I said, but foreigners are not allowed to enter here. Why not? she asked, surprised—she had visited dozens of Hindu temples since being here and had even dipped her feet in the sacred Ganges, among the hundreds of pilgrims washing away their sins—no one had ever stopped her. I explained that this particular temple belonged to a very strict sect that abhorred and regarded as filthy all things foreign. Here, she would be considered cursed and unclean—but no matter, I said, there were many other temples around town she could visit if she pleased. And in this way, I became her official guide—the guide of a foreigner who would be sure to tip much more generously than the stingy, tight-fisted Indian tourists.

Although I took her to three different temples, she still would not forget the one temple forbidden to her—exactly because it was forbidden, she very much wanted to see what it contained. If she couldn't, she said, she would not be able to return home with any peace of mind. I weighed the pros and cons. Perhaps, I thought, if she covered her blonde hair and half of her face with the sari, we could link arms and enter the temple as two pilgrims...

We returned and mixed into the crowd, and then slipped easily into the sanctum. In a flickering light the color of butter, we watched as the ritual was performed. My foreigner's spirit, the spirit of this woman who always seemed to ask why, who tried so hard to understand these strange sounds and these strange ways, seemed to hover and soar with the trilled chanting of the mantra.

But her blonde hair spoiled everything. The flap of the sari covering her head slipped a little and her hair flared brightly in the dim candle light, in the heated gloom, clouded and musky and feverish with incense smoke and the smell of sweat. Everyone in the sanctum froze, staring at this sudden and indecent exposure.

He Ram, (Oh God), it's a heretic! the priest brayed raucously. *He Ram!* I quickly pulled the sari back over her head, grabbed her hand and plunged through the crowd towards the entrance. *He Ram! He Ram!* By now the crowd was aroused, and people were shoving each other. Some began running helter-skelter, while others, thinking the ones running must be the culprit, began to chase them. In the pandemonium, only God knew who the real heretic was.

We escaped to the street and jumped into a three wheeled jitney. Soon afterwards we arrived at her house. By this time I had recognized her—my tourist and her husband were the new tenants who had moved into the villa just outside the entrance to my village. They'd been there for half a month. I knew that her husband was a famous British archeologist, in India to direct the excavation of ruins from the Ganga civilization at a site about 30 miles from my village. She didn't know or care much about ruins, and refused to go with her husband to the dig, where she'd be burnt by the sun and have to look at broken relics all day. She was more interested in discovering the living India, she explained—that was why she'd had the inspiration of disguising herself in a sari and wandering among the Indians.

As soon as we reached the villa, she insisted on inviting me inside to try a glass of the apple cider she had brought from London.

After all, I was the man who saved her—and moreover, it turned out I was her neighbor and a fellow villager also. Come in, she said. Sit. What's your name? Navin? What does Navin mean? Nothing? Just a name? Well I'm Katherine Robson—but you can call me Kitty. It's also just a name.

She began to show me some stone statuettes she'd bought since being in India. One was a small Ganesh, sitting happily with his pot belly thrust forward, his navel exposed, his trunk dangling over both. But why did he have an elephant head— what was that all about? I told her the story—how he was the son of Shiva and Parvati, how his father had left his home when Ganesh was still very little, how when Shiva returned, many years later, instead of seeing his consort waiting for him, he saw Parvati standing and talking happily with a handsome young man and immediately drew his sword and struck off the young man's head. Oh my God, didn't you recognize our son Ganesh, Parvati wailed, and forced Shiva to resurrect Ganesh at once. Shiva brought the headless corpse to life and then promised his son the head of the first creature he saw. As soon as he said these words, the bushes parted and an elephant emerged from the jungle.

Kitty shook her head. What a terrible story—why would Shiva cut off a head just because he saw two people sitting and talking—just as we were now. I shuddered at the bad luck her words could bring. Kitty must have read my expression, for she burst into laughter. Don't worry, she said, my old Brian wouldn't care what we do—as long as we don't touch his precious relics.

She inched a little closer and then casually draped her arm around my shoulders and kissed me. Do you know, Navin, she muttered, you are like that temple—very intriguing, very lovely, and very hard to understand. And why, Navin, don't they want me to come inside? Her embrace tightened, and I knew that what she said was true. It was difficult to penetrate, to understand, the Indian's inner heart. I wondered if it would be better if we were nakedly white, with blazing golden hair and our innermost hearts displayed as conspicuously and shamelessly as fish suddenly exposed when their naked gleaming bodies were netted and drawn up from the Ganges.

Tactfully, I freed myself from her. My late mother had taught me to keep my place in the world, and my life in a village made of complex and interlaced castes had taught me what my exact position in life was. Kitty burst out laughing—a frank, open laughter that made me feel I'd had no reason to shiver and be ashamed. She wanted, she said, only to learn how to cook Indian food. I agreed instantly and went home to get the kitchen implements I'd need to make *chapati* and the spices I needed for chicken *tandoori*.

From that time on, I left the life and irregular earnings of a tourist guide and went to work for the Robson family as a cook. And from the first day, old Brian was delighted that Kitty had finally met a genuine Indian who would now be part of their home, so she no longer needed to wander and explore the country as he went about his work. He was pleased also that the Indian foods I cooked were not as spicy as the food in Indian restaurants, and he could enjoy them. Kitty taught me how to cook Western dishes also, and soon I was making ice cream, pudding and various kinds of cakes. On the whole, my couple was very satisfied—they had no lack of their favorite foods, even in this tropical village, so far from England. Every day, in her spare time, Kitty helped me to improve my district-school English as well. When Brian returned in the evening and sat at a rattan table in the garden to sip his tea, Kitty would give him the notebook with my homework exercises in it, in order to show him what a bright lad I was. Brian read, smiling and nodding, then handed the notebook back to Kitty. Great, he said, only a few unimportant mistakes in diction. Why weren't they important? Kitty said, frowning. He needs to be corrected—to learn from his small mistakes so he can avoid big mistakes. Watching his wife diligently checking my work sentence by sentence, crossing out words and phrases and rewriting them, Brian chuckled gently. The purpose of language, he said, was to understand each other—once we understood, such matters as diction were only blades of grass on which our shoe heels might slip a bit. But Kitty didn't agree. She was determined to correct my very Indian roll of the letter "r" in such words as park, father, fair. She was only doing it, she told me, so that when she and her husband took me to London in the near future, I wouldn't be ashamed or feel belittled because of my pronunciation. I thanked her, but quickly added that even though I wanted very much to travel abroad, I had promised my dead mother that I would never go away and leave her alone.

My mother's tragic death had occurred the only time I was not there to protect her. As she lay between this world and the next, she was plagued by a fear of being alone and tormented by dozens of beasts in human form. With her last breath, she made me promise never to leave her alone again. My father had died when I was very small, leaving her to feed her son by herself. But that was not a reason to be respected in our village. No—an upright woman, it was felt, would have snuck onto her husband's funeral pyre and burned up with him—such an act would have been respected. But we were not religious Hindus and didn't believe in that outlawed custom, and so my mother was scorned and ostracized. Ostracized—but still ogled by the village headman, the police chief and the old moneylender, who tried to flirt with her and touch her at every chance. When they didn't succeed, they began to fabricate stories, trying to smear my mother, and finally they joined together to destroy what they couldn't obtain. I was already grown-up then, muscular and strong, and I always kept myself armed and stayed close to my mother as soon as it became dark. There was only one day when I failed to go fetch her at dusk, as she was traversing the mustard-blossom fields to go home—and it was that day the great disaster occurred. There must have been a dozen of the sadistic, lustful devils involved, but it was dark at the time and I had no clue or witness I could bring before the law. I heaped earth on my mother's grave in the village cemetery and swore to myself I would never commit the mistake of leaving her alone again. One night soon after, the village headman's large house burned to the ground—and no cause was ever found except for a short circuit. But I know for certain that my mother knew what had happened and was happy in the other world.

I didn't forget the promise that Kitty and her husband made, but I didn't think about it either, and I worked just as hard as ever. Anyone could guess what would happen next, with a lady whose husband was away and who stayed about her young cook all day long. And even though I was an inexperienced virgin, I was always vaguely aware of what might occur and, to tell the truth, I both worried about it and wanted and lusted for it. When the event finally took place, Kitty became more attached to me than ever and began to make fervent plans to take me with her and old Brian to London before the end of the month. I would continue cooking for the family and improving my English. If I wished I could go to school in England and obtain my own position in society, or I could become the cook in the Indian restaurant of a famous hotel...in short I could do anything that I wanted with my life. The idea seized me. I felt a kind of lust of gratitude, a need to repay Kitty for her favors, mixed with a dim emotion that I found hard to name. Many times in the past I'd been grateful for my sense of position and place, imprinted on my nature by the thousands of years that the caste system existed in India—a sense which at first had kept me from going too far in my relationship with this lady. But now I had forgotten it all.

Kitty had changed me that quickly. Only a short time before, even though I'd wanted it very much, I'd insisted that I couldn't leave—my mother's grave was here. She'd died five years before, but I'd promised never again to leave her alone. But now I'd discovered my strength as a mature man, and I was overflowing with pleasure and confidence and pride. Everything that had seemed impossible only a short time before suddenly seemed possible. I hadn't been able to go to London because my mother, gasping her last breath, had taken my hand and made me vow never to be separated from her again. But I knew there had to be some way I could keep my promise to my mother and yet still go to London.

An idea flashed in my mind, as dazzling and glistening as a water spout leaping up from the Ganges into the sun. And just in time, too—it was only ten days before old Brian had to book our tickets to London, and I needed to let him know my decision. It took me that whole night to exhume my mother's grave, fill it up again, and wash each bone and every piece of bone in alcohol. Next, I bought a smart backpack—this very backpack, with its black and white stripes —and I knew that from that day on I was free to leave forever that stifling village. I kept this pack with me always—even when we were in the airport terminal, and I went to get coffee for the Robsons. They teased me about my new attachment, but I insisted on always keeping it strapped to my back

Once we were in London, Brian fell ill with typhoid fever. That virus, sleeping quietly for thousands of years in our soil, had awakened to strike him down. Every day Kitty and I went to visit him in the hospital. Sometimes I'd go back to bring books and music cassettes to him. I'd walk alone, down Victoria Street and across Westminster Bridge over the foggy Thames. What a strange country—dim and veiled in fog, its people quiet and cold and dry—and yet ready to open themselves in a wink to the sexual desire of a stranger.

I was feeling guilty, thinking of Brian writhing in the pain of his sickness while I betrayed his generosity and took advantage of his gullibility. When he recovered and came home, surely he would see what Lord Shiva saw: his wife talking intimately with her young cook. I decided to stop myself from going any further than such flirtatious conversations with Kitty. She grew angry, and kept repeating that she would never understand Indians, even though she'd thought she did. It was only after we returned one day from the hospital—both of us happy because Brian had been able to stand up again and even to go sit on a bench in the hospital garden—that we chased each other all over the house, and even romped across the lawn to the pond. We were wet and panting when I finally brought her to my room and I let her knock me down, like an exhausted boxer falling onto his back in the ring, and then, passively and comfortably, I lay back and enjoyed what she was doing to me. It was long and flickering and jumbled up and teetered to the edge and when we thought it was coming to the end, it turned and winged off far, far away. After a time, our patience began to be exhausted. What was holding me back? What was scaring me? I knew I wasn't afraid that the sword that cleaved Ganesh's neck would come down on mine—old Brian was still in the hospital, with just enough energy to grope step by step down the path in the hospital garden. But then whose invisible, reproachful eyes did I feel upon me? Whose glowering look rippled the air around me?

I suddenly understood and shouted, as if I'd been caught red-handed. Quickly, I pulled the quilt over Kitty's body with one hand, and snatched the bedsheet around myself with the other. Wrapped tightly in the sheet, I rushed to the corner, grabbing a big towel on the way. I went to the backpack and carefully draped the towel over it, as if I was drawing a curtain between it and my bed.

Kitty had sat up and was staring at me, her eyes wide and full of questions. I pulled her down and we fell into an hysterical pleasure—that was my answer. But it only invoked a more intense curiosity. How strange women are—they wonder, they pry into everything without restraint, until they finally reach disaster.

Whenever I forgot to curtain off my bed from the backpack, the same would happen: we would go on so long and interminably and wearily that I knew I would suffer a defeat—and just at that time I would suddenly remember. Once, when I was dozing off afterwards, Kitty crawled quietly from the bed and began to rummage through my pack. A yell—sharp and then choked off, like a woman being strangled—woke me, and I sprang up in time to support her, her naked body gone pale all over. She had opened the pack and finally saw what up to now had been hidden.

It took me a long time to convince her that I wasn't a murderer who had hid his victim's bones in his room. But after that Kitty avoided coming to my room, and we had to use a sofa in the living room. But Kitty didn't find it a suitable place for our lovemaking —she preferred my cozy, warm room. She tried to persuade me to rest my mother in the meadow next to the pond on her property. No—I would not let my mother lie in a strange land, desolate and out of my sight. Unable to convince me, Kitty just let out a pent-up sigh and remained unsatisfied on the sofa.

One day, while tidying up my room, I lifted the backpack and was startled to find that it felt feather-light. Even in my panic, I understood immediately what had happened. Shouting curses at her, I chased Kitty, running crazily after her until I finally cornered her on the third floor. I gripped her shoulders and squeezed so hard that she burst into tears; I shook her as if she were a sack of cotton. Unable to bear it, she pointed her trembling finger towards the pond.

I ran to the pond and plunged my hands into the shallow water near the shore, plucking out one bone after another from the bottom where Kitty had dumped them. When I thought I had everything, I began to assemble and reassemble the skeleton on the lawn. I counted the bones over and over. They were all there, except for the phalanges of the fingers. For the rest of that morning I searched the water, dredging my hands through the mud at the bottom, but I could not find anything else. Full of rage, I rushed back to the house and once again grabbed Kitty. This time, however, my hands found her neck, and I squeezed with uncontrollable anger. Kitty quivered, jerked, squirmed and cackled as if she was laughing—cackled just as she cackled when we were making love. It was that sound that saved her, that suddenly brought me back to myself. I released her and pushed her away from me violently.

From then on, I always saw the eyes of my dead and still ill-treated mother staring at me in reproach. Whenever I looked at my backpack, I saw my mother with her fingerless hands, deformed as a leper's. I became taciturn—as cold as the Thames encompassed in its fog. But time gradually began to heal my pain, and Kitty would often implore my forgiveness. In fact, on two or three occasions we tried to make love on the Kashmir carpet in the living room. But when I touched her she hiccupped and then cackled, the way she always did, the way she did when I was strangling her as my mother's skeleton lay incomplete on the grass near the pond.

I was unable to go on.

A natural ending had come. With my backpack on my back, I said goodbye and received a shower of burning kisses all over my face. Kitty told me she'd hoped I would become attached to this house—but if I was determined to go, then she would come with me. I tried hard to make her understand that the problem was not the house, but Kitty herself. Even if she abandoned everything to come with me, that problem would remain. Kitty looked thoughtful, then took a few steps backwards as if to see me better. She stared at me as she'd stared at the temple of that strict Hindu sect—even though she couldn't infiltrate it, couldn't penetrate the mysteries it contained, it was still lovely to her, still attracted her.

I stopped off at the hospital to say goodbye to old Brian. The expression of filial repentance on my face seemed to disturb him. Brian was used to mummies and relics which never repented.

After that, some of my compatriots found me a job as a cook in an Indian restaurant in London. Then I went to Bangkok to be a cook in a hotel. It was a place where sometimes groups of European air-hostesses stayed over after their flights. One night one of them managed to find her way to my room and offered to stay as a provisional guest. She told me that she found Indian men warm and charming, not pale and insipid like European men. However, after we had been intimate, she gave herself the right to find out all about me, the right to check my things, to rummage through the backpack that I'd carefully stowed inside the wardrobe. She stood terrified and speechless, staring at me, until I told her that I had more such backpacks that I kept in different places in my room—each containing a one-night lover such as herself. Only then was she able to take her legs and—not forgetting to snatch her handbag on the way out—run away forever.

*   *   *

Our plane landed in New Delhi at dawn. I gathered up my luggage and cleared customs quickly. I didn't see Navin, and I wondered if he'd been delayed. In any case, the usual pandemonium that boils up before or after a flight separated us and gave us no chance to say goodbye. We would certainly not meet again: it was difficult to meet someone again even on the roads clearly marked on the earth—and seemed impossible on those invisible routes that interlaced in the air.

The next morning, I read a brief news item in the Times of India: "Customs officers at Indira Gandhi International Airport were dismayed yesterday to discover a skeleton in the backpack of a disembarking passenger. The passenger, one Navin, claimed that the bones belonged to his mother, and that he was the sole surviving member of his family. He explained that he was visiting his homeland before proceeding to take a job in the Persian Gulf. The passenger further explained that his plan was to permanently bury the skeleton once he finally found a place where he wanted to settle."

April, 1993
Translated by Ho Anh Thai and Wayne Karlin

The Goat Meat Special

Not only did Hoi finally manage to buy a television, it was even a color set.

One evening his two brats went to visit their grandparents and his wife slunk off to meet with her boss, the manager of the Ban Toc government hotel. Hoi wondered why she was sneaking in and out of the house so much these days. The campaign against corruption was in full swing all over the country. Maybe the two of them were covering something up. Left alone in the house, he turned on the television and grabbed a mystery novel. He read inattentively, listening with half an ear to the TV. His eyes swept up from the book when a fashion show came onto the screen. The models appeared to be amateurs, their movements exaggerated and artificial, their arms flapping loose. They tripped clumsily over their own feet like puppets jerked by strings. The last model was a girl in a two piece bathing suit. She threw a clumsily seductive look at the camera, turned to display her back and turned again. Suddenly something unprecedented occurred. The model tore off her top, dropped it at her feet and began turning round and round. Hoi shouted at the screen, trying to cue her that she wasn't in her bathroom. But it was too late. The girl had already stripped to her birthday suit. A sequence of totally nude shots followed.

Hoi couldn't believe that television was getting so progressive and bold. He told himself to be very cautious when asking about it. The next morning, while everybody else in the office was exchanging gossip, he said casually: "That TV program last night was quite rousing, wasn't it?

"It was ridiculous," a young man quacked at Hoi. "Whenever they were about to kiss, the camera skimmed off over trees or houses or trains to avoid it. That kind of film should be reserved only for pensioners and old managers."

"Nonsense!" Dien, their general manager snapped. "To the contrary, we only like entirely open movies—the kind where everything on the girls' bodies gets entirely opened. We're too experienced and dedicated to be corrupted by such films," he said severely, admonishing the younger man. "While you...If the reins are loosened too much, you'll soon slide into debauchery."

So Hoi came to understand that neither the manager not his coworkers had the luck to see the program he'd watched last night, even though they all hugged their television sets constantly and let themselves be force-fed junk movies, like a flock of hens and cocks being fattened with lumps of steamed rice before being sold to the block.

For the next few nights the programs were very proper, much to his relief. After all, it wouldn't do for parents and their children to sit together enjoying a strip tease.

But now he understood what was happening. Only on those evenings when his wife and children were out and he sat alone in the dark bedroom watching television, did that program flare onto the screen.

And not only that one. There was also a porno film involving some pigs that contained several truly spectacular sequences.

Evidently, these programs only were shown when he was at home alone.

Listening to Hoi's whispered descriptions the next day, his boss Dien was skeptical.

"Really?" He flashed a comradely grin. "Well, maybe I'd better come over and check it out, see if it's true."

That night Hoi gave his children tickets to the movies and found an excuse to drive his wife away. As soon as Dien came over, the two men went and sat in front of the television.

The pig film entranced Hoi. But when he turned to Dien to see if his boss liked it, what he saw in his living room was a goat sitting with its forelegs folded on its chest, its hind legs tapping gently with the music. Hoi screamed and rushed to the door.

"What's the matter with you?" the goat asked in a restrained, polite manner, peering at Hoi through its old man's wire-rimmed spectacles.

The goat still looked very much like Dien. Around its neck was the gold chain the manager usually wore; an Orient wristwatch still circled its left foreleg. The only difference was that the sparse beard on Dien's warty chin had been replaced by a pointy goat's beard and Dien's clothing had been replaced by thick flaps of black and white fur.

"Why have you been put into this pitiful condition?" Hoi asked, gradually regaining his calm.

"What do you mean?"

"I mean you've turned into a goat."

"What? You have the gall to say I've turned into a goat?"

Hoi gave him a mirror. But contrary to his expectations, the goat didn't seem very frightened. It gazed at the mirror for a long time and even raised its fore and hind legs to examine its hooves.

Though the goat seemed to be in silent anguish, it still remained unruffled.

"Well, my life is shattered," it sighed, returning the mirror to Hoi. "Never mind, personal affairs must not interfere with the common good. Listen, tomorrow, managers from the Construction Materials Service will visit our factory. As Chief of Planning, you'll have to welcome them on my behalf. Try to invent a pretext for my absence."

"I can fabricate something for them, but what can I say to your wife?"

"Don't interrupt. Just tell her I was sent for by the minister for some urgent business tonight, before I had to catch an early flight to the south."

"Have you decided to take refuge in my house, sir?"

"Temporarily—just for a few days. Hurry up now, help me find a place to hide."

Hoi had no choice but to lead the goat to the pig shed in the corner of the backyard. Until a short time ago, his wife had often brought leftover food from her hotel, saving the choicest courses for the humans and giving any food that was stale or rotted to the pigs.

But recently the atmosphere at the hotel had become tense and she no longer dared to bring anything home—and so the shed was left vacant.

Hoi came home early the next afternoon. Making certain that his wife and children weren't back yet, he approached the pig shed. The goat, under the impression that Hoi would come home to feed it lunch, had been waiting for him impatiently. The more it waited, the more Hoi didn't come. When he finally did, the goat could barely keep calm.

"There you are, wasting your time boozing it up with those guys from the Construction Material Service, leaving me here to starve to death!" the goat yelled at him shrilly. "I'm almost done for."

"But what kind of care do you need from me, sir? Isn't the grass on my lawn enough for you to gnaw?"

"Grass? For me? Are you joking? Get busy and prepare my favorite courses: pullet with lotus seeds in bain-marie; chicken chitterlings and pineapple browned in fat, some fresh bean sprouts, and—if available—a glass of lizard wine."

"Please—all you need to do is go home and I'm sure your beloved wife will cook those delicious foods." Hoi stuck out his lower lip, pouting, trying to calm down by humming a soft, soothing song to himself. "All right: I'll buy the foods for you, sir. However..."

Hoi bent over the pointed ear and whispered that in the meeting today with the Construction Material Service, he'd like to ask for some books, tiles and cement to be supplied to himself under the pretext of being used for repairs to the factory day care center. "Impossible!" The goat sprang up onto its hind legs, vigorously waving its right fore leg. "That means taking the common property of the people for your individual benefit."

"But didn't you say that you're hungry?"

"I won't let you profit from my predicament!"

Hoi left the goat overnight with its empty stomach. Though it was almost too weak from hunger to stand, it didn't dare bleat for help, for fear that Hoi's wife would hear. The goat knew that if it fell into the hands of that gourmet cook, it would end up as several dishes of half-done goat meat. Unable to bear it any longer, the next morning the goat accepted Hoi's conditions. Hoi laid some documents he'd already prepared on a pinewood box. The goat took the pen, but sat lost in meditation for awhile before it signed. It shook its head in sorrow.

"What humiliation! And just for food."

"Everything we do is just for food, sir."

In no time, Hoi had a heap of renovation materials for his house. Combing through his paperwork, he beat his brains trying to figure out what he could next gain from the goat by forcing it to starve.

He had not yet carried out his plans when one morning Toan, Dien's wife, burst into the house.

"You can fool everybody but me that my husband went to the South—I've just met with the minister who said my husband had no urgent business he knew about. Obviously, you're an accomplice in some affair he's having with some bitch."

Suddenly Hoi's calmness struck Toan in the face like a dash of cold water. Beneath his calm she saw the chilly soul of a cold-blooded killer. She felt panic-stricken. But she was also accustomed to being loudmouthed and arrogant: whatever was on her mind flowed out uncontrollably.

"Or likely you killed my husband by hacking him into pieces and threw them into the pig shed, isn't it? Oh hell, he was wearing his gold chain and watch and his gold-rimmed glasses."

At the mention of those precious items, her greed and regret at their loss stoked her anger and she became fearless. She turned and rushed impetuously to the backyard, and to the pig shed.

Hoi had no time to explain or to stop her. Well, let her see, he thought. But at first, Toan couldn't see anything in the dilapidated shed. Finally, when her eyes got used to the dim light, she stared for a long time at the goat. Suddenly she trembled.

"Is that you?" she asked pityingly. "Have you been living in this shed all this time?"

The goat didn't answer. It bowed its head, as if admitting to a fault. Toan noted that it still wore the gold chain, the watch and the gold framed glasses.

Surprised, Hoi asked her: "How did you recognize him?"

"Why not?" Seeing that Hoi was sympathetic, Toan poured out her heart. "I saw him for the first time like this on the very day he came to ask me to marry him. My parents and siblings were all full of praise for him: he was so handsome and so talented, a General Manager and barely over 30 years old. Only I saw that coming into our house that day was a sharp bearded goat, insensitive to human beings. But I was a spinster of 33, and he was my last chance. For over twenty years now we've shared our lives, and I always see him as he is at this moment, in this pig shed."

The three were silent for a long while. Finally, Hoi asked:

"What are your plans now?"

"Let him stay here—take care of him for awhile. I have no place to feed him in my house, and besides, we're having guests from the country. I'll provide food for him, and you'll be paid for your trouble."

"But you'll have to arrange for his return as soon as possible. If my wife discovers the boss," Hoi jerked his chin at the goat, "she'll take him to the Ban Toc hotel, sell him to the Specialized Dish Section."

That evening Toan brought a jute sack and they put the goat inside it and strapped it to the luggage carrier of her motorbike. Soon the goat was back in its own room, with its own table and favorite books. Toan had carefully prepared a welcome home party for her husband, including champagne and his favorite foods.

After a glass of whiskey, the goat's eyes grew damp and his

face grave. In a choked voice, he said, "Hitherto I nurtured a hope. But today it was completely shattered. You two need to start spreading a rumor that after returning from my urgent project, I was so weak I couldn't continue working. And you, my wife, will need to file my application for retirement."

"Why should a goat care about retirement?" Hoi asked.

"Don't say that. My career, full of satisfaction in every respect, demands a smooth and honorable withdrawal."

"I understand you," his wife nodded. "We'll need to invent a contagious disease for you, so nobody comes to check. All right—I'll tell the Personnel Section of your factory that you have AIDS."

The goat sprang up in anger.

"You'll smear my honor and prestige. A man with my reputation can't fall back on a filthy disease like that as a reason to retire."

Finally, Hoi and Toan settled on hepatitis and pulmonary tuberculosis. Under that pretext they would file the applications for his retirement.

Hoi came home tipsy. Nearing the house, he remembered that his two children were away this evening, attending a meeting of neighborhood teenagers. His wife would be home alone. He suddenly wondered what kind of program she would watch on his as-you-like-it television.

Hoi glued his eye to the gap between the door and the jamb.

The room was dyed with the pale sickly light of the television. He strained his eyes for a long time before he was able to make out a figure on the screen: a graceful man displaying his back and chest, spinning like a fashion model. Suddenly, within a second, he saw the same model parading around without a stitch on his body.

Hoi banged angrily on the door. He even threw himself against it. His wife quickly opened the door, not even deigning to switch off the television. On the screen Hoi saw the same man, with the same graceful smile, now spinning round and round and displaying new fashions. The change of sequence didn't deceive him.

"Be careful," Hoi scowled at his wife, "I know someone who turned into a goat by watching that kind of film."

His wife calmly returned to her chair.

"People only say one thing turns into another," she said firmly. "But you're wrong—nothing changes into itself."

Hoi stood transfixed for a few moments before he caught her meaning.

"You mean human beings are like goats?"

"No, not 'like.' They are goats. All I see around me is a society of goats. The houses and the streets are swarming with goats. Goats riding bicycles and Honda motorbikes. Goats sitting in Toyotas."

"Why have you never said this before?"

"Because I would have been thrown immediately into the Bo Dung Mental Hospital. Instead, I greet the male goats as uncles and brothers. And the females as aunts and sisters. Though it's quite different with the flocks of goats delivered each day from the suburbs to my hotel. There I slaughtered one goat, imagining it was the Director General of the Hotel Cooperative who didn't give me permission to visit France, skinned and carved up another that resembled the woman from Personnel who refused to hire my brother. And I prepared half-done dishes from the meat of that old satyr, the Assistant Manager."

Hoi shivered. He wanted to ask his wife whether she had always felt she was sharing bed and board with a goat also. But he held his tongue. One always remains happier when one doesn't force another to confirm something they both already understand.

*   *   *

After a time no one remembered the unexpected retirement of Dien due to a serious disease. It was said, though, that once a neighbor came in through the open door of the house, looking for Toan. When she didn't see her, she proceeded to Dien's study where she saw a bespectacled goat writing at the table. In front of the goat was a thick pile of paper, with the huge word MEMOIR written in capital letters on the top sheet. Dismayed, she rushed around the neighborhood, spewing out what she'd seen until she was finally committed to the Bo Dung Mental Hospital.

As for Hoi's wife, once again she began bringing home leftover food from work, including his favorite goat meat. But every day before eating he first carefully read through the Obituary Notices in the newspaper. Only when he was fully confidant that Toan hadn't announced her husband's death, only when he was certain she hadn't sold Dien to the Specialized Dishes Section of the Ban Toc hotel—only then could Hoi calmly enjoy his half-cooked goat meat.

August, 1988
Translated by Ho Anh Thai and Wayne Karlin

A Sigh Through the Laburnums

When she turned sixteen, Neelam became such an object of infatuation for the village boys that they would fall off the path and into the field, or off the shore and into the pond, whenever they caught sight of her. Even when one boy played his flute for her, he only dared to do it from far away, under a banyan tree, and so the music that reached the beauty's ears sounded like the wild chirping of crickets.

After the monsoon season that year, upon the advice of an acquaintance, her parents sent Neelam to the state capital to study nursing. She and another girl rented a room from a landlady who believed strongly in preserving the virtues of family and custom. Once she received her first month's rent, she could be relied upon to act like a policewoman, or a hen which fluffs out its feathers and spreads the shadow of its wings over the chicks she has hatched—to protect them from the claws of crows or the teeth of the rats that might carry them off.

In the room next to the two girls' were two university students. As is not unusual, when they had been at home these boys had averted their eyes and didn't dare to look at any of the girls passing by. But living away from home had turned them into two hungry tigers. Both of the boys had the same hungry, searching eyes. The only difference between them was that one set of eyes just stared longingly at Neelam, while the other seemed to undress both girls.

Neelam's roommate denounced them to the hen. The old

lady immediately went to one of the other rented rooms, knocked on the door and called out for someone named Ravi. Ravi opened the door and came out. He was a man with deep eyes, a neatly trimmed mustache and a clean-shaven chin, and every step he took was full of self-confidence. Keep an eye on the two university students, the landlady told him, and do whatever is necessary to protect my two girls. And so a border was created. The two students stalked the two girls; Ravi stalked the two boys, and the landlady watched everyone. Finally, at the end of the month, she kicked both of the boys out.

The following Sunday morning, Ravi asked Neelam to go to an American film with him. By agreeing, she committed two sins. First, a village girl was not allowed to have a boyfriend before her marriage, and especially could not be seen with a boy in public places. Second, a village girl was definitely not allowed to see American films. Up to now, Neelam had only seen Indian movies, with their songs and dances, with their heroes who sought revenge or to save a captured maiden. But in the American movie to which Ravi took her, the hero didn't deserve to be called a hero, and instead of dances with merry songs, there were nude scenes that gave her gooseflesh. Neelam did not know why she shivered and clung tightly to Ravi's shoulder. He calmly took her hand and didn't give it back for a long time, until he was certain she had calmed down.

But the next Sunday they saw neither American nor Indian movie.

Instead they walked in a park full of laburnum trees, as dense as a forest. It was the season the laburnums blossomed and all around the two of them, laburnum flowers were hanging down like clusters of bright yellow, translucent grapes. All of the laburnums in the woods had brightened with the strands of flowers that flowed down around each tree like the golden hair of sleeping beauty. Suddenly Ravi drew close, his cheek pressing against hers. Neelam shut her eyes tightly, fearing she would be forced into the lips-bite-lips scene she had seen in the American movie. But Ravi just let the tip of his nose touch the tip of her nose, and then the two Indian noses, two of the Creator's greatest works, crawled over each other, each slipping along the high ridge line of the other. At just that moment, both noses caught the same breath. Ravi began to quiver all over his body, and he sprang away from her and sat up, and then they leaned on each other, like two squirrels caught in the rain, until the quivering stopped.

That evening, Neelam's roommate suddenly asked if Neelam thought Ravi was a good man. Was he? Really? And was a good man allowed to go to the red light district? What was the red light district? Neelam wanted to know. The girl whispered an explanation in Neelam's ear that made her tremble. It was the place where kidnapped Nepalese and village girls were coaxed with honeyed words, promises of good jobs in the city that ended with them selling themselves to pay what they owed their procuress. Earlier that evening, the roommate had seen Ravi going into a brothel a few blocks from their place. Neelam calculated in her mind and discovered that, if Ravi had really gone there, it must have been just after they had said goodbye.

The roommate didn't want Neelam to think she was only a gossip who made up stories. That evening, she rushed into the room and dragged Neelam down into the street. The two girls furtively stalked Ravi, who was worming his way through the dark streets. They watched him approach a dimly lit brothel where some Nepalese girls were sitting and waiting for customers, and they watched him go inside.

Neelam returned and then sat and waited for Ravi at the front gate. She waited for over an hour, waited so long that when Ravi finally came in, the tears which had flowed from her eyes had finally dried up. She demanded to know from where he was returning. Ravi was startled at the coldness in her voice. When she told him that she in fact knew where he had been, he was immediately seized by guilt. He was a responsible man, and, as any other responsible Indian man, all he had tried to do was preserve the virginity of his beloved, even when he was caught up in fits of passion for her. Neelam understood. It was an explanation that any Indian girl would find reasonable, even though she wouldn't want to think about it.

One morning not long afterwards, when Neelam was about to go to her hospital internship, her parents arrived unexpectedly from the countryside. Neelam was told to pack her things up within half an hour in order to catch the train back to their village, where she would be married immediately. Her groom-to-be, Raja, was none other than the boy who had been too shy to play his flute near her house, and so his music had sounded to her ears like crickets in a field. Actually, this was a match her parents had wanted for a long time, but it was only now that they had been able to finally save up the dowry of 60,000 rupees that the groom's family demanded. The amount was reasonable by the standards of their village, but Neelam's family had to hoard every last grain of wheat to scrape it up, and now they didn't want to miss their chance. If they waited another few years, it would be impossible to marry her off for that cheap a dowry.

Now her life was moving as swiftly as waves overflowing a flooded dike, and Neelam had to abandon everything, including her nursing studies. There was only time enough to tell the landlady. Ravi was at the university and would not get back until the afternoon. It had only been days before when Neelam had made him swear before Kama, the God of Love, and Agni, The God of Fire, that he would never go to the red light district again. It would be a difficult promise for him to keep and still preserve Neelam's virginity. But Ravi had sworn that the God Kama would be the witness of his love and the God Agni would set him ablaze if he did not keep his oath.

But from now on Neelam would not belong to him any more. She wanted to send him a message telling him to take back his oath. But no decent girl could send such a message to a man through her landlady.

The wedding party was held hastily, only three days later. Raja went mad with happiness. He led his friends to the base of a hill and crept into the bushes where he drank up two bottles of whiskey that he had snuck past his parents. Then, roaring out a song, tears streaming down his cheeks, he rode on a white horse to the swearing ceremony before the God of Fire. By custom, both brothers and friends of the groom were allowed to sing and drink as much as they wished at weddings. But not the groom. Moreover, the groom was not supposed to shed any tears. Raja was pulled off the horse, the tears wiped off his cheeks, and his makeup repainted on his face. But still he kept droning out a song. His relatives, fearing the bride's family would hear him, stuffed rags into his mouth. Then Raja refused to remount the horse. Instead, he jumped into a circle of his friends, singing, dancing and laughing as if he were a guest attending the wedding of a friend.

The news of his behavior winged its way back to the bride's family. The chosen groom had turned out to be a guy who drank himself into a stupor. Who refused to ride a white horse. Who acted as if he were denying he was a groom. His procession was halted midway by representatives of the bride's family. Shouting angrily, they flocked to the groom's house and told Raja's family in no uncertain terms that he was persona non grata in their family, as far as they were concerned. The groom's family was overwhelmed with anguish, struck as if by lightning with shame. Their child was definitely in the wrong. But how could they cancel the wedding and preserve their family's honor? Please reconsider, they begged. They were even willing to reduce the bride's dowry to 55,000 rupees. But to save 5,000 rupees on such a soiled product meant the shame would pass onto the bride's family. There are many ready-made garments crowding the market place, and although their prices were reduced by 50 or 60 per cent, even ghosts wouldn't deign to look at them.

The nerve-center of the groom's family was totally paralyzed. However, the sight of a single finger wriggling can give new hope to someone looking at a dead body. That finger was Amar, the son of Raja's young uncle. Amar whispered in his great uncle's ear and his words were like a life-restoring elixir poured into the mouth of an ashy gray corpse. As if he were a medium caught up in a trance, the uncle repeated every word he had heard from Amar to Neelam's family. We will withdraw Raja and bring him home to teach him a lesson. But Raja has two younger brothers, aged eighteen and twenty, and with Amar there are three available boys in all. We beg you to choose one of them in place of Raja, and we will reduce Neelam's dowry to only 50,000 rupees.

Neelam's family felt that there was no choice but to accept. An astrologer was sent for to cast the horoscopes of the three potential grooms. At first it seemed Neelam would be suitable for any one of the candidates. But in the final calculations, Neelam's Pisces mercilessly eliminated Raja's two younger brothers and turned out to be only compatible with Amar's Virgo. The quiet Amar, who everyone praised as being gentle and kind, had suddenly acted as the head of the household, and then had even leapt up on the white wedding horse and saved his family's reputation.

And so Neelam came to be the bride of Amar's family. But since all the brothers and cousins lived in the same house, she was not able to avoid facing Raja. Every day he played his flute. But now the sound was near her, right inside the house, and it was so bitter and so terribly sad that Neelam, speaking to Raja when there was no one else around, told him that if he continued playing the flute in the house for another month, she would go mad. Raja didn't reply. He silently left the house and went to sit by a temple some distance away. The sound of his flute reached her from there only as the buzz of mosquitoes.

A week after the wedding Neelam was still a virgin. There was no extra room in the house to give to the just-married couple, and the custom in such a large family was for the men to sleep in men's rooms and the women in women's rooms. Neelam shared a room with her mother-in-law and her two young sisters-in-law, all of whom stared and glowered at her. One day, the two sisters-in-law went to the field to reap mustard seeds, leaving Neelam alone with her mother-in-law. At mid-morning, Amar came home suddenly from his sundries shop. Saying he had a headache, he went into the men's room and laid down. His mother, seeing that the house was deserted, knew that his chance had come. She told Neelam to boil a glass of milk and bring it in to her husband. But Amar's head felt fine. He locked the door, swilled down the glass of milk, then pounced crudely on Neelam, as if she was a hen in a courtyard. There was no lips-bite-lips as in the American movies. There was no gentle touch of noses such as she had had with Ravi. There was only the sound of Raja's flute, lamenting in the distance.

Time passed. Still the men slept in the men's rooms and the women slept in the women's rooms. Still Neelam would come to lay in a man's bed in anguish and shame, lay motionless as a body stabbed to death. It always happened at mid-morning, after a scheming glance between Amar and his mother, after Amar had guzzled a glass of hot milk, which people regarded as an aphrodisiac. And always the sounds of Raja's flute flowed and wandered like the song of a drunken man, even though he never drank a drop.

Neelam gave birth to a daughter. This meant the family would have to begin a strict regime of saving money for her dowry, in order to marry her off after ten years. Everyone uttered discontented sighs at this bad beginning. Amar's two younger sister were now at the age of marriage. But even though the family had long been letting the village know of their availability, no one came forward to propose. With two daughters, the amount of their dowries had to be divided between them, whereas if they had only had one daughter, surely they would have gotten someone to marry her. And now, to rub salt into the wound, the family had a granddaughter. Neelam was humiliated, mocked as the kind of woman who did not know how to give birth to a son.

Now the family began to make other calculations. Adding up the golden necklace, the bracelet, anklet, rings, earrings, television set, some household appliances and even the motorbike Amar had gotten, they figured that Neelam's dowry had only came to 40,000 rupees. They were furious. If her family couldn't afford the dowry they'd agreed upon, they should have kept her at home. How could they be so unfair and dishonest. Confronted, Neelam's family confessed that they had had to save a long time to come up even with that sum. Would Amar's family please be satisfied for a while until they could save the remaining 10,000?

Neelam was big with child again. Her mother-in-law hung around her, complaining loudly. Surely this one would only give birth to females. Even though she came dirt-cheap, her swindling family had still cheated them of 10,000 rupees. What an honorable family they were! They had crawled out of mud and turned from worms into human beings, and thought they were so stuck up, but now she would send them back into being mud and worms again. Hearing this, Neelam could not remain silent. She and her mother-in-law began going tit for tat, each cursing the other back into worms. But all the gods had witnessed how she had had to join her husband's family, and she would not make it so easy to be pushed away.

Her mother-in-law regarded this as a declaration of war. Two days later, the fighting had escalated to the point it was driving both women mad. Neelam became so angry that she fainted. But the angrier the mother-in-law got, the more alert she would become, and when she saw Neelam swoon, she jumped up immediately. Half conscious, Neelam was vaguely aware of her body being splashed with what she thought was Ganges water and placed upon a pyre. Fire flared up violently around her. She jumped up and ran into the courtyard, crying for help, only to see her mother-in-law throwing away a petrol bottle as she ran by her. Raja, sitting in the distance, dropped his flute and swiftly ran to the house. He snatched a bed sheet from the clothes line, wrapped it around Neelam and rolled her in the courtyard dirt. Then he lifted her up and quickly ran out and waved down a vehicle to take her to the hospital.

Neelam was transferred from the district hospital to the state hospital, the same hospital where she had once studied nursing, where its director had been her teacher. She lived, but her face had been disfigured. Raja, who came to visit, stared at it, fixated, for a long time. Then he buried his own face in his hands and began to laugh uncontrollably. He went out into the hospital courtyard. Soon the sounds of his flute, its sound twisted and insane, cackled and writhed in the air until he was dragged off and thrown out of the hospital.

Neelam was prematurely delivered of another daughter. Another girl who the family would have to marry off in ten years like her older sister. Another girl the family would have to pay

50,000 rupees, or whatever the equivalent currency would be by then, to get rid of. Another girl to be haggled over, to have kerosene thrown on her body so she could be burned away completely, without troublesome questions being asked or legal procedures imposed. The hospital director was a social activist who felt she had a duty to console all her downtrodden, poor patients. What's your name, your age, your native village, your family situation? she asked Neelam, not recognizing her beloved student behind the seared crater of her nose, the jagged and variegated ridges and crags of her flesh. Have you named your daughter and filled in her birth certificate? she asked. Neelam shook her head. She sniggered through her torn lips. A girl in this world didn't need a name and why waste a birth certificate?

When the director had left, the woman in the next bed, who had just given birth also, patted Neelam's shoulder lightly, to calm her down. She was a woman with twenty years of seniority in the vice trade—with the girl she had just bore, she had had five daughters. She was a machine producing products for the Indian brothels. It was nice to have daughters, she said; they were soft and sentimental, not ungrateful rogues like boys. Her eldest daughter had already started to have customers, earning money for her mother and younger sisters. The woman gave Neelam a glass of whiskey, along with a sympathetic look. It was the first time Neelam had ever had alcohol. Suddenly she understood that it was guiltless and should not be condemned for anything. Suddenly she understood why Raja had gotten so boozed up he had lost his rights as a groom.

She drank two glasses of whiskey. It was dark outside now. She picked up her daughter and, staggering, carried her out into the corridor. So that was the life that awaited a girl, she thought. She could be burnt by her in-laws into a deformed ghost, or praised for dutifully helping to feed her family by turning tricks in the red-light district. Neelam approached a rubbish bin. She was suddenly aware of a shadow behind her. She turned right, went on, and spotted another bin. Again she glimpsed a flash of white robe, someplace behind her. She bypassed the elevator and took the stairs up to the next floor. Another rubbish bin.

This time she could see nobody, not before her or behind her. She shrouded the infant's face with a wet face cloth. It was startled and began to cry. But its muffled cry could not be heard after it had been placed in the bin and Neelam closed the lid.

She staggered away, but had only gone a few steps when she realized someone was coming up quickly behind her. It was the hospital director. She opened the lid and took out the baby, still safe and sound, then turned to Neelam. This was not something Neelam should have done in the hospital, the director admonished her. Though she didn't need to excuse herself for doing it. She, the director, was sympathetic. Many of the women who came to the hospital to give birth tried to do the same, and she had been vigilant in Neelam's case, watching her from the beginning. I kneel down and beg you to release my child from her incarnation as a girl in a world of pain and humiliation for females, Neelam pleaded, and then revealed their former relationship as student and teacher. When the director had realized who Neelam was, she wept and embraced Neelam and her little girl.

The next day she drove them both back to their village, reproaching Neelam along the way for not having come earlier to the hospital to have an amniocentesis examination—the baby could have been aborted immediately once it was discovered that she was female. Because of her hospital's success with this method, thousands of families had been released from the disaster hanging over their heads, and it had only cost them 500 rupees each. She admitted that there had been some newspapers which had run exposes on the practice, calling on the authorities to ban it and to punish "the witch who committed genocide." But was it more humane to let the girls be born, feed them until they were adults, save enough money to push them away onto their in-laws, where they would be abandoned to a life of abuse? Of course she herself was lucky enough to have only had a son—he was a doctor now—and just after giving birth to him, she had had herself sterilized because she didn't dare to take the chance of having a daughter.

When they were near the village, Neelam asked to be let off. The director gave her 500 rupees: enough to pay for an abortion if she got pregnant again. Neelam went immediately to a beer and liquor stall, extended 50 rupees over the counter, and asked for a bottle of whiskey. But the shopkeeper refused to sell alcohol to a woman. She searched through the market for a long time before finally finding another liquor stall. This time Neelam was finally able to buy the bottle, after pleading with the clerk that she was doing it for her husband, lying ill at home. She took the bottle and the baby and climbed up a bare, high hill. There she could look down and see the entire village. She could see the roof of those contemptible people arrested by the police and then released because she told them that she had burned herself; she hadn't been paying attention while she was cooking, she'd said. She could see her parents' house where she was determined not to return as a handicapped daughter. She drank half the bottle of whiskey then poured the rest onto her cotton face cloth and pressed the soaked cloth on the infant's face. She dug a small hole with her knife. The child squirmed for a little while and then gradually stopped. She seemed to have left the world meekly. Good. The meeker she was, the better it was she did not live in this venomous and wicked world that would clip her wings. Neelam laid the warm body in the hole and covered it up. She prayed to Yama, the God of Death, to take her child to heaven. She prayed to Vishnu the Preserver to shelter her child. And she prayed to Shiva the Re-creator to grant her child a next incarnation as a boy.

Then Neelam extracted a laburnum seed from its long pod and put it in the earth of her daughter's grave. She buried another seed in a small heap of soil nearby. This was the grave of the beautiful, undisfigured Neelam who had once existed and who now was dead.

She climbed down to the base of the hill and there erected a small hut and cleared a little patch of land and planted mustard and sold its seeds to the processors of mustard oil. No one could convince her to go back and live with her parents. She knew quite well it was a humiliation for any family to take its married daughter back home. And once when she passed her own daughter on the street, the girl had shrieked in fright and run away when she saw Neelam's face, which looked like an eroded hillside. Amar's family told the girl that Neelam was Raksha's demon, and used that story to threaten her whenever she sulked.

Soon after, Neelam was asked to help a neighbor who had gone into childbirth before she could be taken to the hospital. The whole family was stunned when she delivered a chubby girl who weighed over four kilos. This would be the fourth daughter in a family without any sons. The mother entreated Neelam to take the infant away and release her from this world. The father silently offered Neelam a bottle of whiskey. Neelam took the whiskey and the baby and, just as silently, disappeared into the darkness.

It was far. And it was windy. Neelam reached the foot of the hill and found that the soaked cloth that covered the baby's face had dried up. What a strong girl—she writhed and struggled as if she were trying to remove the cloth from her face, trying to see life. Neelam opened the cloth a little bit and let the infant see a sky as black as tar. But after the girl's face had been shrouded again, she began to wriggle violently. Perhaps she wanted to see a human being. Neelam opened the cloth, then struck a match and raised it to her face so the girl could see the deep pits and seams, the wasteland of ridges and ruined heaps. This was the human face. To see it once was to know forever what it was. After that, the girl stopped struggling, though she was still breathing evenly. How could Neelam find water to soak the face-cloth on the top of that bare hill? She rolled up her sari, squatted and urinated onto the cloth. Finally the wet cloth was effective.

Neelam did not forget to put a laburnum seed into the infant's grave.

Time flew by quickly, and the bare hill was covered by the shadows of the laburnums, each tree a virgin girl taken to heaven just after her birth. Neelam was always invited in whenever a woman was going to give birth. Every pregnant woman hid a bottle of whiskey under her pillow. If she gave birth to a son, then she would give Neelam a small sum of money and the bottle to drink in celebration. If it was a daughter, Neelam was given the bottle only, and asked to take the baby away. Once a family forgot and gave Neelam some rupees along with the bottle and the infant girl. Neelam resolutely returned the money. Why would she take rupees to do such charitable work?

In the season of the laburnum blossoms, the entire hill brightened and poured a glorious golden light over the village, paling the yellow mustard fields in comparison. The laburnums shed their leaves and the golden clusters of their blossoms flowed down gracefully like the hair of blond seventeen-year-old girls. A man wandered among the trees, sometimes plucking a blossom lovingly, as if it were a succulent yellow grape. Then he would stick its stem through a buttonhole on his shirt, take out his flute, and play. The song he chose was about the chivalrous but mischievous Krishna who teased some bathing Gopis—milk maids—by stealing their saris and then climbing up a tree, so that they had to stay in the lake and beg him to return their clothing. Hearing that flute, one would think it was playing the music of the gods, not of a mortal being. Neelam, drawn, came to the man and was startled to see that it was Raja. Seeing the deformed woman, Raja smiled in confusion and asked her whether she knew where Neelam was. Neelam took his hand, led him past the young-girl trees, and pointed at the biggest one. This was Neelam. This was the laburnum planted on Neelam's grave. Raja knelt and embraced the tree trunk, caressing it and calling out Neelam's name, crying that he wanted her to marry him. Then he heaped up a pile of dead leaves and set it on fire, bent down a branch of the tree as if he were taking his bride's hand, and walked seven times around the fire. And in this way, Agni the God of Fire accepted their marriage and Raja at last had his wedding and his wife.

At dusk, on another day, Neelam had no sooner entered her hut when she heard a man outside asking for a drink of water. When she went out, she nearly dropped the glass. Before her was Ravi, the same refined and composed Ravi she had known twenty years before, though his eyes no longer seemed as confident. Night fell silently. Neelam told him to stay with her, and then tomorrow he could continue his search, for she knew he had been looking for someone for twenty years. She poured out glass after glass of whiskey for Ravi and for herself. This was a glass of heat. This was a glass of bitterness. This was a glass of humiliation and precarious destiny. But it was not a glass of enmity. Ravi had been searching, questioning people everywhere to plow up a few clues. Finally, he had been told to come to this place. For all these years, he had never gotten married, but only occasionally coupled with prostitutes. But now he could no longer control himself, as he had promised Neelam. As he embraced the deformed woman, he asked her if she knew a woman named Neelam in this village.

No lip kiss. No nose touch. Ravi's hands hurriedly groped towards a denouement. The prostitutes had spoiled him. They had not asked for a kiss, or the gentle caress of two noses. But Neelam slowly reined his passion, and little by little the memory of their past tenderness was recalled in their touches. The tip of Ravi's nose, which seemed to have forgotten all, now reenacted its gentle frolics and fumbles on the used-to-be tip of Neelam' nose. But Ravi's memory failed to find the name knit to this intimacy, in the flesh of this woman he was with.

He left the hut towards morning. And Neelam took a shovel and a bottle of whiskey and climbed up the hill like a sleepwalker. She dug a grave for herself, finished off the whiskey, and then lay down in the grave and slowly passed out. She was certain she would die today, in this uncovered grave.

That dawn, a violent whirlwind struck the hill, devastating that golden wood of laburnums. Neelam was dead. All over the village, women who had given birth to infant girls seemed to sigh in relief, and it was as if all those sighs had rushed together and formed the tornado which destroyed all the traces and evidences that had, until now, made the women nervous.

The sun rose. The tornado died down. After Ravi had come into the village, he suddenly remembered what he should have remembered the night before when his nose had frolicked over that woman's face. He immediately rushed back to Neelam. But the hut was devastated. He ran up the hill, straight as an arrow through the fallen, broken laburnum trees. All of the virgin girls lay still around him now, their blond hair flowing. Finally, Ravi found Neelam in her self-dug grave. A blanket of golden flowers covered her face and body, and through it he could only make out the form of a young girl.

Not far away, another man dropped his flute and, lamenting, embraced a fallen laburnum.

February, 1994
Translated by Ho Anh Thai and Wayne Karlin

The Chase

For almost three hours, I had to stand still in the middle of the room. For almost three hours, Bien measured my shoulders and chest, and then hung my pitiful body with the pieces of cloth he had just cut and assembled temporarily with crude stitches and pins. If at this moment—it was around 10 p.m.—anyone walked into the room, he or she would scream out in horror at seeing me. A sixteen year old guy, naked except for a pair of pants, draped in pieces of rags. I looked like a scarecrow watching a watermelon field, except for a copy of the book *Ancient Fortress* that I held in my hands. I'd been reading that book passionately.

That's because there was nothing in that small town interesting to a kid from the capital, except for my uncle's bookcase. As soon as I arrived here and got off the bus, I had rushed to my uncle's house, greeted him and his wife quickly, then ran up to the bookcase as if I was going to miss an express train. That reading-express had carried me along ever since, and I wouldn't have bothered to get off if Bien hadn't come to borrow my foreign made shirt so he could use it as a model to make one for himself. He also informed me that we were of the same age and size and so I had to come to his house and act as a live mannequin for him.

"I've got a pair of tight trousers, just as modern as yours. But this prawn-tail shirt—I'm gonna finish it tonight, for sure."

"That's impossible," I said. I really wanted it to be impossible.

Bien, shocked, glanced towards the inner room. "Please lower your voice to about half that level."

I looked up from the book to Bien, feeling pity for him. Half? One-third? How could someone divide sound as if he were cutting a cake?

"Yes," he said. "Half. Otherwise my father is going to sing a song about how effective it is if you go to bed early and wake up early. During the time of the French, he was a clerk in the taxation department and used to quarrel all day with the fat-mouthed women who collected taxes. Now that he's getting old, he clucks all day like a hen."

My reading-express was not traveling smoothly at all. It was being rocked and shaken, disturbed by this talkative young tailor. But I didn't have time to answer before the "hen" slowly walked in. He nodded to me and then said to Bien:

"If you don't want to go to bed, you should at least shut off the sewing machine and let other people sleep."

"I'll do it right now."

Bien puttered around, rearranging the pieces of cloth as if he were tidying up.

"I'm too familiar with your word 'now." His father leaned over and looked at his watch. "It is now 10:32 p.m. You can stay here and talk to your friend. I just want to take this, and this, and this."

He quickly stuck one hand under the sewing machine and removed the bobbin, snatched up the scissors with his other hand, and walked victoriously back to his room.

I remained silent, but felt happy. I would be free of Bien, free to go back to my novel. In Hanoi, I had more than enough European-cut shirts and tight-leg trousers with inset side-pockets and foreign trademarks. My father worked in one of our delegations abroad and sent them home regularly. What I didn't have was a huge bookcase filled with books that were extremely attractive to a sixteen-year-old.

"I have to have a new shirt by tomorrow, at all costs," Bien said. "Tomorrow is Sunday."

There was some hidden meaning in this sentence I couldn't

grasp. Suddenly Bien's eyes had turned dreamy. They were the eyes of a smitten adult male, not those of a teenager just past Pioneers' age.

"Please wait a minute," he said.

Bien disappeared out of the back door. But "a minute" with my novel didn't really give me enough time to be happy. I heard the sound of chickens quaking from the back of the house. The chickens were so disturbed it sounded like the chicken house was on fire. Bien's father woke up and hurried from the inner room, heading outside.

After a while Bien returned. He winked at me. "Please help me carry the sewing machine to the kitchen, far enough from my father's bedroom that I can work in peace."

In the kitchen, Bien put down the scissors and reinserted the bobbin.

"My father's pretty strange," he said. "On one hand, he wants his children to sew and earn money, but on the other he wants them to be quiet so he can sleep. And at the same time he wants to sleep, he also worries that thieves might come and steal his chickens."

Bien pantomimed reaching his hand into the chicken house, grabbing a bird, pinching it, and then taking another and squeezing it.

"Now my dear father can sit out there getting drowsy and waiting for thieves."

He giggled, removed the pieces of cloth from my naked chest, and started the sewing machine again.

"Some days ago she came here and said to me: 'Even though your father is a tailor, you don't dress fashionably at all.' That's what she said to me, Le did."

As if I lived in this tiny town and Le was my sister. That's what she said to me, Le did! Bien asked me if I knew that young girl with the running nose.

"I wouldn't be surprised if she's your girlfriend, right?" I answered, making sure he saw my derisive mood.

"Please don't joke. She's not my girlfriend nor someone I'm running after, even if she is an object of your desire. Le is the

Youth Union Secretary of my class, and I have no ideas about falling in love with the Youth Union Secretary."

I caught the embarrassment in Bien's face. Suddenly I felt that the hidden thoughts behind his confused voice and clumsy movements might be more interesting than the novel I was reading.

"O.K., I get it," I said. "Le is Youth Union Secretary and she needs to have a blouse to wear, so she came here. You used this string-ruler to measure her body like you just measured mine, and hung pieces of cloth on her body like you just hung them on mine."

Bien glanced at my naked waist and blushed slightly.

"You're joking again. My mother measured her. I'm only allowed to cut the cloth and do the sewing..."

It was as if he had totally forgotten me and had sunk himself into the monotonous hum of the sewing machine, which can easily make anyone fall asleep. Suddenly he looked at me in a cunning way:

"While I was making the blouse, Le came here. I asked her: 'Should I make your blouse with the collar in the "longing for" style?' She covered her laughing mouth and said, 'Come on; who is longing for me?'"

Bien made another line in his shirt. "Come on; who is longing for me?" He imitated the young girl's giggle and her girlish voice.

I got to see Le's face the next day. It was really a beautiful morning to put on newly-made clothes and stroll to a female friend's house, and Bien was proud to have me next to him as we came down the narrow street. Here he was, walking with a friend from the capital, wearing the most fashionable clothes of that time. Both of us felt as if we were already young men who had reached the coveted age of eighteen.

"I really want some ice cream," Bien said. He didn't give me time to say yes or no, but quickly paid for two vanilla ice-creams from the vendor.

"The ice cream from the shop near the park is nice, but I always buy my ice cream here. Once I had an eating contest with a friend of mine; I really thought I could defeat him. I didn't know that after the ninth one, my jaws would stiffen. It was so scary that for days afterwards I shivered horribly every time I looked at ice cream."

He hadn't cared whether what he had just said was overheard or not. But now he came closer to me and lowered his voice:

"Look at the 'Develop and Color It' shop on the other side of the road. Hey, no, don't turn your face that way. Le is sitting at the table where they put colors on the photos."

I was slightly disappointed. Based on Bien's description the night before, I had imagined Le to be much more beautiful and elegant. In reality she looked rather young, perhaps the same age as Bien and me, and was not very fashionable at all. She was giving all her attention to moving the brush on the developed photos and didn't care to raise her eyes to glance at the two young men eating ice cream. I had always been artistic and also knew how to draw a bit, so I wasn't impressed with the aesthetic value of painting colors onto photographs.

"Is she wearing the blouse you made for her."

"It's a pity, no."

Bien said this with sincere regret. We continued strolling and after a while came to the park, where the nicest ice cream shop in town was located. That town was as small as the palm of your hand; during a short stroll you would pass all the main roads. Bien hesitated a bit and then asked:

"Let's have some more ice cream, OK?"

"Sure—let's see how good the ice cream here is."

"No, let's go back to the other shop."

I knew the real reason Bien wanted to eat there, but I followed him anyway. Eating ice cream somebody else has paid for was nicer than paying for it yourself.

This time, I had the opportunity to get a clear look at Le. I realized that she had beautiful red lips and a straight nose. This time, I began to think that gifted fingers were needed to move that brush so skillfully over the photos. And this time, I began to recognize that eating ice cream here was nicer than eating ice cream in Hanoi.

*   *   *

Now, seventeen years later, I still feel regret that the story didn't stop at his point. But it's my fault that it didn't. After that afternoon, hiding my eagerness to see Le again, I told Bien:

"Why don't you dress yourself up in your new clothes. I'd really like to have some ice cream from that shop again—and this time I'm buying."

We were lucky. Le raised her head and her shapely eyes sparkled when she saw us. The street was narrow and the distance between those two boys and that young girl was not great and I was certain I saw that sparkling clearly. Suddenly, both of us felt like real young men. But we pretended we were busy speaking to each other and didn't notice her.

If only after we had eaten the ice cream, if only after that first time we had stayed up until midnight to make a new and worthy shirt, the story would have ended, then that ending would be happy. But once again these two young goats, praising the ice cream they had just finished, had to go to the park to try the other shop.

We were almost there when we saw a crowd of young men dispersing and running in different directions, like a bunch of chickens being chased by foxes. Behind them was a group of policemen in yellow uniforms, and following the police some red-banner men, the municipal forces who helped the police carry out security measures. I was trying to grasp what was going on, when Bien rushed off to one side, yelling: "Run!"

Why should I run? I was a decent young man who had come from the capital to visit this tiny town no bigger than a coin. I wasn't a criminal and I hadn't even been there long enough to cause any trouble. I stood where I was, staring at the people running towards us.

"Are you mad?"

Bien turned back to me and yanked at my arm, forcing me to run after him. We cut across the road obliquely, passing in front of a Russian jeep which had to stop abruptly, its brakes screeching, then ran down some steps, taking them two at a time, pushed a bicyclist out of the way and entered the park. We could see the shadows of the red banner men behind us. Once we were past the trees, we squatted down next to a round flowerbed.

"They cut off kids' long hair and tight-legged trousers," Bien said breathlessly. I shivered slightly, thinking about almost getting caught. That might happen yet, I thought, if we stayed here shivering behind this flower bed. Bien signaled me to follow him, and we ran first to a tree, then to a bench, and then quickly behind a monument commemorating the martyrs of the war. I hoped that the sacred souls of those martyrs would protect these two pitiful people.

After a moment, we noticed that a boy about ten years old was sitting on the bench we had just passed. With a book in his hand and his school bag besides him, he was staring at us with his mouth gaped open. He looked to be an educated kid with an intelligent face, and since it seemed to me that there was some sympathy and compassion in his eyes, I winked at him in a friendly way.

Two red-banner men and a cop were coming close to us. We moved around the monument, keeping out of their sight as they passed, then sighed with relief when they were gone.

"They're over here!" the boy shouted, pointing at the monument.

I was shocked, but I ran immediately after Bien, that silly boy's voice echoing in my head. "They?" What kind of proper education had he had to consider two young men in tight-legged trousers and long-tailed shirts as gangsters or thieves? "They?" His voice had been terrible with disgust.

Rushing out of the park, I bumped into a young man who had hair reaching down to his shoulders. He was being chased by a small group of red-banner men. He fell down, and lay still on the pavement. We turned in the direction of the flower shop, but still had enough time to see the red-banner men trip over him and fall in a heap. We cut through the town square, where a group of young soccer players were also quickly grabbing their clothes and running away. Bien led me into a row of ruined houses. We disappeared behind the shattered walls, under the broken concrete ceiling and twisted iron beams.

"This was our town post office—it was destroyed by the bombing in 1968."

Even though we were being chased, Bien hadn't forgotten to play his role as a native welcoming and introducing the beautiful sights of his town to a stranger. We went behind a hidden wall. I was surprised to see several other young men here. Bien happily recognized one of them, a man about 22 years old.

"Brother Thang," he said. "How come you're here too?"

He proudly pointed at me: "This is Giap, my friend who has just come from Hanoi."

"Nice to meet you," Thang said and solemnly shook my hand. "I apologize but I have to leave right now. Please come see me when you have time. Bye." He looked out to see if everything was quiet, then slunk along against the wall and left us. My introduction to Thang had left me feeling really adult.

Here I was, hiding with these grown-up people behind this wall, linked to them by luck and risk.

"Maybe they're gone," one of them said. Since I was feeling so adult, I thought I'd walk out first. But Bien tugged furtively at my shirt, keeping me in my place. The other three walked out, one after the other, passing through an area of individual bomb shelters, overgrown now with thick grass. Suddenly I heard whistles all around us. The ruins, which were totally silent just a moment before, were now swarming with red-banner men.

All three had been captured. One struggled against a red-banner man twisting his arms behind his back.

"I've been determined to capture you at all costs. I missed you two times already today," the red-banner man said. The young man looked over his shoulder angrily, but then let himself be pushed forward. Suddenly he halted, as if he had just remembered something, and whispered into the red-banner man's ear.

"Is that right?" the man said, and glanced towards the wall we were hiding behind. He made a sign to one of his colleagues.

I couldn't believe it. Just minutes ago we had all shared the same situation, waiting together nervously for bad luck to pass us by, holding our breaths and longing for the situation to be over. Apparently not all those who had reached the grown-up status I had been so eager to assume, knew how to behave like proper human beings.

But in any case we weren't going to let them nab us that easily. Bien silently guided me through some broken walls to the other side of the ruins. We passed a row of thatch houses, then found ourselves at the foot of a giant water tower. It had a round tank, held by four sturdy concrete pillars, an a spiral stairwell leading to the top.

"I didn't have the time before to show you this place," Bien said. "Let's go up there."

We looked around to make sure no one could see us, then cautiously climbed the stairs. Bien had fallen back into his role as tour guide. "This tower," he said, "was built at the end of the last century and it's 25 meters high. On the third of October, 1930, the communist fighters hung the hammer and sickle flag from it in support of the Soviet-Nghe Tinh Movement."

We reached the top. I was astonished at the immense landscape. There weren't any obstacles to obstruct our view. I had known some of the town's small streets and narrow alleys. And this afternoon, thanks to the crazy chase, I had gotten to see the park, the town square and the bombed-out post office. Now, at dusk, I had the opportunity to see the entire panorama of the town, as if I were a commander overseeing a battle. Everything was tiny, and as clear to the eye as the palm of your hand. On the other side of the square, a crowd had gathered in front of the precinct office like a swarm of ants, curiously watching what was happening inside. Along the nearby road, more newly caught youths were being brought in. And in the other direction, the chase was continuing. I recollected how when we were standing at the ice cream shop and staring at the "Develop and Color It" studio, I had thought we were the only two guys wearing the new fashions, the only two. Now I was sorry that I hadn't stayed at home as the "General Campaign" rampaged through every small street and alley, every ruined area.

I suddenly remembered the "Dog Campaign," as we kids used to call it, which had been mobilized on our block four years before. At that time we lived on a street near the bank of the Red River. No one knew why so many dogs infested the river banks. So many—yet no one would claim to own any of them, since at that time owning dogs was forbidden. The dogs hid in the bushes, stole chickens and attacked small children. Everybody said they were feral dogs, but no one dared to do anything. People would wonder if in fact the dogs had owners, and worried what those owners would do if they saw someone kill their dogs.

Then there was a rumor that a fox was seen around the block, threatening the lives of the chickens and ducks our housewives depended upon. One Sunday morning all the heads of households brought sticks, shoulder poles, knives and hammers, and began the "fox hunt." In reality, there had been no fox, but they were hungry for dog meat and there were abundant dogs, peeking out of the bushes as if they were making fun of the people. It was a great chance to get some dog meat without worrying about angering their masters, if they had any. But none of us knew who started the rumor that there was a fox, or who started the campaign of chasing after it. It was all silently agreed upon among a group of adults, and we children had an opportunity to shout, run, and jump around freely. With a belt in my hands, I ran madly through the bushes, whipping at any white or yellow shadow passing in front of me. We shouted until we were hoarse, beat at the bushes and plants until they were tattered. The dogs howled madly and ran panicked everywhere around the buildings.

Here and there, groups of people had built bonfires to barbecue the dogs.

I hit a black dog with white spots. It jumped up, its legs waving in the air, fell down, rolled and rushed off towards the river bank. Pff! Someone hit it with an axe, splitting it from ribs to belly. Its bowels and blood poured out, but it kept running until it jumped into the river, its intestines floating and writhing like white snakes on the blood-reddened water.

I shivered. Was it because the memory of that chase hadn't faded from my mine, or was it simply because we were sitting on top of the water tower that I felt chilled? It was quite dark and the ruins below seemed totally deserted. We struggled down from the tower.

We had made an irrevocable mistake. As we made our way over one of the collapsed walls, we heard howls and cries all around us, and black shadows rushed out from their hiding places: the red-banner men had waited patiently to ambush the last two remaining wild grasses. A marathon race ensued among the debris of broken bricks and over the obstacles of trenches. The two of us jumped up on a wall. At its top, the only escape route we could see was through a dark window. I hesitated. How could we know what was behind that window? It could be a deep hole or a pointed iron bar. But Bien passed me and jumped through. I jumped after him, but exactly at that moment the frame came loose from its jamb and fell down on me, pinning my stomach under it. I tried to move, but the two sides of the frame where stuck on something and I couldn't push it away. From out of the darkness, Bien came back and tried his best to free me. Suddenly a red-banner man had grabbed my thrashing legs and held on tightly, he and Bien pulling me between then as if I were a rope in a tug of war.

Finally the others came and removed the frame and then led the last two victims back to their office. A group of children followed in a line behind us, taunting us as if we were two criminals:

> *With hair like the ass of a duck*
> *And trousers tightened too*
> *They save a little cloth*
> *And waste a lot of shampoo*
> *Vit, vit, vit...*

In the precinct office, a group of young men were sitting in a row on a bench, waiting their turn. In the front of the room one young man was having his trousers cut from the bottom up by a scissors-wielding red-banner man. The youth jumped as if someone had thrown hot water on him.

"Stand still," the red-banner man said to him.

"Sir..."

"You're not allowed to speak..."

"You cut my leg?"

"Did I?"

Just then blood ran down to the young man's foot like a red earthworm. But he turned out to be the luckiest one there because he didn't have to take his pants off, and they were only cut along one seam on each side. The rest had to remove their trousers and then the garments were cut up along two lines on each side. Soon it was our turn.

"I protest. You have no right to do this!" I yelled crazily.

"You're not allowed to say anything yet," the red-banner man said.

The calmer he acted, the madder I felt. Why did all these young men have to bow down silently as if all their tongues had been shortened? They were all about five to seven years older than me, but they were abasing themselves as if they were begging for pity from a group of malicious children. I was the youngest one there. But I felt if I didn't scream out, didn't defend myself, it meant that I accepted I was not yet a man. Besides, wasn't I the son of a respected family who used to travel abroad with his parents, who themselves were the acquaintances of well-known people in the Capital?

I poured all my invectives on their heads. As a result, both of us had our limbs held tightly and our trousers taken off. At that point, it was discovered that we were wearing European cut shirts, so those were peeled from us as well. We were left with only underpants and t-shirts on our bodies.

"I protest this brutal activity!"

Shttt! The fourth gash opened on one trouser leg.

"You'll pay for this!"

Shttt! The seventh gash across both flaps.

Shttt! Shttt! The scissors worked across our two firmly held heads.

The red-banner men worked silently, and silently they put our names and addresses into their notebooks, their faces cold as coins.

We didn't dare walk along the street. That evening the electric lights seemed terribly bright. Maybe our Le was still patiently applying colors to photographs, but both of us were worried about her seeing us. Bien led me into an empty alley behind the rows of houses. I felt my face grow hot as I remembered Bien imitating Le's giggle: "Come on; who is longing for me?" Now, almost naked, groping through the debris of ruined houses, I felt greatly ashamed thinking about any female friend seeing me.

Bien walked slowly in front of me. Suddenly he disappeared into a hole. Before I had time to catch myself, I slid down after him. Before I knew it, I found myself lying on my back at the bottom of an old bomb crater next to Bien. Strangely, we didn't sit up but just lay there, two mute boys feeling homeless and exhausted. I looked up bitterly at the narrow sky above the mouth of the crater and suddenly felt angry with Bien:

"What a coward you are. You didn't even dare to open your mouth once."

Bien sighed, but remained silent. After a while, he said:

"You're lucky. You come here from somewhere else, and you'll leave and go back. You don't have to live here. And you have plenty of fancy clothes and will always have more to replace what you've lost..."

The light above the mouth of the crater reflected off the branches of a flamboyant tree. It was almost autumn and summer only remained held in those few flamboyant flowers. A breeze blew overhead, as if the sky and earth were sighing.

*   *   *

After that summer holiday, I returned to Hanoi and began my new school year. Later I went to Germany to finish my degree and stayed on there to complete my PhD. I got married and had a son.

Bien didn't have any of what I had. He finished school, but his father's biography wasn't "clean," and he didn't get good references from his ward leader either, so he couldn't enter university.

Recently, when I went to visit my uncle, I met Bien again. He told me about his failed escapes. The first time, his boat ran into a storm and crashed back onto the shores of our country. Wearing his worker's clothes, Bien infiltrated into a group of miners on their way to work. The second time, he hugged a piece of plank from his sunken boat and floated in the sea for a day before being rescued by a navy patrol boat. He spent a year in prison. Now he survives by working as a contractor. All of his property was gone as a result of those two attempts.

I sat motionless, listening to his stories, and then I heard the sound of someone giggling and calling her friend. I knew no one in this area anymore, but still the sound shocked me and reminded me of that giggle and those words I heard years before: "Come on; who is longing for me?"

Bien sat silently, not shocked, not turning to look, not looking down. Nothing appeared in his eyes. His face was motionless, unmarked by any trace of reminiscence. And then I understood how much he had lost, in his determined attempts to escape from the past...

October, 1988
Translated by Phan Thanh Hao, Regina Abrami
and Wayne Karlin

The Man Who Stood On One Leg

His name was Ananda, and Ananda means satisfaction and bliss.

One morning he went to the director of the factory that stood just outside his village and asked for a million rupees. This sum, he knew, would be large enough to build a great temple with a unique architectural design, the kind of temple that would lure droves of tourists to the village. Until now, tourists had passed by quickly, as if Ananda's village were located in a wasteland. But the young director—he was the same age as Ananda—refused outright. Wasn't India already overburdened with millions of temples, an abundance of gods, and a shortage of everything else? No, he would only donate a small contribution to the village charity fund. And when he said "small," Ananda knew, the young director wasn't simply being modest—he meant really small. Tiny. And as for the temple fund, the answer was "no." And that was that. And now he should leave the office.

Yet Ananda could not go back to the village empty-handed, since he had promised both the village's old notables and Agni, the God of Fire, that if he could not get a million rupees for the village, he would offer himself as a sacrifice and would throw himself onto the burning pyre that waited in the cremation ground near the river.

That evening, the director got into his car and began the short journey back to his house in the village. The road from the factory gate to the highway was about 800 meters long. In the middle of that road, just a short distance from the factory gate, the director suddenly saw a man standing with his left leg drawn up and the entire weight of his body pressing on his right leg. He recognized this as the posture of God Shiva in the cosmic dance performed to shake the universe. The driver braked the car, and he and the director both opened their doors and got out.

"You again!" the director said. "What are you doing here? What do you want?"

"One million rupees."

Ananda's face was full of holiness and mischief. The director wanted to spit at the holiness, but he respected the mischief. He waved his hand, signalling to the driver, and the two men lifted Ananda up and placed him on the side of the road. Ananda kept standing perfectly still on one leg, as silent as a real statue. Only after the car was out of sight did Ananda drop his other leg and quietly go back home.

From that day on, every morning, just before the director's car brought the director to the factory, Ananda went straight to the same place and stood on one leg: sometimes the left, sometimes the right. And every evening, after the car had left, he returned to his home and ate his one spare meal of the day. His late parents had left him his house and a small grocery which was now being taken care of by a friend. The villagers did not really believe Ananda would ever get the money from the director. Watching him standing on one leg day after day, they had come to the conclusion that he was simply practicing his yoga exercises.

Yet in fact the villagers were not so certain about what to believe and what not. Everything was as possible as it was impossible. The director was not a bad man. He was the son of one of the village's Brahmin families, a family whose influence and reputation had spread as far as England, whose wealth had allowed their children a British education. Upon their return to the village, they had built a new factory for the production of certain latex products. In order to demonstrate his concern and good intentions for his native village, the new director had launched a vigorous campaign, during which he meted out to each family a box containing ten condoms—the factory's new product. He stood up on the reviewing stand, mercilessly thrusting his forefinger into one of the things while glibly explaining how to use it to the villagers. The agonies of our people are caused, he said, because the average man only used one condom a month when he should have used eight. A big flock of children was not the cause of good luck and happiness but rather of poverty and catastrophe. At the end of the ceremony which introduced the new product, he loudly chanted a slogan: *Only shoot/ once a week/if you want/a future/that's not bleak./ Only shoot/on one night/if you want/a future/that's really bright.* "Shoot!" all of the village urchins shrieked out, thinking the slogan had something to do with guns and the army. And as soon as the director had left, the villagers completely and instantly forgot what he had said. Instead of cramming their privates into the condoms, they crammed in their breath. Soon hundreds of pure white balloons flew up over the village and burst like firecrackers.

The village remained as poor as it ever was. As unknown as it ever was. Every day, the luxurious tourist buses continued to come one after the other, speeding straight past on their way to other towns. Over there, an ancient city was spread out for ten miles on the crest of some mountains. A little past that was a Queen's palace, a place popular with visitors for the last ten centuries. And every day Ananda still stood on one leg, watching the convoys of tourist buses streaming past him on the highway. Not even glancing at his village of poor launderers, most of whom he could see from where he stood, over by the river, smashing wet clothes against slabs of stone as if they were not washing but trying to smash the rocks to pieces.

Ananda could see everything that happened over by the river. All day, the launderers would talk and complain loudly to each other. All day, the men would try to bend down behind the women whose saris would billow when they stuck their buttocks up and bent down to strike bed sheets against the rocks. And each evening, the bank of the river would be turned into the place of secret rendezvous for the youths of the village. It was on that bank that Ananda saw Asha, once a little girl who his parents had wanted him to marry, walk hand in hand with a young lad. He watched as they crept under a bush, not far from the place where he stood. He listened as the brazen sounds they made came to his ears. Like everybody else, they had come to regard him as an inanimate object, something like a tree stump standing near the river.

There was one creature, however, that didn't think Ananda was an inanimate thing. This was the vulture who perched on the top of a nearby ashok tree. This ominous bird was black, coarse as a turkey, meditative as a sage, and bald as an austere monk. At first the vulture thought that Ananda was dying, and for a long time has been waiting patiently for his death. In the meantime, it snacked on dead mice and snakes, all while waiting for the day it would have a chance to feast on Ananda's body. Probably it counted the days. Probably it was the only one who could remember how many seasons of hungry and thirsty expectation passed with Ananda standing first on one leg, and then on the other.

One afternoon, the sky suddenly turned red. Houses, trees and everything else were instantly shrouded as if by a reddish-brown screen. Then the sand storm struck. Wild gusts of wind blew in clouds of sand from the desert. Sand whirled over the river bank, making a sound like a cascading waterfall, pushing into the eyes and nostrils of those launderers who hadn't the time to find shelter, making them choke and cough and feel as if they were being suffocated. In the factory, a clerk had no sooner finished closing all the doors and windows of the office, when he got an order to call for the director's car.

"But the storm is still raging, sir. It wouldn't abate for at least another half an hour."

"Call the car for me," the director repeated.

The car crawled out of the factory gate, as if wondering itself at the necessity of this unexpected trip. The driver practically let it drift into that wind on its own inertia. Then, suddenly as a wink, he slammed on the brakes and the director was thrust forward. The car had stopped just an inch away from the living statue. Because he couldn't see in front of him, the driver had believed that Ananda had left his usual place to take shelter from the storm. As a natural reaction, he started to get out of the car with the intention of lifting the man bodily and placing him on the side of the road. But the director raised his hand to stop him.

"That's enough."

The car returned to the factory. The director had found out what he wanted to know.

But that encounter in a cruel storm provoked the driver into playing a cruel joke the next day. Alone in the car, he began to drive at top speed straight at the living statue standing in the middle of the road. Surely, he thought, even a genuine god like Shiva would drop his other leg and run away with his head in his hands if he faced such a wildly speeding car. The launderers working by the river all screamed when they saw the unavoidable accident happening right in front of their eyes. A split second before the impact, the driver knew that the man wouldn't run. He lost his nerve and yanked the steering wheel to one side. The car swerved to the side of the road, flew up over several small hills, shuddered mightily, and landed upside down, its wheels spinning madly over its flattened frame.

The driver was pulled out of the wreck like a heap of rags. He survived, but from that day he was crippled. And since then, on every holiday, the villagers would see a man, bent-backed, one-eyed and lame, come out to Ananda and lay some rupees and a plate covered with flowers he had grown himself on the ground before the man standing on one leg. The curious would follow him, and a crowd of them would surround Ananda.

After the accident, the director had a new cutoff built from the highway to the factory. Now the road did not run straight to the place where Ananda stood, and people no longer had to stop, get out of their cars, and lift that obstacle over to the other side of the road several times a day. Ananda understood that the competition with time was really just beginning now. He and the director were both tireless runners.

Very late one night, Ananda was still standing in his usual position, since he had not yet seen the director's car leave the factory. Suddenly he saw the shadow of a girl moving towards him over the ground. When she was nearer, he saw that her face was familiar. But it seemed to have come out of the remote past.

"Is this Asha?" Ananda remembered at last.

"No, I'm not Asha. I'm Gita, Asha's daughter."

Standing before Ananda now was the result of those sneaky acts he'd watched Asha doing. Gita told him that in those days, her mother had not enough money for a dowry, and so had had to remain single and raise her daughter. Now had come Gita's turn. All of her friends by now had one after the other stained a *tilak* (vermilion mark) between the parting of their hair. But she had no dowry either. And moreover, she had to bear her mother's shame.

Gita embraced Ananda, then yanked at his hand and urged him to come home with her, swearing to live with him until Yama, Death, came to take them away.

"How old are you?" Ananda asked and dropped his leg, giving himself a firm position from which to embrace her.

"Sixteen."

Could it be? Ananda had been lost in another world, and hadn't been aware of either time or the changes in heaven and earth.

"Listen, Ananda, go home. Throw the director and his factory into the rubbish bin. To hell with temples. Our village has always been unknown and let it remain unknown forever."

Gita's talk reminded Ananda of what he was doing. He pushed her away lightly and tucked his leg up again.

"No," he said. "I have to wait for the director."

"Oh, he left a long time ago. I saw him before, sitting in the car of one of the foreign experts."

Ananda had missed him.

"No matter; I'll stay here until tomorrow morning and catch him when he comes back."

"Will you stay here until your last breath?"

"No, not until my last breath. Only until I receive one million rupees."

Every night after that, Gita came to Ananda's house when he returned from the river bank. Yet even the harmony that came into his life from living with a woman could not prevent Ananda from going every morning to stand in front of the factory until evening. Gita still hoped he would change. Anyway, she thought, she would bear him a child, and with that, a family would be created.

But Gita's plans proved premature. One day Ananda spotted her among a mob of the launderers, who were marching past him with stamping feet towards the entrance of the factory. Once there, they prostrated themselves on the ground, buried their faces in the dust, tore their hair and wailed. Then they began to scream in rage and to throw anything they could get their hands on at the factory. Then they began to chant whatever came into their mouths. Apparently they had found out that toxic wastes had leaked from the factory into the river, making any woman who drank from it barren. The factory had never received any Certificates of Merit for its condoms from the Committee of Family Planning. But now its toxic waste was surely worth at least two Certificates.

The ensuing lawsuit was contentious and dragged on and on.

Finally, the launderers were each given a meager cash compensation, not even enough for Gita to have a sufficient dowry.

One morning, exhausted after the lengthy appearances he had had to make in court, the director went strolling leisurely along the river. Suddenly a way to resolve the man-standing-on-one-leg case flashed into his mind. He would make a package deal, along with the compensation to the launderers. He went to where Ananda was standing and politely presented his compromise offer.

"Please accept 10,000 rupees. It's an amount equal to the compensation of five barren launderers."

"But I need a hundred times that much to build the temple."

Ants, evacuating their nest because of the rain, were running like a stream of black dots from Ananda's feet to his neck. He stood perfectly still, his eyes fixed on something at a distance in front of him. The director turned in the direction of his gaze to see a naked white heap on top of a small mound.

"What is it?"

"The bones of the vulture. It was waiting for my death. But it has to give up now."

His name is Ananda. Ananda means satisfaction and bliss.

*   *   *

Early in 1990, I had a chance to make a stop over at Khushi village. When the tour guide told the driver to stop, I expected that he was going to introduce me to something significant. Instead I was led to a crowd surrounding what I took to be a snake charmer. But what the tourists were crowding about was a man standing on one leg. It was said that he had been standing there for a long time, and that only recently he had begun to attract the curious gazes of tourists, as the sole wonder of Khushi village. I managed to find a place in front of him, and he asked me from where I came.

"Vietnam?" He repeated, elongating each syllable as if showing the word to his memory. After a while, he asked: "Which Vietnam? North or South?"

"Vietnam has been reunified for fifteen years."

I looked into his eyes as I told him that. They were the eyes of a man not affected by loss or gain in this world, eyes that could not gauge the movement of time.

"Congratulations to you," he said finally.

"Success to you," I said, and left.

About two years later, I passed that village again. In my uneasy sleep, I was dimly aware that the bus had stopped, and of the driver's raised voice.

"Khushi," he called out.

"There's nothing here worth stopping to visit," I said sluggishly, my eyes still half-closed.

"Are you kidding?" my companion asked, his voice incredulous. "Look!"

Startled, I opened my eyes. There, next to the road which ran from the highway to the factory, stood an enormous temple, with a 30-meter high pyramid shaped tower soaring from it.

The temple was supported by 444 beautifully carved marble pillars, no two of which were alike. Since I already knew the story of Ananda, I assumed he had finally succeeded in getting his money out of the director's pockets.

"Was Ananda a member of the temple administrative committee?" I asked.

"Which Ananda?" the young tourist guide asked in return, the immediately recognized the mistake he'd made because of his lack of experience. He'd forgotten to present the story of Ananda to the tourists.

It turned out that one afternoon, after a heavy storm, the director left the factory and saw Ananda, curled up on the ground in the very place where he'd once stood. At first, the director couldn't believe that this wrinkled and frozen body was Ananda. For years, he had seen Ananda standing upright, balanced on one leg.

After that, the director was often seen wandering around the place where Ananda had stood. Sometimes he bent down, as if he was searching for a footprint left on the very spot where Ananda had been. Sometimes he lifted up his own leg, as Ananda had done. Sometimes he just stood silently, looking down at his feet. Then, one day, he suddenly announced he would donate the money to build a temple right in this very place.

At the entrance, instead of the usual idol of Hanuman, the Monkey God, holding his mace to guard the temple, the director had ordered a carving of the God Shiva, dancing to save the universe, one leg lifted up. And now the tourists had a place to stop and take photographs. Now, thanks to this wonder, Khushi village has become well-known. The villagers themselves now had a place to pray. Now those women made barren by the factory's waste had a chance to come and touch the *linga* or phallus of Shiva, and pray to have children. And often now, a one-eyed old man with a bent back walks trembling to the temple, holding in his hands a plate of gaudy yellow marigolds from which emanates an incredibly chilly fragrance.

May, 1992
Translated by Ho Anh Thai and Wayne Karlin

The Barter

While I was studying in India, I had a German classmate with whom I also shared a room in the hostel. In a word, we were roommates.

The first day we met, he introduced himself with these words: "I am Heinrich, from Bavaria, located in the south of Germany."

I told him I had read the work of the German poet Heinrich Heine, his namesake. He shrugged—nowadays, he said, everyone was writing poetry. I abandoned nineteenth century German literature and mentioned Heinrich Boll and Erich Maria Remarque. He looked at me suspiciously, as if I were trying to trap him into admitting some association with criminals wanted by Interpol.

The only time I saw him express any pride in his German background was one evening when he invited me to go with him to the India International Center to see a solo dancer perform the *bharat natyam*. This dance was born in the Hindu temples of Tamil's Nadu state, where the ritual was traditionally performed at festivals by dancers-cum-prostitutes. We found the International Center on Max Muller Road, and Heinrich pointed proudly at the sign. "Max Muller was a German, and a well-known Indologist," he said. "Germany is one of the first countries to have developed Indology."

Perhaps that was the only German achievement he felt significant. In his country, after all, prejudice still existed against

Asians. Even he, a man from a small farm in the south, had once been mimicked for his country bumpkin accent by some prostitutes in a Berlin alley. Heinrich had gone to the capital to look for work, but finding none, his money nearly exhausted, he had taken to sleeping in parks or in the doorways of shops. On one such night, the inspiration to become a scholar of Indology had broken like a light in his mind, sparked by an newspaper notice—a boxed ad, small as a matchbook—offering scholarships to study Hindi and Indology in India. The next day, without eating, Heinrich took a train back home. He had spent all his remaining money on a Teach-Yourself Hindi book, and several books about Indian culture. A year later, he returned to Berlin and went straight to the embassy of India. The dozen or so Hindi sentences he spoke, and his bit of knowledge about Indian culture were enough to help him pass the interview, and the unemployed German graduate student packed his backpack and got ready to go. Before leaving Germany, he was already infatuated with India. After arriving, he was entranced.

I was the one who had to live with his obsession. One day, I called his name, Heinrich, five times, and he didn't reply.

"Don't you hear me?" I asked in English.

He looked blankly at me, as if he were deaf.

"Don't you hear me?" I asked again, switching to Hindi.

"Yes, I do," he said, replying in the same language. "But Heinrich is no more. From now on, there is only Amar Singh."

Our entire hostel of 40 foreign students was abuzz with the news that "Heinrich is no more." In his place was a guy with an Indian name who wore a *kurta*, the loose-fitting Indian tunic. This Indian guy slept in Heinrich's bed, took Heinrich's seat in our class and in the dining hall, and flatly refused to answer if anyone called him Heinrich, or to speak English to anyone. He told me that the week before he had gone on a pilgrimage to Benares, and had dipped into the sacred water of the Ganges to wash everything he had been away. Afterwards, a priest had taken him through the rituals to convert to Hinduism. He had become a Brahmin, the highest caste, with the Hindu sacred thread draped around his torso, from his right shoulder to his left waist.

"The holy thread is embracing you a bit late, isn't it?" I said. "Usually Hindus don't hold the wearing-the-thread ceremony for anyone over fifteen."

"In the eyes of all the gods and this great civilization, I am only an infant."

"I thought children under nine years old aren't allowed to wear the thread. Aren't you being sacrilegious?"

He regarded this as a low remark to which he wouldn't stoop to reply. Nor would he join in the repartee of our group of foreign students, who often preferred speaking English to the language we were studying. "Amar Singh, may I borrow your book?" someone would ask, but then say "Hey, Heinrich, you have a letter at the school office," just to enjoy watching him deny his new identity as he hurried to see who had written to him.

That winter was chilly. By five o'clock in the morning, the temperature outside would fall to two degrees celsius. Our room temperature, after the heater had worked all night, would reach eight degrees. Amar Singh would rise and open the window wide, and the room temperature would instantly be identical to the temperature outside. Then he would sit in a corner and pray. Before him would sit a large plate on which he'd arranged a handful of red powder, rice, and a *ghee*-fueled lamp, the clarified butter burning with a wavering flame. His prayers usually dragged on until after six o'clock. Every day I complained that he was freezing me out and not letting me get enough sleep. Every day, he practiced his Indian-style stoicism by either acting as if he didn't hear anything, or by saying that he didn't feel the cold at all.

Once, at about one o'clock in the morning, I switched on the ceiling fan and turned it to top speed. The fan roared like the rotors of a helicopter.

"Switch it off," he moaned, sticking his head out of the blanket.

"But I don't feel cold at all," I said, mimicking him.

I knew if we continued going tit for tat it would only be a matter of time before we were both found frozen to death in our room. We were two countries in a continuous border conflict, with no peaceful solution in sight. He did not want peace. One crisis would still remain unresolved, and yet another would come up. I no longer even had to wait until five in the morning for our first clash. One morning at four, I was startled out of my sleep by a series of loud thumps coming from the ceiling. My first thought was that another Indianized Westerner was pounding a stick above my head in order to smash my peaceful sleep. This went on for several more mornings until, unable to bear it any longer, I threw off my blanket and rushed up the stairs, determined to catch the faux-Heinrich red-handed. But it turned out to be the genuine article. And he had no stick—just a coconut he was hurling down on the floor in order to smash its shell. He silently gathered the pieces and then took them to our room, to use as part of his morning worship ritual. I said nothing. I had gotten into the habit of saying nothing. Negotiation was useless. I would simply act. I waited until five o'clock in the evening, when I knew Heinrich was accustomed to taking a short nap after class. I went to the upper floor, directly over his head, and thwack, thwack, began jumping up and down, practicing the karate moves that up until then I had only done in the morning, and in the courtyard below.

The skirmish of the top floor and the battle of the room did not end the war; soon it spread into the domain of the intellect. One day by chance I came across a paragraph from a speech by Indira Gandhi which she had given at the Sorbonne in Paris, in 1981. Gleefully, I pushed the words under his eyes:

"Many in the West, alienated by the acquisitive society, have been turning to the East for spiritual light, even as the young in our countries look westwards, dazzled by its glitter. A barter of deceptions, this spiritualism is no more a consumer good than is technology. Each has to be internalized, through a dedicated period of self-discipline: what we in India call *tapas*, yoga, which is essentially a discipline—physical, mental and spiritual control."

Feeling smug, I watched him read. But all he did was shrug, his complacency unruffled. "I practice my yoga regularly," he said.

You can't have a war if one side doesn't deign to fight. Luckily, our student group was about to be split up and sent off on study tours far away from the capital. The time would allow a temporary cease-fire between the two of us, a chance to rest and replenish our weapons. We were to be divided into groups of four, though some groups would have three students. My group would only have two. I was the first. I waited for the dean to read off the name of the second. Of course.

Heinrich and I went to the southern state of Tamil Nadu. We travelled by train, sharing our small compartment with two Indian men. When one of them told the attendant that he was a non-vegetarian and would like a chicken curry, my classmate immediately retorted that since he was sharing a compartment with vegetarians, he must eat vegetarian food. The man stared in surprise at this blond Westerner who was acting more royally than the king. I was all ready to support him by declaring my desire for chicken curry also, thus creating a two/two balance of forces in the compartment. But the man possessed the Indian talent for self-denial. He contented himself with vegetarian dishes until we arrived in Madras where he went his own way and undoubtedly to his own food.

The university in Madras recommended that we visit a certain village about 100 kilometers from the state capital. When we arrived in the morning, we heard that there would be an auction of *devadasi* dancers—the name means "slaves of the gods"—that evening at the temple complex. These were girls who had been dedicated to the goddess Yellamma-Renuka when they were very small, and then trained to be temple dancers, performing at rituals and festivals. Now they had attained puberty and the temple administrative committee was holding an auction sale. The highest bidder would have the right of "first touch" with the girl, and would become her master until he was satiated with her, at which time he could sell her to another man.

The first four girls were each about sixteen years old. After their preliminary dance, a price of 600 rupees per girl was agreed upon, and they were handed over to their new masters, peasants with long snouts and pot bellies, like sewer rats. They hurriedly paid the girls' parents and, pawing the girls, led them to the dancers' private rooms inside the complex.

Now it was the turn of the fifth girl. She stepped up onto the round platform made of black stone and began to dance the *bharat natyam*. Swift as the wind. Forceful as a bellows. Searing as a flame. All of these elements emanated from the movements of a fifteen year old girl. As in a trance, she became Lord Krishna, became the story of his life, from a mischievous little boy to a brave and chivalrous god who "fought the west and conquered the north," as we Vietnamese say. I had seen this dance many times before, performed by professional dancers in New Delhi. But I had never seen it done with such a naive and fresh authenticity.

Her dance teacher, singing and pounding out a beat for the girl's dance on the *tabla* (a pair of small drums), looked like a bitter man. He had been guiding the girl since she was nine years old, had cultivated the rose bush until it budded, and now another, wealthier, man would come along this night and pluck the rose. As another Vietnamese proverb has it, he was angry with the fish, so he hacked at the chopping block. What he hacked were his drums. Without a pause to allow her to rest, he kept singing and pounding, knowing she had to keep whirling as long as he kept up the music. She danced for over an hour without pause, until the chivalrous and kindly Krishna she was portraying had become an exhausted old woman breathing her last breath. It seemed as if once the dance teacher stopped drumming, she would collapse like a body without a soul.

"I'm going to kill that damned guy," I said, and started to rise. Amar Singh pulled me back. Staring at the girl, he ground his teeth with a grating noise. His face was steely.

The satyric sewer rats began to shout their prices. Two hundred! Three hundred! Three hundred and twenty! Three hundred and eighty! The dance teacher was still singing and beating the drums. He would not spare the girl, even though she was staring at him entreatingly.

"Stop!" I yelled and sprang up.

My sudden shout startled the dance teacher into a different tune, his voice going much lower.

The head priest raised his eyes and asked me: "Noble guest, how much do you offer?"

"Five hundred."

Now it was my turn to be startled, for this amount had been roared out by my German friend. The dance teacher's mouth gaped and so was finally silent. The dancer took this as an opportunity to rest. She pressed her palms together in front of her chest and sank to the floor.

The sewer rats shrank back into a corner. They were clearly offended at this arrogant Westerner driving up the price with his wealth. The angry buzz of nationalism filled the air. One of them shouted, "Five hundred and twenty!"

"Six hundred," my friend said, not even condescending to look at him.

"Six hundred and twenty!"

The price climbed slowly. Seven hundred. Seven hundred and twenty. Eight hundred. Eight hundred and twenty. One old goat even muttered, "One thousand rupees," his voice trembling, as if he feared my friend would not go higher. Finally, everyone emptied their pockets for a last bid. Four thousand rupees. God knows what they all would have done with the girl if they won.

"Four thousand and five hundred rupees," said Amar Singh, and the place went silent.

The deal was struck immediately. My friend paid the dancer's parents, who belonged to the lowest untouchable caste, and then paid another one thousand to the temple's administrative committee, including a fee for a ceremony marrying him to the girl.

The next morning, Amar Singh borrowed all my money, three thousand rupees: it was the same amount his new wife would have provided for her parents over half a year if she had continued to work in the temple as a dancer and a prostitute. He spent it on a farewell party for her relatives and neighbors. Everyone honored and congratulated her parents for snaring a

Western groom who didn't need a dowry paid to him. His wife preened in all her new glory. And the unemployed graduate student who had come from a small farm and who used to sleep on the sidewalks and in the parks of Germany, preened in all his glory as well.

Back in New Delhi, Amar Singh borrowed money from his friends to rent a room for 1,500 rupees a month. He borrowed from anyone he could, promising to return the money as soon as he received it from his father.

One day he came to me. "Our room in the hostel (which was free of charge for scholarship students) would cost one thousand rupees a month if we had to pay rent for it," he said. "Now that I'm not living there, you have it to yourself, which means that you should be paying me 500 rupees a month. Six months from now, when our course is over, that would come to three thousand rupees, which is exactly what I borrowed from you. The way I figure it then, we'll be exactly even—neither of us will owe the other anything."

Although he had become an Indian in all ways, even to changing his name, it seemed he was still very German when it came to matters of money. But by now our relationship was much changed. Before we'd left New Delhi, we had been two neighboring countries with an unresolved border dispute between them. Now we had returned as two friendly nations regarding each other from separate continents. Besides, I was grateful that he'd jumped into the auction and probably saved me from a murder charge, since I had been about to kill the dance teacher with a karate chop.

Sometimes Amar Singh came to see me—particularly whenever I published an article in the weekend supplement of the English language newspaper. He would borrow half of the fee I'd earned for the article. He became my most faithful reader and biggest fan, never missing an article I'd written. I suspected that he scoured the newspapers every day, searching for my byline.

One day I dropped by his flat only to find he was out and only his wife was home. Lalitha no longer danced. The sophisticated managers of the noble capital theatre would turn their noses up at a rustic dancer, an illiterate girl with no gimmicks in her performance. Not that Lalitha missed performing. She was living in the capital with her foreign husband, seeing his foreign friends—things she had not dared to dream about before.

"Isn't Amar Singh at home?" I asked her.

"As usual, he's gone to pray. He goes every chance he gets. Pray and worship, worship and pray. Today he's gone to the temple to prepare for the ceremony of Lord Krishna's birthday."

"Aren't you going?"

"Maybe, maybe not. Whatever. Do you want to listen to some music?"

She turned on the cassette. It already had a tape in it. Michael Jackson.

She tugged at my arms to get me up, and started dancing with me. Once, she said, her husband had gone out to practice his yoga and an American guy named Alan had come over and they had had an entire afternoon to enjoy themselves. Another time, her husband had gone on a pilgrimage to Haridwar, and a Japanese guy named Sojama had come over and they'd had a whole night to enjoy themselves. I got the idea and extracted myself from her grip. I wasn't a lame rooster who took his pleasure in the hen-coop of his friend, I said. Besides, I was still afraid of the gods. Lalitha hooted and said I must not have read the *Bhagavad Gita* carefully, or I would remember the story of the Brahmin priest and the prostitute. The priest was extremely irritated at seeing how customers from all over the world would queue up at the prostitute's door. Every day he cursed the loose woman. Then one day after she had prayed at the temple—the prostitute prayed fervently and often—she met the priest at the entrance. He threatened her with hell and with terrible punishments, threatened her so vividly that she fell down dead on the spot.

The prostitute was taken directly to paradise.

The priest was swiftly thrown into hell.

The prostitute was always conscious of her sins and repented. Her soul was always directed towards holiness.

The priest only threatened others. His soul was always directed towards the obscenity of the prostitute and her customers.

Lalitha finished the story and looked at me as if she had just finished a lofty civilizing mission. My God, I thought, she has just started to learn how to read and write, and begun her lessons in English for beginners, but she knew her classics and epics. Moreover, she knew how to apply them to real life.

*   *   *

Before I left India, I went to say goodbye to Amar Singh and Lalitha. As usual, he wasn't at home. He had opened a yoga class for foreigners, though even Indians were attending it as well. By now Lalitha spoke English rather fluently, though she still didn't know how to read and write. She boasted that English was the only language she could use to chat with the neighboring women, who were just breaking into the middle class and resolutely refused to speak Hindi or Tamil or any of the Indian languages. She disclosed that Amar Singh's father was doing well financially now, and had begun to send money to his son— I should claim the debts her husband had heaped up, borrowing from my newspaper article earnings. As I turned to leave, Lalitha stopped me. Take me with you, she said. She was ready to leave India—she hated the dark brown skin of the Indians. She loved my white skin, loved anyone with white skin.

"I'm not white," I said. "I'm yellow."

"Then I love yellow," she said, without hesitation.

October, 1994
Translated by Ho Anh Thai and Wayne Karlin

The Man Who Believed in Fairy Tales

That morning, waking up in the United States, I was frightened to find that I had turned into an American. Both the bathroom and the bedroom mirrors—two severely realistic rectangles that refused to flatter anyone facing them—assaulted my eyes with the face of a guy with blue eyes and an aquiline nose. The image I saw, if decked out with a wide-brimmed hat and frayed leather vest, could pass anywhere for a genuine cowboy.

I began to feel panicked, since I was sure I was really Vietnamese. I had only come here for a six-month training session. Worse luck, today I had planned to display myself before Nu's family. She was Vietnamese-American and loved the home-country Vietnamese qualities she saw in me. When her grandparents and parents and aunts had heard that Nu was in love with the genuine article, they had agreed instantly to the match. Today the whole family would be gathering to view my true Vietnamese characteristics and merits.

After a while, Nu came in. She was more terrified than even I had been to see that her boyfriend had turned into an American. Luckily she still recognized my voice, and was able to further identify me by some particular marks on my body that not everyone knew about. I rebuked her for urging me to eat so much McDonald's fast-food at last night's dinner—my stomach was still bloated with that damn hamburger. She blamed me right back for listening to two entire Michael Jackson albums before falling into the deep sleep that changed my race and nationality. It was useless to keep on that way since soon I would have to meet her entire family. We decided that I should just go ahead with it, even though we only had a fragile ray of hope that they would approve me now.

We met. Nu's father praised me for being an American who had such fluent command of the Hanoi accent. He asked me which teacher I'd had who had taught me the standard Hanoi pronunciation so well. My situation being what it was, I didn't think I could just plough ahead with some unbelievable story. Instead, I just politely asked permission to marry Nu.

Immediately, her paternal grandparents chorused their refusal. No! She would not marry an American. Not her, not any one of their grandchildren. Not the boys such as Bong (Catfish) or Be (Bull-calf), not the girls such as Nu (Flower-Bud) or Na (Custard Apple). No one! Then her aunt jumped headlong into our drama, like a hostile witness summoned before a court. She would not permit Nu to marry me either. She held herself up as an example of such a disgrace—hadn't she soiled her family's name by marrying an American? Hadn't she been called the "American Office Girl" by people in Saigon, when at that time working in an American office meant being a toy for debauched foreign bosses? Having an American husband was really satisfying, she admitted. But the more satisfaction, the more suffering! Take her as an example. Her niece should not be permitted to follow in her footsteps and stain the family's honor.

In my country, in fact, the aunt's dramatic protest would be called being more royal than the king. Nobody in her day had tried to control who she could love. But now that she had enjoyed herself so much, she didn't want to let anyone else have the same enjoyment.

As for Nu's father, he still liked my standard pronunciation. But he patiently explained to me that the Vietnamese community in this city was so small that it had to be kept pure. As an expert in chemistry, he hated impurities, such as his sister's family.

At least that gave me some understandable explanation. But

at the same time, it shattered my intentions to marry Nu, and also my plans to bring her to Hanoi where I could reintroduce her to the ways of her country. My six month term had finished, and I left America with my briefcase and with my bitter memories of love.

Airport customs and security officers have the reputation of being very strict. However, the Americans, afraid of the illegal resident problem, gave no problems to a Vietnamese with an American face, as long as he was cheerfully leaving their territory. On the other side of the ocean, my countrymen, eager in the spirit of friendship to attract American and Western tourists, smoothed my way also. Of course, in both places I did leave a little tip for the customs' officers' coffee and breakfasts.

For a time after I returned, my parents and the rest of my relatives remained half in doubt about my identity, though finally they recognized me. They simply figured that I had undergone cosmetic surgery in order to beautify myself as a blue-eyed, aquiline-nosed, bearded foreigner. Our neighbors all said that it was as if my family had won a bumper prize at the lottery: with only a two bedroom flat for ourselves, we were still managing to extract money from the well-lined pockets of a real foreign tenant.

One day, feeling lonely, I took a stroll around the Lake of the Returned Sword. Such a stroll had become an extremely adventurous affair for me. With every step I took, I was urged to buy a map or get my photo taken. *Hao a iu, Tay ngo? Oan photo? Oan mep? Khong co ban do, di lac thi chet cha may.** All I could do was look at the Guillotine Building, and then over at the Jaws Building.** Suddenly a man approached me, mumbling English words that were generously helped along by his hands, which would surely exhaust themselves if they got into a conversation of any length. He said he was touched to hear his

---

* How are you, foolish Westerner? One photo? One map? Without a map, you'll lose your way and die with your father.

** Two ugly buildings adjacent to the lake. The building of the Hanoi People's Committee looks like a guillotine. And the South Korean-Vietnamese joint-venture building looks like the shark's mouth in the popular movie *Jaws*.

mother tongue spoken by a foreigner who was obviously entranced by the architectural wonders of the capital city. He said his name was Nguyen Toan Thich. Mr. Likes-It-All. He was by profession an architect and delighted to meet me—a man clearly interested in architecture.

Usually, when one of my countrymen meets a foreigner who speaks Vietnamese, he takes the opportunity to talk much more than he usually would, as if he was accumulating compound interest. So it was now. Likes-It-All informed me that he'd obtained a temporary contract, contingent on approval, to design a large private hotel. He had come up with a high-rise that incorporated French architecture. But the daydreaming pigs who made up the jury of experts that had final approval of the project couldn't recognize French architecture even when it stared them in their faces. Was this the French design for a large building, or was it a design for a crematorium that was able to incinerate their entire families? they'd wanted to know.

Likes-It-All pulled me down next to him, onto a stone bench in the park. Greatly agitated, he drew out the design from his bag and showed it to me. Actually, to me, the building, which included Greek style white marble pillars, Gothic arches, and a mosque-like dome, didn't look like a crematorium at all. In its attempt to reunite and reconcile the architecture of all ages and all nations, it would serve perfectly as the international headquarters of the Architects Association.

Likes-It-All asked me to go with him to appear before the jury of experts. I wouldn't need to speak much. The jury wouldn't take the word of any local architect. Only a foreign expert would be able to persuade them.

Then Likes-It-All complained to me that he had three daughters and his wife at home: four emancipated women who treated him like a yellow-skinned slave. Four wild ducks who quacked noisily if he didn't provide the money for their clothes and cosmetics whenever they needed it. If he lost this contract, they would never again allow him to sit huddled in a corner watching the evening football game, with the television, of course, turned to its lowest volume. If he blew this contract, never again would they let him shout joyfully, like a real man, whenever there was a spectacular goal.

I would have left if Likes-It-All had tried to bribe me with a percentage of the contract. But I felt a kinship to this dominated man. He was a lonely man, as lonely as I was, regarded as a foreigner on my own home soil.

The chairman of the jury of experts had a doctoral degree in architecture. After his appointment as the leader of the nation's architects he, by then a graduate in optics as well, had been sent to our fraternal country of Germany for two weeks to defend his thesis, although he didn't know even a word of fraternal German. The chairman shook my hand in a friendly fashion and took me at once to view a bedsheet sized diagram of Likes-It-All's building design. Dear French comrade, he said, but was interrupted by the vice-chairman, who prompted him that France was a capitalist country. Sorry, dear French expert, he corrected himself, and asked me to judge whether what I was looking at was genuine French architecture. I nodded decisively. Yes, French architecture! The vice-chairman began to question me closely. What age did this piece of French architecture belong to? Smoothly, I answered that it was a good example of nineteenth century French architecture, influenced by the architecture of Greece, plus Rome, plus Western Europe, plus Turkey, as would be seen by Mr. Eiffel. My words buzzed into the ears of all of the experts on the jury, and soon they began chorusing, French architecture, right, French architecture!

The design was immediately approved. The formal contract was immediately signed. Another contract naming me as their expert consultant was also drawn up and immediately signed by me.

Afterwards, Likes-It-All brought me to his house for a victory party. The faces of his three daughters and his wife looked at me like warped shovel and hoe blades displayed in a store selling used farm tools. If I were Mr. Likes-It-All I would have suffocated in this polluted environment reeking of the roll-on underarm deodorants the four women used. The mother, the oldest, was also the one with the gaudiest makeup and the boldest clothing style. Her dress had long splits up its seams, right to the most sensitive zones. Her shoes also came as somewhat of a surprise to me. Their toes were like big oranges, twice as big as their heels. It must have been a new fashion from the south of Britain, so unique and modern that no one else had yet had time to imitate it.

Directly, Likes-It-All and his wife, with the three used hoe blades nodding in agreement, said they were willing to have me choose one of them, free of charge, to become a Westerner's wife. It would honor their family, they said, if I agreed, but only of course on the condition that the couple would love each other and behave with each other "like a glass full of water." Did I understand that Vietnamese saying? I did? Then I must really be a corner ghost.* I knew everything. Swiftly and noisily they ate, and gave me permission to marry one of the girls. Swiftly and quietly they disappeared and left me and the oldest daughter sitting together in the room. She told me her name was Champagne Nguyen-thi. I joked insipidly that her younger sisters' names must be Hamburger Nguyen-thi and Sausage Nguyen-thi. Oh, she exclaimed, I really must be the corner ghost! Since the three daughters had been born during the time of centrally-subsidized coupons, their parents had named them so to assuage their craving for Western foods. What did I crave? she wanted to know. Surely I must like a bold and formidable girl such as herself. When she was just fifteen and her boyfriend was sixteen, they both wore white mourning headbands and rocketed around the streets at night on a Win motorcycle with its brakes torn off. Her boyfriend had crashed into a tree and died on the spot, his head smashed open. She had flown through the air for a distance, then jumped up as if nothing had happened. She had dashed back, snatched her boyfriend's gold chain off his neck for a souvenir, and ran away. Now she only wanted to marry a Westerner like me. A kind, gentle Westerner who would help her strive for self-improvement and accumulate good deeds. A Westerner who would take her to his country and teach her to

---

* The guardian ghost that dwells in a corner of the house and knows everything that happens inside.

speak a foreign language. Or at least to accurately sing some songs, such as *Gioten, tuymen, ongxem (Je t'aime, tu m'aime, on s'aime)*. Would I like to come and sing karaoke with her? She was a vet karaoke singer; vet, that was the chic word people in Saigon used.

I was afraid of *karaoke*. I was afraid of the vet. I was very afraid of the formidable girl. I rushed out of the room, intending to flee this place.

It wasn't so easy. Miss Hamburger had barricaded herself in the next room with a tape measure. She was a seamstress. If I didn't like the formidable vet, certainly I would love her, a soft girl who only threaded yarn into a needle.* Her elder sister sauntered in from the first room, as if nothing had happened. No matter, she said, something that fell through a sieve would eventually be picked up and put back into the washbasin—she would regard her sister's husband as her own, so she hadn't really lost anything. Then she disappeared. Miss Thread-Yarn-Into-a-Needle decided she needed to make some trousers for me immediately. She began measuring my buttocks, hemming and hawing and taking her time with those sensitive buttock measurements. Finally, I had to grab her encroaching tape-measure while I still had things I could take with me as I ran for my life.**

I now hoped I would be able to escape through the front door. But as I went into the dimly lit corridor someone suddenly embraced me. It was Mr. Likes-It-All's wife. Since her daughters were defeated, she said, she was determined to win. Otherwise her family's honor would be stained. I decided to confess to her that I wasn't really a Westerner; I was only a domestic brand who had undergone cosmetic surgery when I was abroad. Mrs. Likes-It-All immediately changed her tune, and began calling me big brother and herself little sister. Big brother and little sister had the same tastes, she said. Little sister also loved cosmetic surgery and had had her nose ridge raised like a

---

* From the title of a popular Quan Ho folk song.
** Allusion to a Vietnamese proverb: "In danger, abandon your things rather than abandon your life."

Westerner's. Her fondest dream was to be turned into a Westerner, inch by inch.

Now I saw a way I could change tactics and get rid of this woman. I reversed myself and said that actually I really was a Westerner, and I didn't like Western style beauty that came from a surgeon. A genuine Westerner liked only pure and original beauty—Giao Chi beauty.* Did I really? Mrs. Likes-It-All said doubtfully. Yes, really, I replied firmly. Mercilessly, she at once removed one shoe, peeled off one sock and laid her bare foot in the most brightly-lit part of the corridor. Look, big brother, she said.

Mrs. Likes-It-All's foot explained why the toes of her shoes looked like large oranges. The big toe stuck out from the other four toes at a right angle of 90 degrees. It was the foot of the ancient Giao Chi, who always had to have special shoes made for themselves.

At this point, my only option was to take advantage of her inattention and flee.

I had to flee for a long time. I had to flee from every place. I could not make people believe that I wasn't a Westerner, that I was only a domestic brand, as domestic as all my neighbors, as all the other 70 million people of my country.

One day, towards the end of the year, as I was sitting sullenly at my window, a neighborhood girl passed by. Why aren't you going shopping for your family's new year celebration, Khoa? she asked me. Khoa is my name. But my neighbors had stopped calling me by it. To them, I was Mr. Westerner Tenant. I told the girl that I was a Westerner and so had no reason to prepare for the Tet festival.

The girl shook her head. Maybe the others on the block thought so, but she knew I was Khoa, not a Westerner and not Chinese. She paused. I remember, big brother Khoa, a few years ago, she said, how you would sing while you were waiting in the line to get water from the block's tap tank. She had learned the

---

* Giao Chi—the original inhabitants of the northern part of Vietnam, 4000 years ago.

songs I sang then by heart. And now she had heard Mr. Westerner singing those same songs while he waited to get water:

One morning, I suddenly felt that life was meaningless;
Though someone was nearby, it seemed he was far away...

The voice she had heard certainly was not the voice of a Mr. Westerner. It could only be the voice of big brother Khoa.

I was stunned. I was puzzled. Anxiously, hopefully, I asked the girl if she thought there was a way I could get back to myself. Yes, she said. Perhaps there was. Perhaps one day a fairy would appear who honestly loved me, not because I was a Westerner or for hundreds of other reasons. Only when I met that sincere love would the curse be lifted to me, and I would return to being who I was before. I had not believed in fairy tales for a long time. But now, secretly, I hoped this one would come true. The girl would ask me to stretch my arms out through the window. She would take my hands and tell me to shut my eyes. I would feel her pulse, throbbing from her hands into my veins. Then I would hear my heart beating lightly. Gradually it would beat more strongly. Gradually, it would beat more passionately.

And I would open my eyes and see that I had been returned to myself.

September, 1996
Translated by Ho Anh Thai and Wayne Karlin

Leaving the Valley

As soon as the wet nurse gave the administrative chief the knickers of the Virgin Goddess, both of the women knew that something very important had happened. Several hours later the news reached the Royal palace. And around five PM the Evening News hit its readers' eyes with a huge headline: *Virgin Goddess Has Her Period and Ends Her Era.*

The people of the capital were relieved to finally get this long-overdue news. After all, wasn't the Virgin Goddess fourteen years old already? That was an advanced age for a girl to begin her menses here, in this country where girls sometimes give birth to their first child when they're eleven. In fact, because of that, the elaborate search for a new living Goddess had already been carried out, and a candidate had been selected. She'd been only three years old at the time and she'd been waiting now for over two years for her turn to become a Goddess.

The ex-Goddess, now considered filthy and unsanctified, was immediately removed from her palace. From now on she would be called by her birth name, Sabana.

There had been other signs before she'd begun to menstruate.

Over the last several days Sabana had been displaying unusual symptoms. During the procession marking the welcoming of the monsoon, the king and the royal family and the Virgin Goddess were driven all through the city, to be applauded and admired by the people. Suddenly, the Virgin Goddess had burst into tears. It was an inauspicious omen. Then the Goddess had insisted on being brought a can of Coca-Cola from a shop by the road. Another inauspicious omen. While the king and the whole royal family often consumed imported goods, for the Virgin Goddess to do so was considered profane. It didn't matter that the Goddess had been drawn endlessly through streets burning in the sun and stinking with the foul odors of the crowd, that she'd been assailed with screams and shouts loud enough to drive her insane. No matter that the Goddess felt a little bit feverish and had to lie down with fatigue. No matter that it had only been when her wet nurse helped her sip a little of that damned gaseous drink that she had been able to sit up torpidly in her carriage.

All that week the Goddess had burned with fever and remained listless as a wet reed. Meanwhile everyone bustled around the palace preparing for the coronation of the new Goddess, for, since the Virgin Goddess is supernatural, she can only remain Goddess as long as she doesn't bleed. In the time before Sabana's reign, one Virgin Goddess had been deposed when she was six years old because she'd scratched her arm with a nail while she was running though the palace. Another former Goddess had lost a tooth at eight years of age and also bled.

Sabana had ruled as the Living Goddess longer than all of them. She'd made it to the age of puberty.

And she'd begun her reign quite early, when she was just four years old. She had been discovered at the other end of the valley, a pretty girl with no infirmity or disease, no marks or scars; a girl who never cried. The capital of the kingdom lies at the center of a wok-shaped valley, surrounded by a rampart of mountains. Most of the population of the kingdom spend their lives in that valley; they never climb the mountains to see the world outside, and so their Gods and Goddesses as well must come from within the confines of the valley. Twenty girls were found during that first extended search. For first trial, the children, aged three to seven years old, were put one at a time into a room. It was midnight. The room's darkness was illuminated only by one flickering candle. It was humid. Stuffy. The girl was alone. She'd take one step forward and then trip over something bulky and hairy. She'd look down and see a freshly severed buffalo head, bloody, wide-eyed and glowering. Then she'd look around and see other animal heads: the heads of buffaloes, goats and sheep, scattered all around the room, sitting in slimy, slippery pools of blood.

Some girls would faint.

Some girls would scream and cry, run in utter confusion, slip, fall, scratch and tear at their hair like madwomen.

Most of them shrieked out for their mommies.

That was enough to eliminate them. Finally, all that were left were the four bravest girls. And Sabana even sat on a buffalo head and pressed her legs to it, as if she were riding a rocking horse.

Then came round two.

Again, one by one, each girl was pushed into a room, and told to select the most beautiful dress in it. The room was dim and reeked of ancient caked dust.

Each of the three other girls picked a brand new sari.

Then came Sabana's turn. In she went, then came lumbering out with a faded and dusty cloak in her hands. She had liked its threadbare, frayed embroidery. In fact, the cloak she'd picked had belonged to Daneju, the first incarnation of the Virgin Goddess. It had been borrowed, after a suitable ritual, from the temple of Daneju, then mixed in with the scores of dresses placed in the room.

The administrative chief, the wet nurse, the entire managing committee and all the servants simultaneously prostrated themselves.

A shower of flowers poured down upon Sabana. The Virgin Goddess had been found.

Sabana had ruled in the Palace of the Living Goddess for ten long years.

*   *   *

By now the ousted Goddesses' parents were no longer alive. One of her brothers was still living in their home village, but he had never taken care of his sister, only continuously petitioned the administrative chief for help in supporting his four small siblings. The wet nurse was unable to accompany Sabana back to her home. During her life time she had already cared for nine other Living Goddesses. Now she was busy with the new Virgin Goddess.

However, one of the middle-aged ladies-in-waiting was ordered to return Sabana to her village. She took the girl to the bus station. Sabana's clothing, possessions and her precious gifts had already been sent ahead, and the child only had one small bag to carry. Instructing Sabana to stand next to the bus stop and hold onto her bag carefully, the lady-in-waiting went to look for the ticket booth.

"Come on, the bus is leaving!" a passenger shouted to Sabana.

Several hands extended through the open door as the bus began to pull away. Sabana quickly stretched out her hand and was pulled inside.

Now, after ten years, Sabana was travelling by bus again. As the Living Goddess she had only been permitted to ride in litters, palanquins or horse-drawn carriages. Only a deposed Goddess could ride in a motor vehicle. Sabana found herself sitting next to an enormous woman whose broad, flat face was densely dotted with moles that looked like black beans.

In fact the woman was a procuress of prostitutes—with one glance she could tell that Sabana would be easy prey.

"Where are you going?" she asked softly. "Choti village? Great, I'm going there too. You can travel with me."

But this bus was not going to Choti village. It would traverse the entire valley and then go on to India. The procuress, having netted three victims, was returning home. She'd gone to a village where she'd conned the people into believing her honeyed words about coming to recruit workers for an Indian textile factory. The villagers had been overjoyed and not only entrusted the three girls to her care, but had asked her to come back with more jobs for other girls. Now the three girls searching for the promised land were sitting in the seats in front of her. She'd sell all three to a brothel over on the other side of the border, get five thousand for each one. She was sure she could get another five thousand for Sabana and didn't hesitate to spend the 80 rupees for the girl's ticket when the conductor came around.

After half a day on the road, the bus was stopped at the border checkpoint. The procuress gathered up her four girls and told them to follow her. She grinned flirtatiously at the policemen. The four "nieces" and their "aunty" had just passed the checkpoint and started reboarding the bus when a tall, stalwart looking man rushed over to them.

"Hey you—procuress!"

The young man grabbed her hand and pulled so strongly that she nearly fell on her back.

She recognized the man. Trying to keep calm, she pulled as hard as she could to get out of his grip and then began running to the bus. As he caught up to her, she tried to shout imprecations at him. But the young man covered her mouth with his big hand and, ignoring her frantic struggling, hoisted her over his shoulder and headed straight back to the checkpoint. Once there, he dropped her like a bomb onto a bench, then began to explain what had happened.

Just last month, this procuress had slinked into his village —his name was Govinda and his village was located beyond the valley. The woman had tried her line there about recruiting girls for factory jobs in India, but the villagers had seen through her. They'd trussed her up and had every intention of stoning her to death. In Govinda's village, such a sin as hers could also be punished by having her head cut off. It was Govinda who asked the others to have mercy on her and let her go. But it seemed her nature hadn't changed.

The procuress screamed loudly. Govinda covered her mouth again and lifted her back onto his shoulder. Just in front of the border post was a mud puddle. He flung that heap of flesh down into it. The procuress struggled and thrashed in the slimy, urine-stinking puddle. Laughter rippled through the crowd of people watching her.

The other three girls knew how to return to their village,

and were taken back to the bus station. But Sabana just stood there, looking around in confusion.

"Why don't you go with them?" Govinda asked.

"I need to go to Choti village."

"Oh, then you have to go in the opposite direction. What you'll have to do is return to the capital and get a bus to your village from there."

Since Govinda was also travelling in that direction, he decided that he would accompany her, place her on the right bus, and then go on his way.

As they drew close to the capital, they noticed that the road was becoming more and more crowded with lorries. From where could so many vehicles have come? All of them were filled with people, waving all kinds of colorful flags, brandishing banners and placards, shouting and chanting and waving as if they were going to a festival.

"There's going to be a big demonstration," Govinda explained. "It's no concern of mine. But stay close—I'm afraid you may be crushed in the crowd."

By the time it reached the city, the bus could no longer advance another inch. When they arrived at the central square, the passengers disembarked and tried to worm their way through the human sea. Govinda, holding Sabana tightly, elbowed his way across the square. Once they cleared the center, they would decide what to do next.

Suddenly someone fired several rounds into the air.

The human sea swelled, overflowed and burst out of one corner of the square. Flags, banners and placards began to fall and people shoved each other aside as they tried to flee. They trampled on the flags and banners and upon the fallen people in their panic to get to the side of the square not blocked off by the walls of police.

Sabana was torn from Govinda's hand and whirled off in a stream of running people. Her handbag had vanished. So had Govinda. And in a few seconds, so had most of the human sea. She was being borne along by about a score of people, running rapidly at a formation of policemen directly in their path. The policemen were armed with truncheons, shield and cane poles. But they also had guns.

For a second the people stopped and stood transfixed. But then, gathering their courage, they rushed headlong at the line of policemen, like eggs hurling themselves against stones. Sabana was struck on the shoulder by a truncheon. As she tried to compose herself, she found that she was being dragged along the road, then lifted up and thrown into a van. The door banged shut after her and the van shot off like lightning. A short while later, she was pushed into a pitch-dark room.

More accurately, she'd been pushed into one of a long row of makeshift jail cells, each stuffed with at least 50 people, the men separated from the women. She was thrust down in the midst of the last group of arrested demonstrators. No sooner did she manage to get to her feet then she was grabbed by one of the women.

"Are you Right Wing or Left Wing?" the woman demanded.

"What's that?" Sabana asked in dismay.

Immediately, a group of women who'd been sitting in one corner leapt up and screamed, "Down with the Right Wing!" Just as quickly, another group sprang up and yelled, "Down with the Left Wing!"

"But I'm neither Right Wing nor Left Wing," Sabana cried.

"Then she must belong to our Liberty Alliance!" a third group shouted.

"Then she must belong to our People's Front!" a fourth group chimed in.

"Down with the Liberty Alliance! Down with the People's Front!" the other two groups chanted.

Cornered, Sabana yelled what she had yelled many times before in the Palace of the Living Goddess when she wanted to get her way.

"I am the Virgin Goddess!"

Although the women were illiterate, they had all seen the public portraits of the Virgin Goddess. For a second everyone stopped dead. Then they all burst into a shout at once:

"Down with the Virgin Goddess. The revolution is opposed to kings and gods!"

They pushed in, attacking Sabana as she cried and struggled. One group punched. Another slapped. Another twisted her arms, tore her hair, pushed her down. Then they chanted slogans and fought with each other, raining blows on each other until they were exhausted. They fell down, bleeding, their hair torn, their clothing pulled ragged.

As a matter of fact, the women in the cell didn't belong to any political group.

When the demonstration had been called, the organizers sent lorries decorated with flags and banners that said "Support the Right Wing" to one village. Everybody there piled into the lorries and off they went. Meanwhile different organizers, with lorries that carried banners saying "Support the People's Front" came to another village, and those villagers also piled into the lorries and were driven to the demonstration. Each villager was given a free box lunch, box dinner and twenty rupees. It was a great way to get a trip to the capital.

That night, the arguments and blows between the women prisoners broke out again as soon as everyone was settled in. Sabana hid in a corner and watched them as they fought and chanted slogans as if the revolution mounted by their leaders, the riot outside, depended upon their energy.

The police were used to this kind of demonstration. Early in the morning, they crammed all the detained demonstrators into police vans, drove them a little ways out of the city and threw them out. If they knew how to come to a demonstration, the police reasoned, they should also know how to find their way home.

Finally, after everyone had dispersed, Sabana was left sitting hopelessly by the side of the road, unsure how she would get back to the capital.

A shadow moved over her.

"Sabana! I must have passed this place dozens of times this morning, searching for you."

It was Govinda! Her savior Govinda!

He had been arrested also and held in the men's area of the same makeshift cellblock. As with Sabana, the other prisoners had demanded to know to which wing or party he belonged, but at last they left him alone and fought against each other. He was too large and stalwart a man to be bullied the way Sabana had been bullied.

"I'm going to take you to your village now," he said. "We can't be sure whether or not another revolution will break out."

As they sat together on the bus travelling to the eastern side of the valley, Sabana thought she should reveal that she was really the Virgin Goddess to Govinda.

"I don't know about any Virgin Goddess," Govinda said. "In my homeland, we don't worship any gods."

"So you're not afraid of me?"

"Why on earth would I be afraid of you? I'm ten years older, and much taller and stronger. And besides, you're so lovely."

Finally they arrived at Sabana's house. It was the most expensive in the village, a gaudy affair located right at the village's entrance. Sanjay, Sabana's eldest brother, was now 25. But no trace remained in him of the innocent boy Sabana had left. For the past ten years, with help from the benefits he'd received as the brother of the Living Goddess, he'd put his energy to building a house, getting married, and supporting his four younger siblings. But his fortune had turned him into someone who constantly worried about losing what he'd gained. When he saw his sister enter, he stared at her as if Yama, the Goddess of Death, in the guise of Sabana, had come into his house.

"Did anyone met you on the way or see you come here?" he stammered, glancing around nervously.

"No one," answered Govinda for Sabana.

Sanjay quickly shrouded Sabana's face in the folds of her own sari and pushed her back outside. "Come with me now," he said. "If you stay here you'll die an old spinster. The entire village knows you were the Virgin Goddess and now no village boy will dare take you as his wife."

People believed that the Living Goddesses' husband would die prematurely and suddenly.

When they'd gotten far away from the village, Sanjay paused and said: "When I received the bags and boxes of your things that they sent, and then the news that you would be coming home, I asked a woman in a neighboring village to take you with her to India. She promised to find you a job there in a textile factory. And besides the job, she'll also find you a husband."

Govinda was furious. "No! I know the kind of woman you mean, and I know the kind of job she'll arrange for Sabana."

They told him about the procuress. Sanjay stood frozen, staring at them, not knowing what to do now with this damned sister who'd suddenly showed up in his life.

"When I brought Sabana back to you," said Govinda, "I didn't think of it as something that would bring you suffering!"

All three of them remained silent, unsure what to say.

"She came here with me," Govinda said softly, "so therefore let her leave with me."

Sanjay sighed with relief. And tears welled in Sabana's eyes.

"My village is beyond the mountains. Vasant village. Whenever you want, you can come there to fetch Sabana."

Sabana cried out and leaned her head on Govinda's chest.

"Aren't you afraid of me because I used to be the Virgin Goddess?"

"I've already told you—in my village there are no gods of which to be frightened."

*   *   *

I met that couple long after they had become husband and wife. Only one mountain range away from them, and just beyond the far slope of the mountains, lay Sabana's native valley. In this wok-shaped valley, surrounded and enclosed by mountains, the people have never seen the horizon. When they look up, all they can see are the dark gray mountains around them. That narrow little valley often erupts in small and large revolutions. That cramped little valley contains small and large brothels. And in that valley, there is always a newly ordained Virgin Goddess to take the place of the goddess who bled. Yet, if you simply leave the valley, cross the rampart of the mountains and go directly to the other side, you will reach a place of fertile fields. And from there you can see the horizon. And there you will see Govinda and Sabana. They work together and love each other.

November, 1994
Translated by Ho Anh Thai and Wayne Karlin

Behind the Red Mist

At three sixteen on that catastrophic afternoon, most of the residents of Building A1 in the Green Meadow Housing Complex were still busy at their jobs in offices, factories and schools. The few people who remained at home were retired folk, a few children who didn't have afternoon classes, and a teacher under treatment for mental exhaustion. Suddenly people felt the entire five story building shift. It was as if from the time it had been erected the building had been sitting quite calmly on the back of a turtle that had turned to marble, and now the turtle had awakened from a sleep of a million years. The right half of the turtle was still stiff from having been marble for so long. But the left half could move, and the limbs on that side were kicking and pushing hard into the tough soil in a rabid effort to surface, to emerge into the sunlight and air of the day. As a result, the building was slipping from the turtle's back and leaning to the left, its canted angle more apparent with each passing moment.

Her head spinning, the mentally exhausted teacher thrust her face deeply into a pillow, thinking her miserable affliction was acting up again. Others felt they were on a pitching deck, with everything on it in danger of sliding off into a corner. Old Mrs. Lam thought, in that wobbly moment, that her body had become one with the massive building, tilting and slipping with it to the left, shaking along with the cracking walls. She shuddered along with the building when she heard the sound of a rupture somewhere to her left, missed a step and felt as though her whole body had fallen to pieces, just like the broken bricks.

Earthquake, she thought, able to conjure up from her memory the shaky sensations of an earthquake she'd experienced some years before. She took one more step towards the main entrance, but where the floor was supposed to be was a void instead, and her right foot slipped into it. She extended her left foot further out, until it touched the tile floor, and at the same moment fell against the wall on her left.

The fact that one side of Building A1 of the Green Meadow Housing Complex had collapsed remained a hot news item for months afterwards, and ignited many disputes about who was to blame for this disaster. But for a person present in the building at the time, such as old Mrs. Lam, the experience was over almost immediately. A mere second later she was aware that she had been thrown against the wall and that the room was tilted to the left. "The black bean pudding I prepared for Tan must have spilled all over the inside of the fridge," she sighed, then pushed herself up to check the refrigerator.

Just at that moment Tan appeared by the door. When he saw her, he went pale. He rushed to grab his grandmother's hands and pull her out into the corridor.

"Hey, where are we going. Let me check the pudding first..."

Tan didn't say a word. Holding her tightly, he led her down the staircase. The old woman felt the 17-year-old's entire body shaking, as though he were not leading her but rather leaning against her to allay his own fear. Grandmother and grandson reached the bottom of the staircase and rushed across a stretch of sand before Tan allowed them to stop so that his grandmother could turn around and look at what had happened to the building.

The old woman had seen much in her life. During the war, she had seen firestorms of bombs. She'd seen young soldiers singing in the morning as she walked past them who were gone in the afternoon, disappeared completely into the craters left by five thousand pound bombs. She had seen tall buildings reduced to rubble by those same American bombs. But to see the building in which she had lived for over twenty years, from the time it had been dedicated, suddenly falling down on one side, was something she couldn't imagine and couldn't look at now.

"Stand right here, Grandma," Tan said. "Don't go near there."

He let her go and started back towards the building. Now it was her turn to grab his arm. She saw that the poor boy was still shaking. Why in the world would he want to go back inside? Don't be a fool, she wanted to say to him: people can always create material wealth, but if you lose your possessions and save your life, you're still lucky, my child. But, as Tan yanked his arm free and ran off, she held her words. She understood she was mistaken about him. No, kids these days were pragmatic and knowledgeable; they understood these things even more than she. Tan was a good kid. When he had returned from school and saw his building shaking and falling apart, the first thing he thought about was rescuing his grandmother, pulling her out of harm's way—not about retrieving any property. He wouldn't be so foolish as to return to the building now because of material things.

The building hadn't collapsed completely; only one side had caved in. Luckily, no one was at home in the apartments on the left side, where the walls and ceilings had pancaked. The people in the other apartments had helped each other get away. But Tan wasn't able to put his mind at ease. He remembered Linh, the little boy who could solve the Rubic cube in a few minutes. Tan rushed to a wall that had cracked just enough for a person to slip through and looked inside. Little Linh's apartment seemed empty. The frame of the main door had twisted under pressure, and a crack had appeared in its green paint. The lock was still trembling as if it were quaking with panic.

Once he was satisfied that little Linh was safe, Tan ran toward the back of the building, where some tenants had cultivated a little patch of soil into a few scraggly rows of spinach. Later, when people remembered the incident, they would say that the fact Tan had run to the rear of the building was an act provoked by his karma. He had been totally satisfied by then that all the collapsed apartments were empty, and there was no reason to rush back into what was still a very dangerous area. But he felt drawn forward, some sense of anticipation pulsing through his veins and brain as he approached those rows of spinach plants still wet from last night's rain.

Suddenly his feet caught in the tendrils of spinach. His flip-flop remained stuck in the jumble of leaves while his foot kept travelling forward, until it came in contact with a wire. It was the live end of an electric cable that had been cut and fallen when the left side of the building toppled.

A cold metallic arrow pierced his heart. All the energy in his body seemed to pour upwards into a final, painful scream. His right foot, which formed the contact point with the high intensity electrical current, twisted in violent convulsions. Tan crumpled, and rolled once, getting clear of the cable. For a split second, he felt his body reviving, bit by bit, as if anticipating a torrent of life. But then the cable jumped, danced in the air, and fell again, its end hitting his bare arm. His half-dead body jerked several times, but he didn't have enough strength left now to even utter a scream. He felt engulfed as in a flow of lava spewing down over a city, turning the sky bright red and everything under it shaking in the intensity of the heat. In the wake of the burning pain, he felt himself turn to ash, float lightly away.

His body spasmed again, jerked away from the cable, and fell motionless on the ground.

In the emergency room, the doctors shook their heads and looked at each other, then turned apprehensively to Tan's grandmother, who had come with him in the ambulance. The old woman said nothing, asked nothing, answered nothing, nor did she understand anything that was said to her. Her face unnaturally calm, she sat motionless on a stone bench in the hospital courtyard, as if waiting for her grandson to come home and eat a bowl of the pudding she'd made.

On that terrible afternoon, the emergency room was crowded with patients. The attendants hastily carried Tan off to the morgue, where his body would wait for his relatives to come and complete the procedures needed to claim the dead. Some time after five o'clock, Tan's parents heard the shattering news and rushed to the hospital. The old woman was still sitting on the stone bench, her face calm, as if devoid of life. Oh dear, she was thinking, the pudding must surely have spilled all over the shelves in the refrigerator. She would have to soak it all up with a rag, then clean the inside thoroughly, and more than once, to get rid of that smell. And what room was her grandson in? Were people trying to save him? Just this morning, before he'd put his tins of food into his bag with his books, he'd said to her: "It's Tuesday—I have ballroom dancing class tonight. Could you please save a cup of black bean pudding for me before I go to class, Grandma?" And she'd said: "Let me cook you an early meal. You'll be dancing until past ten o'clock; you'll get real hungry." He'd laughed at her: "How many times have I told you— it's not healthy to eat when you dance." She had just learned about the boy's dancing class last month. He'd held a strip of film before her eyes: "Look, grandma; I'm holding a woman's hip." She'd put on her glasses, but saw only two strange, tiny figures, their hair all white. "Can you see? That's me; that's my hand, and right here is a woman's hip." She'd taken off her glasses and shook her head: "I can't see what's what. And how awkward, to call your girl friend 'a woman.'" A few days later, he'd brought home a photo and showed it to the whole family. Her daughter-in-law had whispered nervously: "This is the end; our little Tan's in love." "Why should love be the end?" she'd replied. "You and your husband fell in love, didn't you? Why make a fuss?" Tan's mother said nothing, but for the next few days, she went to the school to secretly check out the girl dancing with her son. In the end, she breathed a sigh of relief and said to Grandma: "There's no love story here, mother. That girl is too ugly for Tan to be in love with her." When Tan heard about it, he'd smiled: "I needed a dancing partner, not a girlfriend," he'd said. Then, when they were alone, he told his grandmother everything. His whole class, it seemed, had been swept up in the dancing fad that young people called "birds flying away in pairs." And since this girl was the ugliest in class, no boy would ask her to be his partner. Many of the girls had hoped Tan would ask them to the dance class, but her Tan had gone to this unfortunate girl. Before their first practice session, he'd told grandma, he'd set a strict rule: "Dancing only; absolutely no love." Of course the girl had agreed.

What else could she do? Without Tan, she would have ended up moping around alone at home while everyone else was out having fun.

As grandmother's thoughts drifted from one incident to another, part of her mind whispered to her about a catastrophe and draped her reminiscences with a pain she couldn't bear. At that moment of pain, feeling dizzy, she was faintly aware that Tan's mother was helping her walk, and in fact was shaking and squeezing her just as Tan had done that afternoon as he'd led her away from the building. Where's Little Tan, my grandson? her mind asked. Is that him, under the metal grill on that table, where countless corpses had lain before, waiting to be claimed by relatives? She could see Little Tan's father bowing his head as he stood next to several people in white tunics.

The doctor looked at the old woman, then looked down. Although he normally was able to keep his composure in such situations, he suddenly shuddered as he saw Tan's face. Something wasn't right. He leaned over and put his ear against the victim's chest as his fingers quickly searched Tan's wrist for a pulse. He listened closely, trying to discern in the silence a faint sound, a movement so slight it seemed not to exist. No, he wasn't mistaken. Something was starting to move inside the chest, and he could feel a feeble coursing of blood in the veins.

"He's alive again!" The doctor shot up, unable to suppress a shout. "Quickly, get him back to intensive care!"

*   *   *

Tan kept falling, just like he had once in a nightmare in which he'd fallen from the top floor of the Thang Long Hotel and had woken up just before he'd hit the ground, so happy he could hardly contain himself. But this time he kept falling and falling and he couldn't wake up. Was he plummeting to the center of the earth? He'd read once in a physics books that if people could dig a tunnel straight down from the surface of the earth, cross the center, and emerge through the opposite surface, then an object falling freely through the tunnel would automatically fall back once it reached the other side of the earth. He was free-falling now through that tunnel that bisected the diameter of the earth. The closer to the center of the earth he fell, the higher the temperature; his whole body felt heated as if the blood inside his veins was water boiling at a hundred degrees Celsius, spreading the burning heat to each centimeter of his flesh, each red hot cell in his bones.

Then, magically, Tan was falling in a deep, muddy well. He couldn't see anything in the black void, could only feel his hands reaching out to clutch at the sides. Sometimes he would grab at a clump of dried grass, or a broken brick, or a bent iron rod. He fell blindly through the dark with only one thought running through his mind: either be with the living above the ground, or be forever dead in this bottomless hole. But his sharpest, most dominating instinct was the desire to survive.

He was suddenly at the top of the well, no longer falling. His right trouser leg was soaked and muddy and his foot so stiff he could barely lift it up. It felt like the leg of a clay soldier that had been dropped into water and immediately lost its shape, twisting until it no longer resembled anything. Tan stretched out both of his legs, and held them still for a moment, to relieve the stiffness. Everything around him was quiet and sunk into darkness, with only a few spots here and there lit up. Up ahead were the faint shapes of several structures. Could this be the Green Meadow Housing Complex? But where were the rest of the buildings? Could they all have collapsed like Building A1?

He sat for a while, letting his eyes adjust to the darkness. Slowly he began to distinguish his surroundings. Far away, directly in front of him, was indeed his building, A1, though it seemed somehow different. But that would be natural, wouldn't it, after he'd fallen many times back and forth along the diameter of the earth? Strong winds blew through the deserted field of wild grass. The sharp smell of the grass made Tan believe even more in the reality of the life that surrounded him. Until now, he'd had nothing in his nostrils but the odor of muddy soil, chemicals and ether. He reached out, grabbed a clump of grass, and struggled to stand up. As he did, he remembered his grandmother explaining the way Green Meadow had been named. When the convoys of trucks carrying soil, cement, sand and whitewash had arrived to erect the first building, the A1, this area was nothing but empty fields, filled with frogs and toads arguing with each other all day and all night. Even after they were all given new names, the developments were still called by their old, quaint ones: Red Dirt Path Public Housing Complex, Green Meadow Public Housing Complex. The A1 Building was constructed upon a waterlogged marsh, and since its construction was substandard, it had immediately started sinking and tilting to an alarming angle. But with a housing shortage, people didn't have a choice. They complained, but no one moved away. Where would they go? In a few years, the building had sunk further, the cracks in the walls widened, and the agency in charge of urban construction had to assemble a workforce to reinforce the foundation with concrete, fill in the cracks, and cover the walls with a bright new coat of whitewash. The residents remained fearful though, and from time to time would express themselves by writing letters asking the authorities for help.

Tan started walking, placing his right foot down gingerly. Every step he took shot a sharp pain up right from the sole of his foot to his heart. The pain reverberated in his ears and blurred his vision, so that the darkness around him took on a jaundiced and sickening feel.

"Who's there? Stop!" A girl's voice rang out.

Tan cried out in pain, but continued his progress, stumbling but determined not to stop. To stop meant admitting that he could not control his feet: that his right foot was damaged.

The same voice spoke, this time louder:

"Lie down!"

Tan was startled; he didn't understand what was happening. Abruptly, someone shoved him hard and he fell down on the grass. A ball of fire erupted nearby, followed by a series of terrifying explosions. The earth seemed to burst open and disintegrate into dust. Tan lay absolutely still on his stomach, until he saw a hand reaching down to help him up.

"How careless you are!" the girl's voice scolded. "Bombs going off everywhere and you just go strolling along as if nothing's happening."

The girl's hand was withdrawn immediately when its owner saw the boy's bright eyes. Tan sat up. In the flashes of light he saw a girl's face, partially hidden behind strands of long hair. It was the person who had called to him, pushed him down and then stretched out next to him when the explosions erupted. But the awkwardness he felt was overcome by his shock and curiosity. Why were there bombings in the center of the capital? The days and nights of B-52 bombing were things from the past, fifteen years before when he had only been two years old. If not for the articles he'd read, the photographs and films he'd seen, he couldn't even begin to imagine how it had been. Of course there had been the border war, eight years ago, but that had been confined to the northernmost provinces. What war was happening now? Hadn't the experts proven that World War Three was an impossibility?

"Who is bombing us?" he asked, looking up in confusion and noticing, for the first time, a golden moon in the sky.

The girl had pulled back her hair and fastened it with a metal hair pin. She scrutinized him:

"Are you all right? Do you feel sick? Do you want me to help you?"

Clearly she had heard his question. But she didn't seem to understand it.

"No, thanks. My house isn't very far."

Tan struggled to stand up. His wobbly steps startled her.

"You've hurt your leg!"

Forgetting her shyness, the girl reached forward, put her hands on Tan's muddy leg and searched frantically for a wound.

"There's nothing wrong with me." Tan waved her away, then felt he had been a bit harsh. He softened his voice, hoping for a bit of sympathy.

"I'm not sure why my leg is so stiff today."

The girl stopped what she was doing and blushed, suddenly aware again that she was a young woman and this was a young man. She turned slightly from him and discretely fastened a shirt button that had come undone some time before.

"Are you sure you're not wounded?"

"Wounded?" What a strange girl, Tan thought. She spoke as if it had been a real bombing attack, now, in 1987! He smiled and shook his head, to reassure her, then started walking again.

"You can't walk home alone with your leg like that," the girl cried out and came running after him. She was still hesitant, but couldn't simply leave a person in need without help. She walked up boldly to Tan, then gently took his arm and draped it over her shoulder, making sure to hold his hand in both hers, so she wouldn't have to worry about it falling down to her back or breasts, either inadvertently or deliberately. This way she could help this shaky boy while feeling secure about herself.

Tan gave up and leaned on the girl's shoulder. He was only wearing a thin shirt and, pressed against her body, he felt distinctly warmer. And there was A1! He recognized the path leading to the staircase, even though the surroundings seemed barren and unfamiliar. Where were the scraggly rows of spinach, the bushes that divided the ground-floor apartments? In front of the entrance, he saw a large panel with words on it painted in a deep red. Under the opaque light of the winter moon, Tan could read the neat lines:

> *The war can go on for five, ten, twenty years or even longer. Hanoi, Haiphong, and our cities may be destroyed, but the people of Viet Nam remain fearless. There is nothing more precious than independence and freedom. Upon our victory, our people will rebuild our nation to make it better, more beautiful*
>
> ### President HO CHI MINH

Tan understood vaguely that there was some link between these words and his surroundings, between these words and this moment. But his entire body was feverish, his head was echoing with confused noises, and he could not explain anything to himself. *There is nothing more precious than independence and freedom* was a truth for any age; he could remember several times when his teachers had discussed the sentence in such a way. But today was the first time he had seen it as part of an unaltered paragraph, and he felt he could grasp its meanings in a more concrete context and perhaps understand it more profoundly. "Perhaps" because at the moment Tan could only feel its meaning, without intellectual analysis. But that emotion was strong enough for him to feel somehow displaced in time.

"This is my building," Tan stopped in front of the path to the staircase. "I live in apartment 203. When you have some time, please stop by."

"Apartment 203," the girl repeated cheerfully, gently removing Tan's arm from her shoulders. "Are you a relative of brother Do? No wonder you look kind of familiar. I live over there."

She pointed to a row of nearby houses that Tan didn't recognize; he had grown up seeing two five story buildings in that spot, not the row of houses the girl had just pointed out. But even more surprising was hearing the girl referring to his father as "Brother Do."

The girl walked away so quickly she was almost running. As she was disappearing into the grassy field, Tan suddenly remembered, and called out after her:

"I'm Tan. What's your name?"

"Trinh. I'm Trinh."

*   *   *

Trinh was gone now, and with her withdrawal a sense of something lively and energetic in the atmosphere seemed to have vanished also. Tan felt his body sinking, felt he was melting with fever, then felt icy cold. He leaned against the railing and took labored steps upstairs, and then knocked at the door to apartment 203. No one answered. But the door was unlocked. As soon as he stepped into the familiar atmosphere of his flat, redolent with the scent of the betel nuts his grandmother would often chew, Tan felt at ease. But the furniture and decorations in the house seemed different. The room was simply furnished, with only two beds and a cupboard. On top of the cupboard was an Orionton radio. The Samsung TV was nowhere to be seen, nor was the cassette player. Tan's mind wasn't clear enough to register these changes. The familiar scent of betel nut and the pungent sweaty smell of his father told him he was home. He peeled off his dirty clothes, soaked them in a basin in the bathroom, and threw himself on the double bed, pulling the blanket over his head. He immediately fell into a deep sleep and began dreaming.

A red mist slowly forms over the surface of the river, veiling the scenery. First the islet covered with green stalks of corn, then the areca tree, and the steeple of the cathedral, each fades into the mist and disappears. The mist covers the pristine, flat sandy beach, not yet cruelly disturbed by a footprint in this early morning.

Then comes human voices. Behind the faint curtain of mist are the silhouettes of people coming nearer. One person, two, then a group emerges from the red mist, carrying drills and hoes on their shoulders. The crowd stops on the beach. They point and measure excitedly, then start to dig into the wet sand. The curtain of mist, hovering in a red cloud, drifts in off the river's surface and obscures their shapes...

At about nine o'clock in the evening, a woman pushed through the door and came inside the apartment. This was Mrs. Lam, a supply cadre in the textile factory, coming in late from having to work overtime. Mrs. Lam had poor eyesight and so didn't notice the strange pair of flip-flops at the foot of Do's bed. All she saw was a person asleep under the blanket. Had her son come home so tired from his work that he'd fallen asleep while waiting for his mother to arrive and cook a meal for him? She prepared a betel leaf and chewed on it in order to warm herself up, then quickly took a tray of food to the kitchen. Just as she was stirring the beef into the cabbage, two cold hands covered her eyes.

"Remain quiet: this is the special forces commandos."

The hand immediately released itself, and she heard Do's playful laugh. His nose was red from the cold and he was hopping up and down to keep warm.

"It's so cold in here, Mother. Did you just get home?"

His mother looked at him. She waved a hand towards the bedroom.

"Then who's lying there?" she asked.

She stopped. Both mother and son, surprised, stepped lightly through the kitchen door and leaned over to peek into the bedroom. The person she had thought was Do was rolled up from head to toe in the blanket. At the foot of the bed, Mrs. Lam saw now, was a pair of yellow flip-flops, the color of a chicken's kidney, decorated with black lines. She had never seen a style like that!

"Was he there when you came home?" Do whispered.

"I thought it was you, sleeping," his mother said, lowering her voice also. "I didn't want to wake you up."

"There was an announcement on the radio today that two frogmen from the South were captured near the Hai Ha beach."

He calmly slid out the knife lying next to the bowls; his mother picked up a stick, ready to help her son. At that moment she noticed the laundry basin. There was a set of unfamiliar clothes floating in it. She touched Do and pointed them out to him. His suspicions strengthened.

"Stand by the foot of the bed," he ordered in a low voice.

Quick as a cat, he slipped around to the head of the bed, thinking: look at this guy—he's found himself a nice warm place to hole up. But he saw that the intruder was sleeping with difficulty, his breathing heavy, belabored.

Gripping the knife in his right hand, ready to raise it and bring it down swiftly and precisely, Do gathered a corner of the blanket in his left hand and yanked it away in a sudden swoop. He imagined the sleeping man would bolt up, throw the blanket towards him and jump to avoid the knife, a scene he'd often seen in spy movies. But mother and son froze in shock. The person kept sleeping. He was a young man, Do saw, his features radiating a kind of angelic purity against the pillow. Yet his eyebrows were slightly knit, as if to prove that even if an angel, he was struggling in his sleep with some kind of difficulty. The mother gently set her makeshift club down on the floor and approached the head of the bed, staring in shock.

"He looks exactly like you did a few years ago," she whispered, and her son, suddenly feeling the knife in his hand was totally illogical, walked back to the kitchen and replaced it.

"Hey, young man," the mother gently shook the boy's warm shoulders, "young man, wake up...."

The boy opened his eyes. Even if he wasn't feverish, the mother thought, those eyes would be brilliant. There was a far away look in them, as if he wasn't able to see the objects or people directly in front of him. A moment later, as he looked closer and his eyes focused, he saw a person at once both strange and familiar.

"Oh, Grandmother," the boy cried out in a tired voice.

"No, call me 'aunt'," Do's mother corrected gently.

Call her aunt. No, that would be too strange, for here were his grandmother's lips, with the tiny betel colored cracks in them and half of her left eyebrow, gone white some time in the past. But when did she get that black satin blouse? Why is she dressed so youthfully, so strangely? And why is she telling him to address her as aunt?

"What's your name and where did you come from?"

"But why are you asking me that?" The boy wanted to just sit up and grab hold of her and swing her around once, as he usually did when he came home from school. But his fever-weakened body stayed glued to the bed.

"It's me, Tan," he said. "I live here."

"Tan?" The mother, looking worried, turned to Do. He shook his head, indicating he had no idea either. It would be another three years before this room would welcome a newborn child named Tan at birth, Vu Tan. But at this moment, neither mother nor son knew anyone of that name.

Do approached the head of the bed and stood next to his mother, so that for the first time Tan realized that there was a man in the house also. But who was he? He stared closely. Of course, it was only his father. He had smelled the pungent odor of his sweat, the smell of his skin, since his birth, since he had been held in those arms. It was his father; he knew it, even if the tired lines of his 43 years were not yet etched on his face from spending half his life taking all the worries of his family onto himself. But at this moment, his face exuded enthusiasm and love. For Tan it was as if a miracle had taken place that had given back their youth to both his grandmother and his father.

"Dad!" Tan called out, almost moaning. He felt a need to be childish, a sick boy.

"My name is Do," the man felt uneasy at the way Tan addressed him. "Do we know each other? You can call me elder brother, if you wish."

Sure, it would be awkward to call someone five or six years older than myself "Dad," even though he is my father, Tan thought sleepily, and then he no longer thought anything at all. A red mist drifted over him, drawing across his face, concealing the others in the room. He fell asleep.

Do only woke him up when he brought the evening meal to the table. His mother gave Tan two cold tablets and a glass of warm water. She spoke apprehensively:

"Take these pills, then come eat. The weather these days is making a lot of people sick."

Tan slipped on the warm clothing Do handed to him and moved slowly to the dining table, feeling a sense of familiarity when he saw his family's favorite dishes. Perhaps, he thought, people change more with time than the dishes they've always liked to eat.

"Aren't we going to wait for Mom?" Tan asked, as he picked up his chopsticks.

"Did you come here with your mother? Where is she?"

Mrs. Lam had forgotten that she'd promised herself not to remind this strange youth about matters that might stir private memories with which he wasn't comfortable. Then she almost lost control of herself. She could too easily guess the terrible fate that his mother might have suffered in time of war.

Though he was still feeling confused and groggy, Tan couldn't help laughing.

"Who's my mother? If you've forgotten, Grandma, then I'll remind you: my mother is Madame Yen, lecturer at the Teachers' University. And my dad is Vu Do, an official of the Ministry of Transportation."

With that sentence, Tan glanced covertly at Do, as if to recruit him as an ally to tease his grandmother. But Do put down his bowl and sat stiffly, looking back and forth from Tan to his mother and feeling both surprised and embarrassed. This boy had just clearly identified not only Do's own name and job, but the identity of the girlfriend Do had left only an hour ago. He'd never introduced Yen to his mother and he wanted to signal Tan to be quiet, as if he was a friend who had just inadvertently revealed a secret. But he was too late. Luckily, his mother didn't notice his awkwardness. She was still concerned about the whereabouts of Tan's mother. When Tan was distracted, she leaned to Do's ear and whispered:

"What did the boy say about his mother? I couldn't hear him."

Do turned away, covered his mouth and coughed; he had not been able to shake the feeling of being caught red-handed at something:

"I didn't hear him either."

From that moment until the end of dinner, the three ate in silence. Tan could not fight off his drowsy, sick feeling, and went back to bed as soon as he finished his meal. Once again, Do's mother approached the bed and admired the youth. She and Do felt an inexplicable closeness to this boy; they trusted him and also felt a need to protect him. It was a natural feeling for a mother to have, but seemed strange in a 23-year-old man like Do, who had not had his own children yet.

"This boy—he's so cute." A trace of sadness crossed the mother's kind face. "Maybe his parents met some disaster; otherwise why would he end up here? There was a man I saw today...his wife and kids all died in last week's bombing attack near Phuc Xuong. He was wandering around totally lost, telling anyone he met: 'Last night, my kids appeared to me, telling me that they were dying, that I had to dig real fast.' He was wandering all over the place with a hoe, digging into any pile of debris he found until he was exhausted."

She stayed silent for a long moment, then turned to Do with a warning:

"The boy's still sick and confused; don't ask him too much. He's here, and here he should stay. When he's fully recovered, you can tell him what he needs to be told."

*   *   *

Mrs. Lam planned to stay home for a day to take care of Tan. But the next afternoon, Tan's fever broke, and she felt she could leave him alone at home when she went to the factory. She needed to get a few things done there: it was war time and almost all the young men had enlisted, so the burden of production work had been placed on the shoulders of their mothers and sisters. She didn't like taking time off from work just because someone in the family or even she herself got sick. She would have liked even less to have to explain to people that a sick young man had suddenly turned up in her home. It would be as if she was asking to be admired for a good deed. Caring for the boy was simply what anyone would do; it was nothing to boast about.

Tan sat alone by the window, feeling comfortable. Everything around him seemed fresh, as if it had just been washed clean by a rain. A breeze cooled his face and ears and penetrated his shirt, refreshing him also. The ruby leaves spreading from the *bang* tree next to the window reminded him of a plate of sticky red rice. He couldn't recall ever seeing that tree before. How could it have grown so fast, sprouted its red leaves, just in the time he had been sick? And where had that block of apartment buildings gone, leaving nothing but this field of green grass and that marsh? Before he had taken sick, his complex had been right in the middle of the city; now it seemed to have been pushed to the outskirts.

Something was not quite right in his head. It was as if a corner of his mind was stiff and heavy, as if his brain were enveloped in a sheet of corrugated tin. His ideas emerged slowly, like a flood of people surging towards a narrow door that only allowed a single person at a time to push through. He could register all these unfamiliar sights around him, but he could not yet explain them to himself.

"Is Aunt Lam home?" a voice called. "We wanted to ask her for a few betel leaves, just to warm ourselves up."

The door opened and two women entered. They both looked familiar, but Tan couldn't place their faces. One was about 60, her hair mostly gone white, her expression warm. The other was in her forties and had deeply set, very animated eyes, which gave her a sharp look. When she saw that Mrs. Lam wasn't at home, the woman smiled at Tan, and walked to the betel nut container next to the small radio as if she was familiar with the apartment. She opened the container and quickly prepared two pieces of betel leaves as if performing a daily routine. Ignoring Tan, she picked up the conversation she had begun before entering the door.

"I must carry the incense bowl on my head and pray sincerely. If I don't, if I get preoccupied with everyday things and forget to say my prayers, then my headaches inevitably return. When that happens, I just light some incense, say a few prayers, and I feel comfortable again."

The white-haired woman wasn't really paying attention.

"I'm going senile," she said. "I no longer have dreams about good things; at night all I see are bad things. God forbid, there are nights when I see myself visiting an old friend, and when I get there I see my own little Hoi lying wrapped in a burial shroud."

"Worship and abstinence will see you through, auntie."

Tan could see that the woman had said these comforting words in order to turn the conversation back to her own pet topic. But the old woman slowly continued, as if speaking to herself:

"Last night, as soon as I closed my eyes, I saw little Hoi again saying, 'this time I leave without being sure that I'll ever see you again. That's a situation you are going to have to come to terms with.' Then he disappears, going deeper into the jungle, swimming away across a stream made entirely of red blood..."

The woman's voice wavered and she pressed her fingers into her temples and sat as still as if she had turned to stone.

"Why are you so worried?" The other woman finished preparing another chunk of betel nut and plopped it into her mouth along with the first piece. "We all have a destiny, and our deaths are not meaningless."

Tan had pretended not to be listening to the two women's conversation, but just as he was starting to feel badly about the old woman's tale, he couldn't help laughing at the way each woman remained absorbed in her own concerns while trying to draw the other's attention, pulling and yanking back and forth like a tug of war. He had to turn and lean out of the window so they wouldn't see him laughing. The bright red leaves of the *bang* tree, splashed with yellow, suddenly reminded him of the glory days of victory: the colors of the flags, the brilliant flashes of sunlight reflected off the medals on the shirts of the officers marching in the victory parades after the nation had been reunified. A light burst in his mind. Of course. No wonder he had found the old woman's face somewhat familiar.

"Ma'am?" he asked "Your apartment is on the fourth floor, right?"

The old woman turned sadly to Tan, looking at him with dull eyes:

"That's right. I live in room 424."

Tan gave a sharp cry, and kept talking:

"Then I'm right! That's the apartment of Uncle Hoi, the colonel. After Saigon was liberated, I remember how he came back and gave me a bag of sesame candy from Hue. During the parade, I saw him on television with a chest full of medals."

The old woman's eyes brightened. She trembled as she stood up and took wobbling steps towards Tan's bed.

"Are you saying my son will stay alive until reunification? You're not lying to me, are you?"

Tan laughed and took the woman's wrinkled hand:

"How can I lie to you; it's a fact. But, excuse me; how are you related to Colonel Hoi?"

The woman couldn't speak. Her moist eyes were trained warmly on Tan. The other woman answered for her:

"Mrs. Mau here is Uncle Hoi's mother."

"You're Mrs. Mau? I'm sorry, but how is that possible—didn't she pass away at the end of 1976? I remember it very distinctly—it was the day I completed my first week of school. There were more than thirty cars and two hundred wreaths at her funeral. Lots of people Uncle Hoi knew from the ministries and the army came to pay their last respects, and I remember how my family climbed on board the Hai Au bus to escort her out to the Van Dien cemetery..."

Mrs. Mau seemed to have gone into a coma. Tan's words had made her forget everything around her and plunged her deep into an unexpected happiness. She felt her worries lift from her. Even the news of her own death didn't trouble her: she knew that in war time, one could be sitting here today, buried in a bomb crater tomorrow. But now she knew she would live through these terrible years of bullets and bombs, she would live to see her son return, and then she would die and have a proper funeral and a satisfied soul.

"You're Mrs. Mau?" Tan said again. He seemed hypnotized, his mind pulled into a sudden whirl of chaotic thoughts. "Yes," he said. "It's true; you are Mrs. Mau...I recognize you now...I remember, before I even started school, how you used to set a banana or a piece of candy aside for me...Once you even yelled at a kid who had beat me up for no reason."

Both Mrs. Mau and Tan seemed lost, drifting in some far off realm, both of them a long way from reality. Mrs. Mau didn't ask Tan where he came from, what family he belonged to, why he knew what would happen nine or ten years into the future. Neither did Tan ask Mrs. Mau why she was still here when she had died eleven years before. Each accepted the reality of the other and didn't trouble their minds with the small, contradictory details of their meeting.

Only the other woman, standing outside and observing the two of them, kept a clear head. Here was an opportunity for her to realize a long held dream! Ignoring the frozen Mrs. Mau, she lightly shook Tan's shoulder:

"Where did you come from?"

"Right here. This room. Apartment 203."

"Whose son are you?"

"My dad is Mr. Do, my mother Mrs. Yen, and I'm the grandson of Mrs. Lam."

Staring at Tan's distant and dazed expression, the woman dropped a simple sentence:

"Got you."

A money-making scheme had just hatched in her head. Good God, she understood about people being reborn into the next life, but she had never heard of a case where someone from the future had been reborn to live among his ancestors in the past. "Got you," was all she could say, when what she felt like doing was dropping down on all fours and bowing to her lucky saint. "Got you," she had said, as if speaking to someone who would soon have to serve her, be controlled by her. But her mind worked coldly, calculatingly; she realized she would have to play it smart.

*   *   *

Sometimes people fall into a puzzled state, as if they are floating in a void, immersed in a soft curtain of mist with everything in their lives passing in front of their eyes like a film that is sometimes blurry and out of focus, other times clear in both image and sound. Tan is in such a state now, feeling absorbed in some obscure movie, unable to make sense out of long segments of what he sees and hears, but drifting along semiconsciously, without feeling the need to clarify anything completely.

Suddenly a calm cold voice booms from the p.a. speaker attached to the *arjun* tree:

"Attention, everyone: American planes are twenty kilometers

southeast of Hanoi. Armed forces, prepare to fight back. Self-Defense forces and People's Militia, start moving people down into the air raid shelters."

American planes? Hadn't they learned the lesson of Viet Nam yet?

Tan stands stupefied in the center of the room. The curtain of red mist in front of his eyes begins to tear, to be blown by a wind towards the horizon. All that is left is a desolate winter meadow, an *arjun* tree with its red leaves, a funnel shaped p.a. speaker. The droning sound he had first heard from afar reverberates now like cold metal lances piercing his ear drums. Either by instinct or because of the lingering memory of the pain he'd experienced the other day, shooting up now from his foot through his chest to his head, Tan dives to the tile floor. The ground shakes, the floor quakes, the building trembles and heaven and earth quivers. A deafening staccato of thunder pounds the mountains, loosens a surge of rocks onto the city, pounding both tall buildings and tiny living things. His stream of consciousness entirely torn, Tan passes out as if his earlier pain has returned. Everything is buried beneath rocks and dirt.

When he comes to, he has the sensation of waking up after a long night's sleep. Outside his window, the red-leafed *arjun* still stands, looking fresh, as if in an early morning light. A touch of cold wind chills his hands and refreshes the skin of his face. He feels a nightmare has ended, yet he can not escape from the scene in front of him or the memory of the things he has witnessed. Where is he? It is a question that until now had not seemed logical to ask, and from the moment he had stepped into this house, he had not raised it, had not attempted to answer it. Everything had seemed clear. This was his house, his father, his grandmother. But now this is no answer at all. This is his house, but still he feels the need to ask: where am I? The physical location where he finds himself, the family with whom he finds himself, are not the answer to this question. He feels, vaguely, a need to locate himself in time.

As he turns his back towards the window, Tan sees a block calender that had fallen to the floor moments before, when the bombs had rained down on the city. On the front of the calender, a "Hanoi Self-Defense Woman," gun slung over her shoulder, beams a triumphant smile at him, an unfamiliar square insignia attached to her hat. Below the photograph is a caption, small but clearly legible: THE YEAR OF THE ROOSTER, 1967, and on the date block: NOVEMBER THE 9TH, WEDNESDAY.

Tan feels dizzy. Something seems to be pounding him bluntly on the head, as though a drummer in a marching band is whamming his head unceasingly instead of his cymbals.

The march ends, the tired drummer abandons his sticks. Tan suddenly understands everything. In the murky light of the winter afternoon, he holds his head in his hands and sits down on the floor, next to the calender. Once before he had been lost: on the afternoon of the 30th of April, 1975. His mother had taken him downtown and they had stood, as if their feet were planted in the ground, in front of a huge display map, hearing the news of the liberation of Saigon and following the arrows indicating the army's advances. People were swarming everywhere, and everyone had a flag—either the red and yellow star national ensign or the half-blue, half-red flag of the National Liberation Front. Too excited to stay put with his mother, he had broken away, following a man selling paper flags. When all the flags were sold, he had watched a string of firecrackers going off on a second story balcony, then trailed a group of youngsters singing and dancing on the flatbed of a truck to the "Viet Nam - Ho Chi Minh" song. In this way, he had ended up all the way down at the Mo Market before he suddenly realized he was all alone and began to cry. A security officer carted him back home on the back of his bicycle, after Tan had given him his address between sobs.

But now he hasn't gotten lost at the Mo Market, nor in Hai Phong, nor Da Nang, nor anywhere else on this planet. He has gotten lost in the year 1967, twenty years before the period in which he was living. He has no way of remembering the means by which he has travelled here. He can remember his last moment in 1987, when the A1 Building of the Green Meadow Housing Complex had collapsed and he helped his grandmother run out to the lawn, and then returned. His last sensation was when he had lost the flip flop from his right foot and he had felt a burn in that foot which sent a sharp pain all the way to his heart and mind. And afterward there had been the flight inside the earth, through a windblown tunnel. But how could he ever return?

This is truly his home, and he is truly here with his grandmother and his father, but they are not the same grandmother and father he knew. He is suddenly seized by the memory of all the afternoons when he had come home, and had a shower, and eaten some black bean pudding, and then went to fetch the homely girl to go dancing. He suddenly misses the evenings when he sat here with his family watching television, commenting on the shows, arguing passionately about the people on the screen. His father's voice: "Such a funny thing, you prance around a little while and in the end you fall in love." His mother adding: "Too bad the actress isn't all that good looking; it spoils the film for me somewhat," and then glancing at Tan, though even without that glance her meaning was obvious: she wouldn't accept a girl whose appearance was below average. Grandmother, always on Tan's side, admonishing her: "How can talk that way—how can you teach your son to judge people by their appearance." But don't worry mother, Tan thinks, I'm not in love with my friend Thu. I only feel sorry for her because she's so ugly she doesn't have a boyfriend she can hang out with...

All of it running through his mind as if it is happening now, the family together after a hard day's work in the year 1987 and yet that was in the past and it was 1967 and just as he always wanted to return to the days of his childhood he wishes now to return to that past which waits in the future.

*   *   *

All day Do was obsessed with what happened during dinner when the youth had stuck Yen's name onto his like a married couple and cast them as his parents. Just an hour before that, he had said goodbye to Yen after they'd watched the film *The Captain's Daughter*. Or at least attended it. They felt the poet

Pushkin would understand why these two lovers could not remember any of the plot.

Earlier, when his team was busy collecting the equipment it needed for a salvage project on the river, he had seen a girl in a red dress leave the main street of the town and turn onto a path that was bordered by white sandalwood trees and walk towards Do and his companions. It was Yen. They had just said goodbye on Sunday, and Yen had bicycled back to her school in the refuge area. But it was only Tuesday now—what had brought her back so soon to the city? It was war time, and anything that stepped out of the normal routine would set people's hearts racing. Something terrible could happen at any time.

"My dear Do," Yen said.

She was happy to see Do standing among the crowd of young men chatting her up and teasing her. She got off her bicycle, but then simply smiled and stood by a white sandalwood tree instead of approaching him. Her expression calmed him. He told his friends to tie their equipment to the back of their bikes and return to company headquarters. Then he and Yen went in the opposite direction, walking their bikes along the river.

"How did you know to look for me here?"

"I ran into a guy with a beard, over at the company office. He asked me which Do I was looking for, Gravedigger Do or Skinny Do. When I gave him your full name, he said: 'That's Gravedigger Do. Go out to Phuc Thinh beach, you'll find his team for sure.' What a terrifying name they've given you guys."

The Gravediggers Team was the facetious name the guys at the River Transportation Company had given to the men who were searching for a particular French boat sunk years before. The team had only been formed the week before, and included the company's top men, under Do's leadership. He hadn't told Yen about it, and she didn't ask.

As they had walked past a group of children diving into the river, Do turned his wrist to check the time. Twenty-five past five. The gesture reminded Yen of her plans:

"I returned to Hanoi for one thing, and I almost forgot about it. Let's go see a movie, honey."

Do shrugged and extended his arms: a gesture of helpless obedience to her will, just like one of the foreign actors they liked to watch.

"Sure. But how can I go in these clothes?" He brushed at his dusty, purple coveralls.

"There's a war on; nobody is going to take notice. Come on—we have barely enough time to make it to the theatre."

"Look, it's O.K. to wear this, but at least let me take a quick bath."

Before Yen could protest, Do jumped behind one of the bushes by the river bank. Yen sat down next to another one and pulled a book she had been reading from her purse. It was dusk now, and the dying sunlight of this bright winter day somehow had made Yen feel warm and complacent. She was a compassionate and empathetic person, and she saw the dormant beauty held within this sorrowful and desolate stretch of river beach. She heard the sound of Tan fumbling with his clothing behind the bush, and then the sound of him diving into the river and splashing around.

"Hurry, Do, my darling."

"Almost done. Tell me what film we're going to see."

"*The Captain's Daughter*. It's from a Pushkin story."

"Pushkin? That 'I remember forever that magical moment' guy?"

A moment later she heard again the sound of someone splashing, then the rustle of branches, and Do's voice, imitating a radio announcer issuing an alert:

"Attention, citizens: no turning around, and cover your ears and close your eyes for fifteen minutes."

It was probably no more than five minutes when she heard the sound of his footsteps behind her. She was debating whether to turn around when suddenly a pair of wet, cold hands covered her eyes. Before she could move away, she felt a warm breath blowing on her cheek, a pair of lips touching her own. In a second, she dropped her book and was enveloped in Do's arms.

"Fellow citizens, it's so cold," Do said.

Yen turned quickly around. There was nobody near them.

The frolicking kids had left some time before and there was only the desolate beach disappearing slowly behind a curtain of mist the color of ash. She pushed Do away and picked up her book:

"Well, if you're cold, then we definitely can't stay here. Let's go before it gets to be too late, darling."

The two had arrived at the theatre at eighteen past six, just in time to buy some tickets and find their seats. They sat looking straight ahead, neither tilting their faces towards each other, nor rubbing each others' cheeks, nor placing their arms around each other. People weren't accustomed to public displays of affection in those years; if one wanted to express one's love, there were more appropriate places than a movie theatre. Yet for Do to search out Yen's hand in the dark and hold it tightly throughout the film was something that didn't bother anybody.

They had known each other since last autumn. In the late afternoon light of a fall day, a strong wind had shaken all the yellow leaves off the trees and hurled them into the air, where they twisted in the wind and then dropped onto the surface of the river, forming a thick layer, like dead butterflies floating on the water. Do had already boarded a small rice boat from Sanh port, when he realized he had no cigarettes left. He left the boat floating amidst the fallen leaves and ran to the small shop under the ceiba tree. When he came out with some Truong Son cigarettes, he saw a young woman in a red tunic only a few steps ahead of him, walking towards the dock. He called out two lines from a poem, teasingly, flirtatiously:

> *I saw a woman in red saying goodbye*
> *To her husband in the sunlit flower garden**

The woman had slowed down and turned to look at Do with a slight smile:

---

*from a poem by Nguyen My

"It's true, I just said goodbye to my husband. That's why I'm so late getting to the port."

She had pretended to speak with a peasant's accent, and also like an older woman, but the words "my husband" somehow sounded artificial in her mouth. Her sharp and playful eyes, her entire appearance confirmed that she was a student, coming to Sanh port to catch a boat back to Hanoi. Near the port was a Teacher's Training College that had been moved from the capital to be safe from the bombing. While riding on his boat, Do had often seen groups of young women waiting for the ferries, giggling and talking excitedly.

"Look I'm sorry," Do was suddenly genuinely concerned, "there's no evening ferry back to Hanoi today."

"You're not kidding, are you?" The young woman said in her normal voice.

"Didn't you know that one of the ferries took a rocket and sank near the Duong bridge, just two days ago?"

"Yes, I knew, but I didn't think it was one of the boats that came by here." The young woman looked directly at him. "Was anyone killed?"

"It wasn't a passenger boat, only a rice carrier, like mine. But my company had to divert one of the passenger ferries to replace it. Three friends of mine were on the boat that was hit..."

They stood on the dock. A moment passed. The speaker had ceased talking, and his listener knew that anything she said would be superfluous and meaningless in the face of that loss. Suddenly they heard the direful cries of a crow that flown down from a hay pole, right near where they stood. It had tried to steal an egg from a nest, but the hen had pecked it on the head. The crow thrashed its wings and nearly fell into the stack of hay before regaining its balance and escaping into the air, cawing. It was enough to make the young couple burst into laughter.

"So my friend," Do said. "Shouldn't you go back to your school and pick up your bicycle? It will only take you two hours by bike, right?"

"I noticed after classes let out today that both my tires were flat. I kept pumping them, but they wouldn't fill up. We only have a handful of boys at the school, and they had all slipped away to Hanoi this morning, so there was no one to patch up the tires for me."

"Are you thinking of asking me to patch them up for you?"

"I wouldn't presume. But if you'd let me catch a ride..."

"Do you think this is a passenger boat?"

"No. I'd only get on if you'd let me."

Do pretended to hesitate. He looked at the red dress, then at the yellow bag in the girl's hand:

"We're in the middle of a war and you're a display of deadly colors. Giving you a ride would be like sending an invitation to the American pilots: 'Please, Sirs.'"

"You can hide me in your cabin," the girl suggested, then awkwardly corrected herself: "I mean...would you please let me stay in the pilot's cabin?"

She was on board and the boat was a few yards off the dock when she caught sight of a friend running onto the dock. The girl raised an envelope, waved, and called out:

"Yen, wait!"

"Here, over here!" Yen leaned her whole body out of the cabin port, waving both her arms, then turned and yelled over the engine noise to Do, as if he also knew this other girl. "It's Lan. Let her ride with us."

Do's face grew stern and he looked away from her, over the bow of the boat.

"Do you think this boat is just reserved for our use?"

Yen scrambled to pick up her bag and rushed to the other side of the boat:

"I don't think anything. If you don't want to take both of us, I'll just get off now."

She was about to step over the low railing. The distance between the deck of the boat and the surface of the river wasn't great, and it was rather shallow near the embankment. Even if Yen jumped off, she would only get her clothes wet, and would be able to easily wade ashore. But Do quickly reversed the boat anyway, and backed it against the dock.

"Hurry up, Lan," Yen called.

"No, I'm not going home: I have guard duty at the college. Could you please give this letter to my mom and ask her to send me some salt and the book *The Steel is Here*."

"No problem; you'll have everything by tomorrow afternoon. Oh, by the way, would you bring in my shirt from the clothesline before it gets soaked with dew."

The girls chatted for another moment before Yen hurriedly returned to the boat. It finally left Sanh Harbor then, gliding on the reflection of the autumn sunlight shattering in the waves.

Love followed that simple beginning. Each Saturday afternoon, Yen rode her bicycle from that place she had been sent to find refuge from the war to the town. On the days when she knew for certain his boat would land, she would wait at Sanh harbor from early morning. On other unexpected occasions also, like this day, she would sometimes be able to meet Do on a weekday.

"We had our psychology class this afternoon. After ten minutes, when the professor hadn't shown up, I closed my eyes and prayed: 'if the professor is sick, I'll head for Hanoi right away.' My prayers were answered. A few minutes later, the administrative office announced that our class was cancelled. The professor's son had come down with pneumonia and had to be taken to the hospital."

It was the end of the afternoon and the two of them were walking their bicycles leisurely along the sidewalks near the Thien Quang Lake. Listening to Yen innocently telling her story, Do couldn't help smiling:

"We were the same way: always happy to get a few hours off from school. There wasn't one of us who didn't wish that our teachers were sick or had gotten into an accident on the way to school, or had been caught in a big rainstorm. Of course, we'd go on and wish the teacher would soon recover or be safe."

"It would be wrong otherwise," Yen smiled.

A wind blew across the lake, and she shivered in the cold air. But she was in no hurry to return to her warm room. She would miss the moments when she could walk next to Do. Early the next morning, she would have to rush back to be in time for her first class at seven. She smiled slightly, imagining how she might fall asleep in the classroom: not a pretty sight.

Abruptly Do stopped and sniffed, as if trying to catch a last breath of fresh air. His gaze seemed to pierce through the branches above his head.

"What's the matter, darling?"

He didn't reply, but continued to concentrate on whatever it was he had scented in the air. Then he picked his bicycle off the ground, turned all the way around, and began walking slowly, looking this way and that as though searching for something. Confused, Yen turned her bike around to follow him.

"Right here!" Do cried out happily, as though he had found something he'd lost.

Yen lowered her eyes to look. In the dim light of a distant street lamp she could only see an individual air raid shelter, round as a well. Its cover of reinforced cement was set at an angle on the roots of a *xa cu* tree. There was nothing out of the ordinary. Yen turned her eyes upwards. Do laughed and leaned his bike against the tree, then placed yen's bike next to it.

"Not there. Attention, citizens; close your eyes and breathe in deeply."

Yen followed the order obediently. In the flow that slowly filled her nostrils and lungs, all she could feel distinctly was the cold, rather damp air. But then, mixed in with it, she detected something very familiar, very pure, but so delicate she couldn't sense it right away. Keeping her eyes closed, she took hold of Do's arm and struggled with tight lips to discern the faint perfume.

"Oh!" She let out a cry as if in pain, and then the joy that rewarded her earnest search made her rest her head on Do's chest, unable to speak for a moment.

It was the scent of the *sua* flowers.*

The tracing fragrance of those rare flowers only lingered faintly in the narrow space where they stood. If they had walked five or seven steps ahead, they would lose the fragile perfume

*The *sua* (milk) flower blooms only for one month during autumn in Hanoi.

and would not know there were still some *sua* flowers left in this winter season. They breathed evenly, slowly enjoying the scent as if sipping it bit by bit.

"Don't I get any credit for finding this place?" Do said finally.

"I think I deserve the credit," Yen teased. "If I hadn't returned you'd be sitting at home right now, instead of standing here with me, smelling the scent of the *sua* flower."

"You're right," Do said sincerely.

And along with his sincerity, he bent down and placed his lips lightly over Yen's parted lips. For a brief moment, he felt those lips were responding, yearning for his. He felt feverish and could no longer hear the wind blowing through the rustling leaves, driving away the scent of the *sua* flowers, then returning it more potently. Suddenly he heard a sound, from somewhere near their feet, and Yen's lips flew from his like the wings of a shocked butterfly. He didn't understand. Then he looked and saw that Yen, leaning backwards, had lost her balance and tripped over the shelter cover. That solid cover had fulfilled its duty as a grim reminder of reality.

As they parted company near the gate to Yen's house, Do felt an ache of regret about the disrupted kiss. A sudden thought filled him with anguish. He might die tomorrow under an American bomb, there was no guarantee it wouldn't happen, and he had so much to lose now.

*   *   *

Up to this point, Do was still unable to understand why Yen's mother disliked him so much.

The first time Yen had brought him home to introduce him, he was still wearing his dark blue worker's coveralls. Yen had been waiting for him at the end of his shift; he had seen her by her bicycle waiting as he came out of the company's gates. He hadn't had time to go home and change into more suitable clothes, and Yen felt there was no need anyway to worry too much about appearances.

After a week in the refuge area, away from her mother, Yen couldn't control her happiness. She leapt off her bicycle and embraced her mother, telling her excitedly how much she missed home. A flicker of emotion passed over her mother's face, but then, realizing she had a guest, she assumed a flat, cold expression. She pushed her daughter away and looked at Do with a guarded smile.

"This is Do, my new friend," Yen introduced him.

"Your new friend?" The mother repeated the words with a distinct emphases that surprised both Do and Yen, Her question, her tone, seemed cold and resentful, as if Yen had presented her with a *fait accompli*, trapping her to accept a situation without bothering to get her approval.

"Yes, Aunt," Do said evenly. "We just met at Sanh Harbor."

The mother's eyes glinted with a hint of sarcasm, as if to say: what an appropriate place you people chose. But she covered her reaction under a veneer of proper manners. Watching her prepare and pour the tea, Do had to admire her skill in making someone feel awkward about his disheveled and common appearance—with the utmost politeness. Yen had mentioned when she introduced her mother that she was the deputy manager of the Business Bureau. If he had to guess, Do would have thought she had been born into a bourgeois family that had lived for many generations in an urban area.

"What do you do, my dear Do?"

"Dear aunt, I'm a boat captain, working with the River Transportation Company," Do said, and immediately cursed himself for announcing his title, when the mother hadn't even asked. But the mother betrayed no reaction, simply let her upright posture in her chair indicate her superiority to this conceited person in front of her.

"A boat captain? How romantic. A lover in every port, no doubt, and if one is really lucky in love, sometimes even several wives."

Do understood that beneath the obvious sarcasm was a mother's sincere fears for her daughter. But it would be impossible for anyone to detect sincerity under that falsely polite tone of voice.

"Those stories are exaggerated, dear aunt." He felt called upon to correct these false popular notions about his occupation. "Out of my entire team, only six men have taken a second wife or a lover, and every one of them was expelled from the Party and disciplined."

"Only six you say?" the mother said, smiling sweetly, raising her cup of *ngau*-flavored tea to he lips, taking a delicate sip. Her whole manner showed she had come to see Do, in that moment, as shameless for daring to so casually admit the vices of his profession.

Yen wanted to defend him, but she didn't know how. She was perceptive enough to recognize a deep dislike for Do in her mother's demeanor. She heard, buried under those cold, polite words, the sentiments of a superior person towards an inferior: a predisposition that could never be erased.

Do felt the same, but was also angry at himself for allowing her to agitate him to the point where he had lost his self-control and spoken indecently. But, in truth, faced with the mother's quietly disdainful attitude, it was hard to maintain his poise. Do felt he no longer had the courage to interact with Yen's mother.

The following Saturday night, knowing that Yen had returned, Do went to her house but didn't go inside. He walked through the gate, looked around, and certain that there was no one home, decided to climb up the *arjun* tree to look through the window into Yen's room. He caught a glimpse of a shadow, but was unsure whether it was Yen or her mother. Suddenly a sharp voice rang out in the night:

"Who's that in the *arjun* tree?"

Do trembled. Yen's mother had just pushed her bike through the gate, but Do had been so engrossed in peering into Yen's room that he hadn't noticed her. Standing frozen as a corpse on the tree branch, he had no choice but to answer her:

"It's me."

He wanted to wait until the mother had gone inside before climbing down. But she didn't walk away. Instead she stood quietly and watched Do climb awkwardly down. It was clearly her moment of triumph.

"Is that you, Do?" she asked sweetly. "Why don't you come inside, properly, and have something to drink? You'll get bitten by insects if you keep sitting in that tree."

It wasn't until then that she brought her bicycle inside, all the while still talking as if she was truly concerned about him. But Do was sick with the realization that his relationship with her was beyond saving. She refused to try to understand him or to be more charitable. Shortly after the incident, Yen told him that her mother had said: "That man will not amount to much. He's like all of them—out of every hundred sailors, ninety-nine will be womanizers. Can't you see it—even when he came to our home, he still spoke indecently." Yen wanted to argue with her, but each of her mother's words were as assured as a nail pounded into a pole, and her voice rang with the power and conviction of an orator. She was an intelligent person who always felt that everyone else was beneath her, and who always spoke carefully, supporting each statement with impeccable reasoning, a sophisticated style, and an air of high-mindedness, even when it was based on fallacious logic. Both Yen and Do sensed the same thing, but neither could find the exact words to describe it. And in truth, they did not dare.

From that day on, Do absolutely avoided Yen's mother by not trying to see Yen at home. Each Saturday afternoon, when she rode her bicycle home from the war-refuge area, Yen would wait for Do at the gate to his company office. Do felt more comfortable that way, but he was also pained by the situation. One way or another, the day would come when he would have to face the mother, and raise the issue of his relationship with Yen. As long as he kept away from her, he couldn't be sure if that day would go smoothly, or if he would be accepted.

And yet, at last night's meal, the strange youth had talked about a married couple named Do and Yen, and claimed to be their son. After that moment of awkwardness and embarrassment in front of his mother, Do felt happy. There was something weird about the certainty of that feverish person, like the assurances of a fortune teller. Could it be true? Would Yen become his wife, even though they were facing such harsh obstacles from Yen's mother. The young man had talked about it so naturally and sincerely, it was hard to believe it wouldn't happen. Thinking that, Do had to laugh out loud at his own superstition.

Nevertheless, he couldn't resist a compunction to further question the youth. After dinner, Do invited the youth to walk with him to the main gate of his company office. The two walked on the sidewalk past the *sau* and the *xa cu* bushes. It wasn't easy for Do to start talking. He reached into his shirt pocket and handed Tan a *Tam Dao* cigarette.

"Have a smoke."

Tan remembered how he had once tried to filch a cigarette from his dad, but was caught immediately and forbidden to smoke. From then on, he hadn't. It seemed his dad was much more easy going in his younger days. Tan still didn't want to smoke, but he couldn't refuse such a friendly invitation from his father. He took the proffered cigarette, tilted his head toward the lighted match which Do held in his cupped hands, inhaled and exhaled pleasantly. They walked in silence past several houses with locked doors. Under the light from a street lamp, Tan could read a line scrawled by some kids: *Dad, if you're home on leave, look for us at Doan Ha, the village of Nhan Nghia, the Doai neighborhood, the home of Old Am.* Some kids were waiting even now for a soldier-father who might unexpectedly pass through the capital. And in his *now*, in 1987, his grandmother and mother and dad were waiting for him to return, and he was still lost, walking through this quiet streets next to his father, who was not yet his father.

"My girlfriend, sheltering in the village of Che, is also called Yen," Do began timidly, as if hoping to start a dialogue. Tan understood from the phrase "also called Yen," that his father hadn't forgotten last night's conversation, when, still feverish, he had said that his mother's name was Yen. Clearly his father hoped to dig further into his story, to reinforce what he wanted to hear. But he wouldn't say anything. Even if he explained it, this younger version of his father wouldn't believe him, and in the end he would surely be considered mentally ill.

"Did you say Yen, elder brother?" he said cautiously. "It's a nice name."

Elder brother! It was the first time his mouth had formed that appellation to call his father. Even though it was unnatural, Tan still felt somewhat elated. Who ever gets to address a father as brother, to talk to a father as though to a brother?

Tan's easy compliment encouraged Do to open up. No longer maintaining his decorum, and for the first time since he had met Yen, Do told everything about his love affair to this friend. He could see that Tan was a man just coming of age, and someone he had just met, yet for some reason he trusted him completely. He didn't even conceal his regret about the disrupted kisses.

Tan turned his head slightly towards the houses. He didn't want Do to read the emotions on his face in the light from the street lamps. His dad was showing himself to be an open-minded and funny guy, but he was used to a serious person who always spoke in measured tones. How had this man's soul gotten so tired and somber in the course of time? Could it be simply that his father had labored to give that impression to his son so that he might have the authority with which to raise him? The thought made Tan feel badly for his father, resentful toward the Do who was now kicking pebbles on the sidewalk. At the same time, in a sudden rush of emotion, he only wanted to hug Do and whisper: "Dad."

Tan didn't notice that they were now walking along the lake. Do stopped abruptly, a strange, chagrined look on his face. Tan halted also, sensing it was inappropriate to question the reason they weren't continuing their walk. The two stood still for a few minutes, until the lights from the houses blinked out and the streets suddenly went dark. The sound of an alert wailed from the public speakers. Do quickly raised his hand to cover the ember of his cigarette, and caught a last drag before throwing the butt on the ground and stepping on it.

"Hey, over there: put it out!" someone shouted from behind a tree.

It wasn't until then that Tan realized he was still carelessly holding the lit cigarette in his hand.

Do reacted more quickly than Tan, squeezing the burning end of the cigarette and pulling Tan to crouch down by an individual shelter with a round cover that looked like a tray.

"Do you sense it, elder brother?" Tan asked.

"Sense what?" Do looked around in confusion, thinking that something had happened on the streets.

"The scent of *sua* flowers in the air."

Do laughed softly. "That's exactly why I brought you to this street. We have to be standing exactly here—even a few meters away and we wouldn't be able to smell anything."

They stayed silent for a long time. Everything around them faded into the night and there were only the two young men, immersed in the scent of the *sua* flowers. But it wasn't only the sua flowers Tan sensed in the air; there was also the faintly lingering redolence of a vaguely familiar perfume.

"Last night Yen and I stopped right here." Do had lowered his voice, as if talking to himself.

And then Tan understood that the familiar fragrance, mixed with the fragrance of the *sua* flowers, was his mother's, was the perfume she had worn when she was young. Only he, a child she had carried in her womb, and only Do, although he didn't say it, could detect such a scent. Both young men were now feeling a longing for the absent young woman, and more than ever Tan could empathize with the worry that was rising inside Do's heart.

"Don't worry, elder brother. I have no doubt that you and this woman will become husband and wife."

For Do, this was not just a statement of consolation. He heard in its tones the echo of a joy that had been sent from the future to the present, and he believed it, believed it immediately. He squeezed Tan's hand, which was shaking slightly because of his dismay at the words he had just uttered. *You and this woman?* Would he forever have to speak of his parents as if they were acquaintances? *You and this woman?* When and how would he return to his real family, so he could call his dad, "Dad," and his mom, "Mom?" In his seventeen years, Tan had known very little sadness. Only once, when he was in seventh grade, had he lost a friend, when a girl he liked had to move with her parents to Ho Chi Minh City. Tan had helped take her bag to the Hang Co train station and he had grieved for several days afterwards and for some time, he would receive postcards with scenes of Saigon on them. He would stare at them, but after a time, his sorrow had dissipated.

But now he understood that those years of insouciance and innocence had ended. His sorrow grew heavier and heavier, as though pressing down on a corner of his heart. Dad, I'm your son, he wanted to say. I'm the witness that you may believe that your love and mom's will come to its desired end. But you can only believe it by instinct, and if I were to say it, you'd just think I was demented. And this is the grief that has started to weigh on my heart.

*   *   *

The bombs struck on the eastern side of the street.

No one had had the time to hear the alert on the radio, or the sirens, not was there any announcement on the militia's portable speakers. In a flash, the airplanes were already directly overhead. Their roar and the high-pitched scream of the falling bombs pierced his ears. Tan had just time to leap into an individual shelter but before he could pull the cover over his head, the shock wave blasted through like a storm. The earth shook. Branches, earth and pebbles rained down. Something like a piece of paper flew into his face and fell on his lap. At first he thought it was a dried leaf, but when he looked closer, he realized it was a butterfly, with black spots and green lines arrayed harmoniously on its wings. The butterfly was dead, as fragile and still as if it had been pressed into a book. Tan picked it up and examined it, his eyes glued to this tiny insignificant creature whose life force had been extinguished in a fraction of a second. Were the lives of the hundreds of human beings in this neighborhood equally light and insignificant?

He didn't know yet that hundreds of people had just been killed under the American bombs. All he was doing was staring at this elegant and fragile butterfly, but somehow it told him of the heavy casualties. He immediately jumped out of the shelter and rushed after a group of people heading towards the river. The crowd halted in front of a three-story villa that had been built during the time of the French. It had been cut in half. Surrounding it was a torn up courtyard full of broken bricks, metal debris, cabinet doors, table legs. At the very end of the street, a column of black smoke covered a corner of the sky.

"Please disperse. The enemy planes will return," a man's voice boomed from a portable speaker.

"No, no, my children are still in there," a woman cried out. "Hung, Huong, where are you?"

Several young men in red armbands had to band together to pull the nearly mad woman away. The self-defense fighters formed themselves into a human fence to block the frantic residents trying to return to the collapsed building to search for people. Only the civilian defense forces, army engineers and sappers were allowed in to carry out their duties.

"Where are you going?"

The old man who had just been halted lowered his voice to plead:

"I'm in charge of the preservation room. Only half the house has collapsed; you must allow me to get in to remove state property. It's very valuable, comrades."

"We're looking for a five thousand pound bomb beneath that house. Whatever valuables are there can't be weighed against human life."

The old man stepped back, his face crunched up. Tan followed the others to the flower garden on the other side of the street.

Perhaps because the bombs had become as familiar a feature of their days as their daily meals, people stayed across the streets to watch the search and rescue efforts. Tan stood with them, watching for a long time. He was startled to recognize the gray-haired man carefully carrying a tea set and two porcelain plates towards him. With an air of great satisfaction, the man carefully placed the items he had just recovered from the part of the house that was still standing onto a stone bench. His movements were full of care and reverence.

"I had to go around to the back and then crawl inside to get these," he smiled and pointed to the white dust partially covering his chest. "Fortunately, even though the glass on the display cabinet was shattered, these were still intact."

Tan reached out and touched the edge of a delicate, floral patterned plate.

"Don't touch, don't touch," said the old man: the automatic response of a curator. But as Tan respectfully withdrew his hand, the old man apparently decided he could be trusted.

"Watch these for me, nephew. They're relics from the earliest days of Thang Long (Hanoi) as a capital. I have to go back and save some more pieces."

Tan let out a cry that startled the old man.

"Uncle, did you forget there's still a five-thousand pound bomb in there?"

"Two carved dragons from the Ly dynasty are what's still in there," the old man interrupted, and then, as if he knew exactly who Tan was and where he had come from, he lowered his voice as if delivering a message to future generations: "Man will turn to ash and dust tomorrow, but we cannot afford to lose these objects. They are the proofs of our ancient civilization."

Tan sat on the grass, holding his chin up with his fist, staring at the relics on the stone bench. Had he seen similar things in a museum, or perhaps seen these very objects? And what of you, my dear old man with gray hair, he thought: in the world of twenty years from now, I have met no one with a face like yours.

Someone quietly approached and stopped next to Tan, perhaps to look at the antiques, which were arranged as if for sale. Tan kept his chin on his fist and didn't look.

A girl's soft voice rang out: "Hey, my friend. Is that you?"

Tan looked up. At first he only faintly recognized the face.

Then a light flashed in his mind. A warm memory of being held while a girl was helping him to walk. He recognized her, but needed a second.... *Trinh. I'm Trinh.* Her name echoed from his memory.

"Hello, Trinh," he said. "Where have you disappeared since that night we met?"

"I was about to ask you the same thing." Trinh put the baskets in her hand down on the grass and looked over the items on the stone bench with an amused air. "Are you an antique dealer now?"

As if to answer Trinh's question, the old man returned with more of the objects he'd had to crawl through collapsed walls to recover, then called for a pedicab and loaded it as if he were bringing an injured person to a hospital. He was satisfied that future generations would have a chance to admire these precious objects in museums, without ever knowing about today's bombing.

Tan and Trinh sat on the stone bench. As if to contrast the dismal scene across the street, the weather was fair, the winter atmosphere made brighter by the light sunshine. The sun turned the lawn into a yellow carpet, and in a corner of the flower garden, a woman was selling beer next to a kiosk with a peaked roof.

"Didn't you go into a shelter at your school?" Tan said, destroying the silence with the question. He guessed that Trinh was still a student.

Trinh looked down at her baskets with a sad face.

"I had to temporarily abandon my studies to take care of my mom. I doubt she'll make it through the next few days."

Tan felt awkward that he'd carelessly reminded Trinh of her sadness.

"What about you, Tan?" she asked. "Did you have to abandon your schooling also."

"That's right." Tan felt a sharp pain inside his chest when he was reminded of this: both he and Trinh were bereft, both yearning for sympathy. "My family is far away."

"Where, Tan?"

"In 1987."

Trinh sighed.

Not in Thai Binh, Haiphong, or even in Quang Binh or Vinh Linh, but all the way in 1987. He had wanted to say the year, to let her know how far away he was from home, wandering, as it was in time of war, with so many people driven from their homes and scattered all over. He saw that Trinh wasn't shocked by his strange reply, but instead maintained a sympathetic silence. For a brief moment he felt he had to explain his real situation to his friend. But Trinh spoke first:

"You're staying temporarily with Do's family, right?" Trinh lifted her baskets and stood up, but didn't walk away. She waited for Tan to stand also.

"Yes. But I will have to leave, go back to find my family."

He rose and left the garden with Trinh. The two walked along the road parallel to the Red River dam, on their way back to the Green Meadow Housing Complex.

"I'd like to leave also, go away, far away," Trinh said longingly. "But not right now. Right now my mom is in a critical situation."

In fact her mother was in the last days of her life. Not two months ago, she was a healthy and active cadre in the Power Plant Union, and Trinh was still a sophomore in an school relocated to a safer, rural area. Then, suddenly, she had received word that her mother had been hospitalized with leukemia. Realizing that Trinh would have to give up her education and return to the city to take care of her, he mother had urged her many times to go back to school.

But since the family only consisted of mother and daughter, there was no other solution. With her illness worsening, and the certainty of death near, the mother could not even go to the countryside where her daughter's school was. If she were to die in some kind peasant's home, it would bring bad luck to his family. But allowing her daughter to stay in the city to take care of her upset her even more, for she feared that because of her, her daughter would perish under the American bombs. She silently prayed that her death would come soon, so that Trinh could return to safety. Her only regret was that she had neither seen her husband nor heard anything from him; he had left for the Zone B battlefields three years ago and had disappeared since then.

Trinh's family had a room of about twenty square meters in a tile-roofed house that usually held a dozen families. Now all the other family units had been evacuated and the entire building was frightfully silent. Since the day her mother was discharged from the hospital, Trinh had placed her bed in a shelter bunker dug under the front courtyard. It was a public bunker, nearly ten meters square and dug deep into the ground, with only its roof, which looked like the back of a turtle's shell, sticking above the ground. All day her mother lay still, and Trinh handled everything, from cooking to changing the sick woman's clothes, to washing.

Now Tan followed her down the dirt steps to the bunker. It was relatively bright inside since there was a ray of sunlight coming at an angle through the rather large opening. In a corner, a flickering oil lamp stood atop a wooden box, spreading a yellow light upon the forehead, cheeks and nose of the woman lying flat in the bed. The mother made a vague movement when she saw her daughter had returned, a gesture so weak that Tan barely noticed it.

"Mother," Trinh sat at the edge of the bed, opening the baskets and calling out their contents, "Look, I got you some *tao pho*. It comes all the way from up at O Quan Chuong."

She took a tea spoon, scooped up portions of beans suffused in jasmine and mixed it, while her mother murmured a question

"Oh, this is Tan, a friend of mine. He's Do's cousin. Do's the one who was in charge of the youth unit when I was in second grade, do you remember, mom?"

"How wonderful." The mother spoke as softly as a breath when Tan came nearer to greet her.

Trinh started excitedly to tell a story:

"The old Chinese man selling *tao pho* who used to come by here only had a leg wound. He's doing fine; he only limps a little now. He sends his greetings and his wishes that you recover quickly."

Tan sat as if frozen on a small chair, fearing that if he moved just a little then he would lose control and let out a painful cry at this scene he was witnessing. He understood Trinh was talking so animatedly and cheerfully to suppress the sobbing that could rack her any time. She knew that her mother couldn't live much longer. This morning, her mother had asked Trinh to go get the *tao pho*, a dessert she really liked. Until then, Trinh was still hoping for a sudden miracle. Only before she left with the baskets did she understand that her mother had felt death very near.

When Tan said goodbye to the mother and climbed out of the bunker, Trinh followed him.

"The people in all the apartments around here know about my mom's condition, and they're all prepared to help with the funeral. Tan, when she does go, I'll ask for your help also, OK?"

Tan's heart was pained. This young girl had already to think of her mother's passing, and to plan everything out exactly. It shouldn't be the responsibility of a young girl. The war had pressed upon her shoulders duties that should have belonged to much more experienced people.

"Don't worry, Trinh," he said. "I'll come and be with you every day."

Why did he say "come be with you?" That wording should only be used for a promise between lovers. He should have said "I'll come here to help you, my friend," but in his shocked state, he had twisted the words around.

But neither he nor Trinh really paid attention to the inexact nature of his words. More importantly, Trinh felt a sincere affection from Tan, and she worried a little less about the moments when she would have to be alone and watch her mother pass away.

"You know, Tan, I feel as if my dad's on his way back. He'll be wading streams, crossing through jungle, then getting rides in cars and trains. Maybe he'll get back in time to be with mother."

Trinh whispered this, as if she were talking to herself. Her longing eyes turned towards an invisible mountain range all the way at the end of the horizon.

*   *   *

Tan had almost forgotten Mrs. Si when she suddenly appeared again, this time unaccompanied by Mrs. Mau. Again she opened the betel nut container, prepared two pieces, and began chewing them at once. It wasn't until then that she pretended to remember she had something to ask Tan:

"My dear, I have a favor to ask of you. You could come see my place at the same time."

He had no desire at all to go to the house of this person he barely knew, but Tan felt he couldn't turn down her request for help. He closed the door and followed her. As it turned out, Mrs. Si lived in the A3 building, the same as Binh, a friend of his from tenth grade. But Binh would not be born for another three years.

"My dear," said Mrs. Si, in a friendly tone, as they walked up the stairs, "I know you have the ability to tell the future. I want to ask you to talk to sister Hong. She's a neighbor of mine."

Tan nearly laughed out loud. To tell the future. What was he, a fortune teller, a wizard? He was reminded of Teo the Blind, whose house was next to the gates of his school. He had round, dark spectacles and a bamboo stick he waggled in front of him to find his way—and told fortunes also. What did this woman think he had in common with Mr. Teo? Then he remembered the conversation he had had with Mrs. Mau. All right then, he thought. If I can help alleviate someone's worries, and if it's only for people I know. But still Tan couldn't help laughing to himself as he watched Mrs. Si striding in front of him with the quickening pace of a blind yet calculating believer.

Mrs. Si was the sixth child in a family whose father was a driver during the French occupation. Her mother's occupation was debt collector, and at the end of each year, even on holidays and Tet, she would throw herself on the ground in front of someone's house so that the owner, fearing bad luck, would sell off his belongings to pay up whatever debt he owed.

The year Si turned eight, her parents sent her to live as a maid for Ms. Nho the Medium, who on her earnings had built a two-story villa, complete with a glittering temple attached. Each day the young girl swept and cleaned eight rooms, and a large yard full of bushes thick with *ngau* and *mau don* flowers, as well as two orchids that had grown almost as high as the roof. She helped the Medium with everything, from small tasks to receiving incense, flowers and money from those who came to pray at the temple. The girl did this scrupulously and earnestly, never daring to touch any portion of the offerings to the spirits of the temple, for she believed they would punish her. She had seen how Nho the Medium went around with the dazed look of someone who was nearly blind, and the exhausted appearance of a sick person, tottering around as if she were disabled. Yet in an instant she would throw on her turban and her many layered tunic, hold a paddle in front of her, and pirouette around it in an intricate dance. The flaps of her tunic, made of strips of silk the colors of lotus petals, plum and amaryllis flowers, would whirl about swiftly. Her singing would become strident as a bronze bell. And when she spoke, her voice would no longer be her own, but instead would intone the proclamations of such female saints as Thuong Ngan, Thuong Thien. Many times, witnessing this, young Si would faint away as if her breath had been choked off. She worshipped this sickly woman, who after her trance would be nothing more than a heap of discarded fabric. She dreamed of becoming someone like Nho the Medium, with sharp, bright eyes, screaming out the words of spirits.

After a few years, when her family's situation improved, Si's parents asked to have her back in order to take care of things at home. But the echoes of Nho the Medium's trances didn't die in her mind. If anything, she was even more inflamed with her ambition. Every once in a while she would escape from her parents and gather a group of her friends into a corner of the garden. There, dressed in one of her mother's long tunics, a torn towel tied across her stomach, and a bamboo stick clutched in her hands, she would sing the words she knew by heart: *Oh, ah, uh, ah, the spirit is here, now she's here, she bestows fortune and good luck, she builds golden towers, la, la, la...* This game of trances hadn't gone on for too long before Si was caught by her father. As long time nonbelievers who nevertheless made their living threatening their clients with curses in order to recover debts, Si's parents were determined that no one like Nho Medium would emerge in their family. And after that incident, the young girl seemed to change completely. From then until the time she married a National Guard soldier and moved to a liberated area, the seeds of the channeling compulsion within Mrs. Si seemed to have been eradicated.

But it was only an outward appearance that she cultivated. Inside Mrs. Si, an aspiration was still burning, an aspiration to turn herself into someone who existed on a higher plane than mere humans, who would act as an interpreter between the supernatural and the temporal worlds.

Following the liberation of the capital from the French, the husband, now a public security officer, got Si a job in a sewing factory. Their life seemed devoid of anything to complain about, until one day the husband returned unexpectedly from a distant mission and caught Si whirling about in a crazy trance as if she was Xuy Van. Her husband, who still carried fragments of a bullet in his head, threw a crazed fit himself, grabbed the paddle and whacked it over his wife's head as she was in the middle of speaking a dead person's words. The dead soul flew away in shock, while the living Mrs. Si fell down in a pool of blood, and ended up getting several stitches in her scalp, and some scars she still bore to this day. From that point on, young Mrs. Si became secretive about her channelling, partly out of fear of her husband and partly because the campaign against spiritual practices had reached a frenzy all over the north.

Yet, Mrs. Si still nursed the hope of taking Nho the Medium's place. On the one hand, she knew she would have to be careful. On the other hand, if she wished to win over a group of believers, she would have to have a great reputation. Once she whispered to a factory colleague whose husband had died just the year before: "I feel you have more ying than yang; he is still disturbing you greatly."

"How do you know this?" the other woman said, trembling

in fear. "It's true I see him every night, but he wouldn't say anything."

Later Mrs. Si transmitted her friend's dead husband's words during a simple ceremony she had organized clandestinely. The other woman was full of praise and admiration for her, for only her husband could say such things. She passed the word to a few close friends, and Mrs. Si began building up some credibility she thought would help her future plans.

Now Mrs. Si was just 40 years old, but she had in fact asked to retire: she had been ill for two years and received a pension of 36 dong a month. Her husband, following the incident when he beat and nearly killed his wife, was now more even-tempered; in any case, he had been promoted to captain, and no longer paid much attention to family affairs. Mrs. Si felt that a golden opportunity to build up her reputation as a medium had arrived when she had unexpectedly met Tan during her conversation with Mrs. Mau. My God, even she had been dazed with admiration at that seventeen-year-old kid. The things he'd said were obvious, but no one could check them out, and the kid had spoken about them with an almost unbelievable smoothness and sincerity. Today she'd test him out one more time. She had invited Ms. Hong to her house, and just before going to get Tan, had intimated to her that she was about to bring over a "disciple" who had the ability to look into the future.

Tan, walking casually into Mrs. Si's house, knew nothing of her plot.

Waiting at the table was a woman of about 26, her cute face tightened as if she were ready to dispute some matter not to her liking. Even though she was twenty years younger than the woman Tan knew, he recognized her right away.

"Elder Sister Hong," he said, greeting her with the proper form for her age. Just a month before, he had greeted her as Aunt Hong.

"Yes," the woman heard her name being called and shot up as though someone had pressed a critical point on her body. "Yes, I am your niece Hong."

"Is Elder Brother Ta still beating you?" Tan asked with concern, but then realized he had confused future and past— she would be beaten up only in the years to come.

"Is my dear uncle saying my husband is beating up your niece?" Hong asked respectfully, then twisted her lips bitterly. It hasn't happened to me yet, she thought, but who knows; it may happen tomorrow.

How miserable this young woman already was, unfortunate in love, married to the brute Tan knew, so dazed and in need that she would address a young man as uncle, call herself niece. Tan remembered how once, when he was walking past the couple's refreshment stand, which was located in a three-roomed tile-roof house next to the gate to the apartment complex, he had seen a crowd of curious people looking inside. The husband's eyes were blood red, and he was flailing his arms about and screaming at his wife: "You devil, you witch, I'm gonna have to break your skull just to get payback for the dowry money I spent bringing you here." His wife, this same Hong, was holding up the shirt her husband had torn from her chest, while struggling to free herself from the people trying to hold her back, and screaming madly herself: "You phony; you jellyfish-faced, petrified liver; you drowned-man's face, putrid liver, I don't believe you really spent a dime—even when we go out for a bowl of noodles we spend my money!" But just like a pair of first rate actors in a popular opera, a half hour later you could see Hong sitting there and minding the store, tears streaming down her cheeks as her husband, ignoring the customers, wiped her eyes with a huge towel. Their fights occurred on a regular schedule, and always ended the same way. Tan, whenever he saw them, would feel bad about the way ignorant people could bring grief upon themselves. Now, abruptly, he wanted to tell Hong everything he knew, tell her about the harsh years and months that would await her.

"Elder brother Ta will drink until he's completely drunk, and there are days that he'll pass out in the gutter. He'll also love to gamble. You should caution him to stop now."

Tan knew that this statement was useless; no matter how

much Elder Sister Hong warned Ta, twenty years later he would still turn into a miserable man. Reality had already proven it.

Her tears flowing, the woman believed completely this forecast of her future life. Unable to hold back her regrets, she began to tell Tan how this situation had started: "When I was still a single girl, many people fell in love with me, dear uncle. But I ended up marrying that burden. Who can escape destiny..."

Hong wasn't lying. There had been a professor of literature, an electrical engineer, a party committee secretary, and a university student five years her junior who had all given her warm kisses. The engineer had even sent Hong some playful poems alluding to his wish to live with her, and since Hong had an inclination for poetry in her blood, she immediately responded with poems of her own. This young woman from the watch repair factory had filled notebooks with poems and love songs. But fate had arranged for Hong to meet Ta and fall for him the first time she laid eyes on him: a tall young man with a face like flower petals, skin like milk powder and a pair of eyeglasses that made him look quite intellectual. Only after they had gotten married was Hong shocked to find that Ta was not a high-ranking engineer at the rubber factory, as he had told her, but was in fact a porter whose education had ceased after the sixth grade. The clear eyeglasses she had admired so many times had turned out to be a laborer's protective goggles. No wonder when she had lent him a copy of *The Barefooted*, months had gone by without him returning it. Hong always enjoyed debating the contents of such stories, but when she tried to get Ta's opinion, he would only grunt, then switch the talk to flowery words about stars, the light of paradise, the warmth of love... "In fact, he's never read a book in his whole life," Hong said bitterly. And that wasn't all, she continued: many times when, still thinking he was an engineer, she had urged him to transfer to the factory's headquarters, he had said firmly, "They definitely wouldn't let someone with such high-level skills as I have transfer—there are only a handful like me in the entire factory." It wasn't until after they had married that she found he had no specialized skills at all.

"If that were the worst of it, your future life wouldn't be that miserable," Tan said. "But it's not. He will also gamble, and play *de...*"

"Dear Uncle, what is *de*?"

Tan explained how that curse for hundreds of thousands of people worked, even drawing a diagram with a hundred squares on a piece of paper to clarify it. Once, when Ta had lost at *de*, the man had to sell his TV, his refrigerator, and even had to climb up on his roof, remove his tiles and sell those. Afterwards, he even pried up his floor tiles and peddled them as well. Husband, wife and kids had to crowd into a corner of the house just six meters square to keep dry. *You feed your* de *father instead of your own/you live in the gutter, and not in your home* went the ditty people would sing in the future.

"My God, that's terrible," Hong said. "I have to divorce him. I will divorce him."

Tan shook his head, and looked at her with sympathy. "You'll cry out the same thing many times. One time, just as you start shouting at him, he will yank a bench out from under two customers and throw it at you as you run away. You'll have a broken leg, you'll be in a cast, and have to stay in bed for over a month.."

"How miserable. I'll just die," Hong moaned, holding her face in her hands.

Tan didn't see Mrs. Si frantically signalling him to stop. He was releasing all of his pent up anger at Hong's violent husband.

"You won't die. You'll try to hang yourself, but he'll come home just in time and cut the rope. And with the same knife, he'll slash your back on another occasion."

The woman jumped like a beast hit by a bullet. She screamed and shot out to the corridor, her curses fading with her footsteps as she ran home. A little while later Tan and Mrs. Si could hear the couple screaming at each other and the footsteps of the people rushing in to stop them. Mrs. Si ran out to the balcony. Tan followed her. A crowd had gathered outside the apartment of the couple with a bleak future.

"This is terrible," Mrs. Si said, shaking her head reproachfully. "What are we going to do now?"

"I only spoke the truth," Tan said meekly. But he was full of regret.

"The truth? Do you think when people ask to get their fortune told they want to hear bad things? That girl is so angry now, she'll spill everything."

She could get in trouble because of this.

But Hong didn't do as Mrs. Si feared. Her superstitious belief in the person who had foretold her future made her keep her mouth shut about what she had heard. And Mrs. Si had some other real concerns as well. This young man was saying things with an undeniable sincerity and giving out very clear details. Should she really believe he was a messenger from the spirits? He didn't look all that abnormal, didn't seem ill, and didn't have the usual fiery appearance of a medium who lived in an excited mental state.

The crowd in front of the couple's apartment suddenly began to scatter. A man wearing a helmet and knapsack had just arrived and told the people to disperse and prepare for an American bombing. Miraculously, the couple, who had been tearing at each other's hair, immediately released each other and turned to listen to the man's authoritative comments. Tan suddenly recognized him. It was Mr. Tuu from building A3, rumored to be the leader of the construction team that had built Tan's A1 building.

"Do you want to know about Uncle Tuu?" Tan pointed to the man. "I know him."

"No, no." An alarmed Mrs. Si shoved Tan inside her apartment. "He's involved in neighborhood security. If he found out about what just happened in this apartment, you and I can both be sure we'll be invited for tea at the district office."

*   *   *

The door had been left ajar, but the person who had just arrived knocked on it lightly, rather than pushing it open. Was it a stranger? Tan slipped the shirt off his coat hanger and put it on before going to the door.

Standing there was a young woman with large eyes and an abnormally small nose and mouth.

"Excuse me, is this Do's house?"

Tan opened the door wider and stood to one side. "Please come in."

"No, please." The girl pulled a sealed envelope out of her bag and handed it to Tan. "This is a letter from Yen to Do. Would you please pass it on to him?"

The girl said goodbye and left. On the envelope was a picture of a liberation soldier in a bush hat, marching through the Truong Son jungles with a rifle slung from his shoulder and a staff in his hand. The handwriting was indeed his mother's: straightforward, the letters round. The two had just seen each other on Tuesday, and they would see each other again this afternoon, Saturday. Why was Mom writing to Dad? He wanted to open the envelope, read the words that might reflect some problem between the lovers. He also wanted to understand a little more about his mother as a young woman through her letter. He sat contemplating the envelope for a long while and then decided to get on a tram and go to the Phuc Thinh construction site and deliver the letter to his father. It was likely that if he waited until the evening, the message might arrive too late or be unnecessary.

In fact, outside of the usual things that lovers write to each other, Yen's letter contained a simple message: she wouldn't be coming back to Hanoi on Saturday afternoon as planned, but really hoped Do could come and visit her on Sunday morning. However there were also some things Yen didn't explain. The truth was she hadn't stayed at school because it was her turn at guard duty, as she implied. Just before saying goodbye to Do on Tuesday night, knowing she'd be getting home late, Yen had thought something that turned out to be quite accurate: "Mother will never let me hear the end of it."

She had prepared an excuse, but when she saw her mother

in front of her, her stare drilling through to her heart, Yen's words had lost their confidence. "I needed to use the book *Western Civilization*, but I left it here," she said weakly.

Until that moment, her mother had not spoken. She had merely looked at Yen as if seeing her for the first time. Then, maintaining her cold silence, she had turned the tea pot in her hands upside down and poured the tea leaves out into a chrysanthemum flower pot elegantly displayed in the living room. The action frightened Yen.

"When did you learn to tell lies, young woman?" her mother asked finally.

It had taken her a few seconds to speak, as if she wanted her daughter time to suffer in her silence.

"I...missed you; that's why I came back," Yen stammered, and nearly burst out crying at the lie.

"Who, what miserable person taught you to lie?" her mother shouted angrily, like a general suddenly throwing a tantrum in front of her troops.

Her struggle to create an excuse collapsed. Yen sobbed. The gap that separated her mother from Do seemed to her at that moment to have grown deeper, and she felt even more desperate.

Her mother didn't console Yen, but left her to curse herself, to feel sorry for herself and think about her unforgivable behavior. How dare that girl ride her bicycle into the city to meet a man, and not come home until ten at night? And in the middle of a war! Silently, the mother went into the kitchen and warmed up some food, her heart aching. A woman could be wise for three years and then foolish for an hour. How could her daughter be so sure she wouldn't lose her purity, hooked up the way she was with that no-good sailor?

Yen cried her heart out. She was troubled by her mother's long silence. Was it a warning about the storm that was about to come? When her mother came from the kitchen, Yen didn't dare look up.

"Come, eat." It was a stern command.

Although Yen was hungry, she didn't feel like eating at all.

Yet she stood up as if someone had grabbed her arm, pulled her to her feet and yanked her to the table. She ate as if suffering a punishment. When she was finished, her mother cleared the table, washed the dishes and then came back.

"Now you will tell me the truth," she said.

Yen had to recount everything, down to the last detail, like a pauper pulling the last coin from his purse. The mother stared down at her miserable daughter the way a rich and powerful lady might look at her maid. Occasionally, when she heard details she considered obnoxious—the well-worn techniques of a man out to seduce a foolish girl—her lips would twitch. In truth, she was filled with anger both at that man and at her stupid daughter, who she had raised so carefully, only to see all that education wasted, like water poured over the head of a duck.

"Listen to me, young woman," she said in a steely voice, "from now on when you come back to Hanoi, you're to come directly home and not go anywhere else. Even if I'm not home, it doesn't mean I don't know what's going on."

It was a superfluous warning. Yen knew her mother had the ability to make any of her children tremble whenever they lied, betraying themselves with their own reactions.

She kept her head down, staring at her fingers, locking and unlocking them. She felt completely lost, unsure how to defend herself and clear her lover's name. The mother stayed silent, letting her own anger abate.

"My child," she said, her voice going tender now, but no less firm, "it's going to be another year before you graduate from the university and start out in life. If you haven't built up your career and your reputation, how will you succeed? You're still a foolish young girl, incapable of distinguishing between a good or a bad person. If you're going to fall in love and get married, you should let me choose the man and make the arrangements."

Yen knew she could not accept this view. But the sincerity of her mother's tone and her own dislike of the melodramatic robbed her of her defenses.

"I hadn't thought about getting married," she said awkwardly.

"Good. If you listen to me, your life will turn out better. And if you don't, then we're no longer mother and daughter."

This Yen believed.

Her mother had been a brave cadre, during the fight against the French. She was the daughter of a patriotic lawyer, an educated woman with a baccalaureate degree, when she met and married Yen's dad, a mechanical engineer who had studied in France. The young couple had become revolutionaries when a fighter from the Capital City Battalion, unable to withdraw with his unit, had taken refuge in their house. They had hidden him there for two months, an event which led the couple to carry Yen, then a three year old girl, into the liberated zone in 1949. There, the husband worked at the military machine plant and the mother threw herself into the campaigns to recruit women. During party meetings, sometimes in front of thousands of people, this intellectual woman with fiery eyes had raised her voice to exhort the crowd and to explain the tactics of the resistance. Depending on the subject of the talk, she could switch from a caring and confidential tone to a steely and vengeful one. Along with her altruism, the young mother also took a private pride in her work: the satisfaction of knowing she stood out from the others. She wore the brown shirt of a peasant, but with her tall frame, her well-proportioned body and her fair skin, she appeared elegant in that simple short-sleeved brown blouse. She shook hands and embraced the other women in an egalitarian and open manner, but in her heart saw this as a generous gesture from someone of superior rank. After peace came, she returned to Hanoi, and accepted a series of important posts from this agency and that department, deliberately creating herself as someone with a hardened yet proper attitude, distinct from the other female cadres who still spoke with provincial accents and occasionally displayed peasant-like habits. She started to demand that her husband participate more in Party activities and duties. He was a man who was passionate about his work, and her claims on his time became a terrible burden for him. In truth, these demands had started back when they were both in the resistance, but in those days his participation wasn't so critical to her. But now she wanted a husband with a prominent position in society, and besides she enjoyed the feeling of power at arranging his career, shaping his direction in life. The rupture between them began when he resolutely refused the title of chief of staff in the Ministry of Industry and Metallurgy. From that point on, she looked at him with condescending eyes, the eyes of a sharp and savvy women regarding an insignificant man, without reputation or career. The disdain and resentment she felt towards him boiled inside of her, her anger flaming up day by day until she could no longer endure him. They separated. He returned to his parents' house on Tran Hung Dao street. She stayed on in the house on Hai Ba Trung with three children.

But even such a hard woman suffered secretly and had moments of loneliness and need, especially after a tense day at work, or after having stood at a podium and given a speech ringing with enthusiasm, only to return home to a manless house. Once in a while, late at night, the husband would come and knock on the door. She would push the peep hole cover to one side, look through the opening, which was just like the circular opening to a pigeon's cage, and see him standing there. She would bite her lips in displeasure, not wishing to open the door. But in the end the woman in her won out against the propagandist. He was allowed in the house, allowed to look at his children, sleeping in their beds, allowed to share the matrimonial bed. But still, the next morning, she would look at him and again see a failure. She was disdainful of men without prestige or career, and was never softened by their words of courtship. She would look at her husband in a way that revealed her disgust to him, and he would leave the house in despair. Until the next time, when he would come in the night and she would reluctantly let him in, and he would leave again the next morning...

And if you don't listen to me, then we're no longer mother and daughter, she had said to her daughter, and Yen, knowing her father's experience, believed her. Until now her parents still hadn't gotten divorced and lived just a short distance from each other, but there was no reconciliation date. It seemed her mother had created for herself a defined attitude, an unswerving standard, a single direction, and she was determined not to stray from this path. Whoever did not cooperate with her would be left behind, even if it were her husband or her child. It had been like that all of Yen's life, and all of the lives of her siblings. When they were mere toddlers, they had been trained severely by their mother. At the age of five, Yen had been forced to sleep alone in a single bed in order, her mother said, "to build an independent and brave character." When the lights went out, the little girl had felt the distance between her bed and her parents' was infinite. "Mother," she had sobbed quietly, knowing her mother was not too far away, but not daring to cry out too loud, for she feared her mother more than she feared the dark. Her mother had stayed silent and forced her husband to not respond either. After a while, the girl fell asleep. The mother's educational theory had yielded results.

Once, Yen's younger brother Hai had a slight flu and asked his mother if she would talk to his teacher and let him stay home from school that day. His mother felt his forehead, gave him some medicine, then took him to the *pho* stall at the end of the block and made him eat a bowl of beef noodle soup so hot it made him sweat. Then she said sharply: "Now you will go to school. I'll come by this afternoon to check with the teacher and see how you're doing."

The boy, who had been thrilled to have an unexpected bowl of noodle soup, had to go home immediately, get his books and go to school, full of pity for himself because his mother had no sympathy for him. But the mother was very pleased. Only in this way would her children become strong and know how to overcome the weaknesses that would otherwise keep them from their goals.

But if she thought that this method of child-raising would turn Yen and her siblings into strong individuals, she was wrong. Instead they had become docile sheep, at least at this point in their lives. The mother had firmly believed they would accept her manipulations and go forward to build their reputations and careers. That was why she was secretly horrified at the relationship that had sprung up between Yen and that man Do, and was determined to break it up. Yen was the oldest child, and if she defied her mother, she would provide her younger brothers with an example, a way to tear down the mother's protective fence and escape from her sphere of influence.

Yen fell into a tense sleep at about two in the morning. She woke up very early and began to prepare for her return to school. But her mother had risen earlier still and had already prepared a green bean and sticky rice dish for Yen. She packed a bag of fried meat for her to take along also.

"Leaving so early, my child? It's still very dark."

Yen looked at her alarm clock: it was a quarter to five. Outside the window, it was pitch dark, and sometimes the northern wind would blow through.

"You don't need to come," Yen said hurriedly, when she saw her mother putting on a coat, wrapping a scarf around her head, and pulling out her bicycle from the corridor. "At this hour, the defense and militia troops are all over the road, and I can walk by myself."

The mother didn't reply. Once she had made a decision, she never questioned it or allowed it to be contradicted. The two women rode their bicycles past a brightly lit *pho* stall, the charcoal glowing under the pot of steaming broth. Her mother suddenly, almost timidly asked if perhaps Yen wanted some noodle soup.

"You're funny, mother. I'm still full of sticky rice."

Yen understood her mother was feeling badly about her roughness the night before, and that her suggestion to have the noodle soup was a gesture and not one of her mother's cold and certain decisions. They went on. Many times Yen urged her mother to return home, but she patiently pedaled on through the coldness of the early morning. She didn't stop until they had gone some ways beyond the outskirts of the town and the morning had turned a little brighter.

"Go on," her mother said. "And make sure you don't turn back and try to see him."

She turned her bike around and pedaled away towards the

city, confident that Yen only had enough time to get to her school
and make her first class.

After three days of deliberating, Yen arrived at a decision:
she would not return to Hanoi on Saturday afternoon. If she did
come back, she would go straight home; otherwise she would
have to go through another interrogation like the one she suffered
on Tuesday. Remembering that, Yen felt ashamed, and hated
herself for her weakness. No, to return to Hanoi without being
able to see Do would be unbearable. She would send a message
asking him to come meet her at school. This, she felt, was beyond
her mother's control.

*   *   *

Do's "Gravediggers" team had finally found the boat that sank
60 years before.

At the beginning of the century, a few local capitalists had
risen very quickly during the time Vietnam was colonized and
called Annam by the French. French nationals and other foreign
capitalists had a complete monopoly over all areas of Annam's
production, business and transportation. The number of
indigenous capitalists was still small, but they quickly established
a presence.

Among them, Banh Te Bay was one of the most influential.
Among his projects was a line of passenger ships which
competed with a French owned company, Laurent and Sons.
The owner of that company looked for various ways of strangling
the young Vietnamese upstart's company, but failed each time.
There were even skirmishes between the employees of both
companies as they competed for passengers. One day, ironically,
the Annamese capitalist's river boat *Hong Bang* had just left
Hanoi at a leisurely speed, and hadn't gone very far when the
French vessel *Palace* caught up with it. The French captain at
first just wanted to show off a little and have a laugh by passing
the Annamese boat. But suddenly he was seized by a desire to
demonstrate French superiority. The *Palace* pulled a half-boat's

length ahead of the *Hong Bang*, then veered right, trying to force the Annamese river boat to turn towards the embankment. If that happened, the *Hong Bang* would either crash against the embankment or run aground in shallow water. The passengers on both boats poured outside, fighting each other for the best places on the upper decks, cheering loudly. The *Hong Bang* increased its speed, struggling valiantly to maintain its forward direction. The other river boat surged forward also, intent on achieving its goal. The passengers shouted and clapped their hands, with the Annamese on the French boat roaring their support for the *Hong Bang*. But the situation, which had started out as an arrogant game, ended tragically. The *Palace* continued to force the Annamese boat towards the embankment, and the *Hong Bang* continued to increase its speed. Suddenly there was a terrible crashing sound. Everyone assumed the Annamese boat had been hit because it veered off. But no, it maintained its speed and surged forward, leaving in its wake the sound of the Annamese passengers, still shouting and laughing and triumphant. Then, in full view of the shocked people watching from all of the boats along the banks of the river, the *Palace* began to shudder and fall to pieces: something had exploded inside of it. Water poured into the cracks in its hull and the ship nose-dived and sank to the bottom of the river like a boxer that had just taken a knockout punch. Just at that moment church bells on the shore rang out, as if tolling for a departed soul, and the morning light turned murky, as if it was dusk. The fishermen along the banks rushed to the scene in their sampans and were able to rescue the passengers and the captain.

Although the owner of Laurent and Sons instigated a law suit, it failed, and he didn't bother to try to raise the boat, but had simply accepted the insurance payments. For a time afterwards, the smoke stack stuck out of that part of the river, and served as a diving board for children. Then more time passed and even the smoke stack sank completely, and in the swift course of events during the war of liberation, people forgot all about the once famous French river boat.

One of the kids that had stood on the bank to cheer on the *Hong Bang*, and who later dove several times down into the wreck, playing hide and seek with his friends, was now an old man of seventy. By coincidence, Do had allowed the old man to sit in his captain's cabin while he was on a job towing a barge back to Hanoi. During his lunch break, the old man had unwrapped his rice and told Do the story of the confrontation between the two ships that had happened over half a century before. Immediately Do was struck by an idea: why not salvage the French river boat and restore it—wasn't his company in dire need of boats since there were so many old or bomb-damaged vessels to repair? He made repeated trips to the old man's house, in a village on the outskirts of the city, and probed the old man's memories about that area of the river where the boat had gone down. Calculating from the distance the old man estimated, adding the river bank's extension by twenty centimeters each year due to the buildup of alluvial soil, Do decided that the boat was buried under about two meters of sand right under the river beach. He presented the facts to the company's management, along with a map of the area where he thought the boat was buried, and suggested that a team be formed to search for it. The proposal was accepted and the Gravediggers' team was born.

From the time the river bank was still obscured by the morning fog, until darkness turned everyone's face into charcoal, the search team dug up the area indicated on Do's map. After nearly a month without seeing a hint of the boat, some people began to despair, and the old man, who had come along, felt terribly guilty. The beach and the foliage were no longer the same as they had been, so there was nothing he could use as a landmark. He feared he might have pointed out the wrong location and made more trouble for the team members. One day at noon, most of the digging detail had left their equipment and washed their hands and feet to get ready for lunch. Only two of them were still working, getting in their last shovelfuls. Suddenly, the blade of one shovel hit a hard object and clanged loudly as if it had struck a rock. Then it slid, making the agonized noise of metal grating against metal. The group of men sitting around the edge of the sand pit, which looked like a small bomb crater, didn't pay any attention. Only the men still digging paid attention: they began to work in a frenzy, like gold prospectors who had just caught a glimpse of the precious metal.

"Here we go. We've found the dragon's mouth!" yelled one guy. He dropped his shovel, picked up a handful of sand and threw it at the men who had just opened their lunch packs. Everyone bolted up and jumped into the pit, where they stood staring at the part of the smokestack that had just been exposed. The entire team went mad then, punching and wrestling each other, hugging each other and jumping up and down. They even dragged the old man, with his beard that looked like a fishing line, into their dance, howling like a pack of savages.

Do sent a man back to report to the company, asked that another team of workers be mobilized, and suggested that the village leadership might get some additional help for them. Meanwhile the rest of the team, including the old man, dug eagerly in the sand.

When Tan brought Yen's letter out to the site, the faded tent was empty and the only people he could see were digging down in the pit where part of the deck was beginning to show. Do climbed to the edge, took the letter, opened it and read it immediately, and his eyes brightened. Tan considerately walked away from him, going closer to the edge of the pit so he could take a look. One man, his naked back glistening with sweat, looked up at him and smiled:

"You're Do's younger brother, aren't you? Come on down here and help us out and later generations will recognize your work at this historic moment."

Tan jumped in cheerfully, thinking: *the later generation is here, digging along with you.* The river boat, thought to have gone to eternal sleep under the sand of the beach, considered to be content with its past, was now being excavated and would become useful in the present. And in the future also, for Tan remembered that in 1987, the boat his father's company had named *Victory* was this very same river boat once called *Palace.*

*   *   *

On Sunday morning, Do took Tan on his Reunification bicycle to Yen's Teachers' Training College. After a night of confiding to Tan about his feelings for Yen, Do felt there was no longer a distance between him and the youth: Tan had become a close and trusted friend. Perhaps Do still felt a blood link to Tan, but he couldn't explain the reason for it to himself. As for Tan, he happily and immediately agreed to go with Do. Since the other day, Tan had only heard about his mother, had only felt the touch of her warmth on the street of the *sua* flowers. But he had not yet met her. He very much wanted to meet and know more about his mother as a young woman.

Do steered the bicycle handles to the right and turned into a street that ran between two rows of sea pines. It was full of pot holes that knocked the two of them about. On one side a field of sugar cane obscured the river; on the other was a ditch separating the street from the freshly harvested field, thick with the exposed roots of wheat plants. Suddenly a young woman rushed out of the sugar cane field, waving her arms vigorously. Tan dismounted as Do stopped the bike.

"Which one of you is Do, please?" asked the young woman, confused when she saw the two men who resembled each other so much. Before either could answer, she recognized Do as the older man and turned to him. "Yen asked me to come here and warn you not to come to the school gate. Her mother came early this morning and she's sitting in the office. If you don't know the back way yet, then follow me."

The young woman pointed to the sugar cane field, then took off first. Do began to follow her, then suddenly realized he shouldn't lead Tan into some possible trouble. He pushed the Reunification bike towards him: "Don't bother coming along. Just wait here, and we'll be back."

The Teachers Training College consisted of four long thatched roof buildings forming a rectangle around a yard. The only entrance was through the front gates. Behind the buildings were fields. Yen's building faced the main office and the offices of the teachers and administration. If she walked out of the front gate, her mother, sitting in the administrative office, would see her and become suspicious. Since she had seen her mother arrive, not knowing what she said to the head of the administrative office, Yen had not dared to show her face. She had worried that things might get more complicated if Do stepped through the school gate, and so had asked her roommate to intercept Do on the road and let him know.

Yen had been naive to think that she would be able to escape her mother's eyes by meeting Do at school. After the discussion between mother and daughter on Tuesday night and early Wednesday morning, when Yen had not come home yesterday, as on other weeks, her mother became suspicious. It could very well be that if she blocked one tunnel opening, they would sneak out of another. She was ninety per cent certain that they had agreed to meet on Sunday morning when "that guy" was off from work. But a brave and sharp woman would not be beaten by two kids. She would block the remaining tunnel opening, and strike a superior blow by first letting the school administration know the situation, and then informing that guy's company. She rode her bicycle to the school early that morning, full of determination to punish those who had so blatantly dared to challenge her. The head of the administrative office, who had planned to take advantage of the day off to build a chicken coop, had to put away his boards and receive a deputy agency director. He listened to her talk about the romance between Yen and Do, constantly nodding his head, though in truth he couldn't understand what the big deal was. He had seen Do a couple of times when he had come to visit Yen, and he seemed like a rather nice guy.

"I suggest that the school take appropriate measures to stop such unhealthy relationships within the student body," the mother said. "I suggest that Vu Do be forbidden to continue his relationship with my daughter." These commands were issued in a warm, soft tone. The mother had cultivated the art of using certain qualities of voice whenever she issued a request or instruction. In this way, she avoided making listeners feel they were being ordered about and instead allowed them to feel persuaded by her sincere and confidential tone.

"Forbidden?" The head of the administrative office was startled. He wondered if things between the couple had become more serious than the mother was willing to divulge. "Did you say 'unhealthy,' dear comrade?"

"Our country is at war, young people are petitioning to be allowed to volunteer to shed their blood at the front, and here is Do, drifting about at home, falling in love. Is that something you consider healthy, comrade?"

The mother noticed that every once in a while, the office head would glance discreetly at a pile of wood and tools in a corner of the school yard. This displeased her immensely. Nonetheless she softened her voice, as if asking a favor: "The comrade should go ahead and finish his work. I only request to be allowed to sit here and wait for him to arrive."

The head of the administrative office, concealing his delight, rose and took his leave, struggling to keep his feet from rushing too quickly, struggling to keep from appearing like someone who has just escaped an ordeal.

In the meantime, Do was being led by the young woman across the sugar cane field, then sloshing through a recently harvested rice paddy, the water coming up to his ankles. They approached Yen's building from the rear. She was already standing at the window, waiting for him.

"My dear Do," Yen said, letting out a sigh of relief that the confrontation she feared between him and her mother would not happen after all.

"Darling," Do said, moved by her words. He reached for her hands on the window bars. "Come out here, my darling."

The window, with its upright bamboo bars, separated the two. They looked at each other through that window like a prisoner and a visiting relative.

"I can't, sweetheart. The moment I step out of that door, Mother will see me."

One of her three roommates was mending a shirt button. She looked up suddenly. "What if I pretended to carry the water container to the well to wash my clothes, and you hide behind it, slip out back?"

Yen shook her head. "It wouldn't work. My mother is too sharp and alert."

The other roommate, who was copying poems into her notebook, dropped her pen, slapped her hands together and cried out: "It's simple. Give him a knife, cut through the bars and take them out. Then she can fly through the window and be with him."

Yen, Do, and all three roommates shouted. Yen quickly raised her hand, signalling them to keep silent. If she heard unusual noises from the room, the mother could very well come and check.

Do worked fast. He used the knife to saw through the tops of the window bars, then adroitly shook and pulled them out of their bases. Only two bars had to be removed to give Yen enough space to climb out. She took her copy of *The Old Man and the Sea* as a present for Do to take back with him to Hanoi. When she was out, Do replaced the bars, using shards of bamboo to secure them into the base. They waved goodbye to their three allies, crossed the flooded rice paddy and disappeared behind the sugar canes. Do held onto Yen's hand with one hand, and with the other he reached out and pushed away the long sugar cane leaves that were ready to whip across their faces like swords.

"We've escaped!" Do called out, as if it were a joke, but in fact he and Yen felt as if a weight had been lifted from them. They stopped and looked at each other, both of them still panting. At that moment, Do remembered that Tan was waiting for him on the other side of the sugar cane field.

"Yen, I have a new young friend—you're going to get to meet him now."

He recounted briefly how Tan had suddenly appeared in his home, and then whispered in Yen's ear what Tan had said about them being his parents. Yen blushed, and, pretending to be outraged, said, "That's something you definitely made up."

Still, she was somewhat curious now, and followed Do to

Tan. She didn't know what to ask or even what to say to this strange youth. She couldn't very well ask him if he had really said what Do told her he'd said, or if Do had only been joking. Nor could she ask the normal questions a person would ask at the beginning of a friendship about his home and family. Do had warned her against asking any questions that might awaken painful memories. In the end, she remained silent, and just smiled at Tan, sweetly and affectionately.

As for Tan, he was struck dumb in front of this 21-year-old woman, so full of lively charm. Was this his mother? The same mother that twenty years from now he would teasingly call *Madame* Yen? Dear *Madame*, looking the way you look now, if you were thrown in with the young women of your age twenty years from now, you'd be considered a country bumpkin, someone who definitely belonged to the "old guard." But right now, this young woman's freshness seemed lovable and fitting and Tan stood awkwardly in front of her, unsure as she was about what to do or say.

"You must have been worried, waiting so long for us," Yen said finally.

"Oh, no," Tan said. He could wait much longer for these two lovers. He could wait twenty years.

"Yen's mother was waiting in the office to catch us," Do said. His tone was joking, but edged with bitterness. "That's why we had to slip out and take the back way."

Tan looked at the two of them, unable to conceal his pity. They were not afraid of death: one stayed in the city to work under the rain of bombs, and the other bicycled each week along a national highway that was the target of American attacks. Yet they did not have the courage to face Yen's mother. Why should they have to run and hide? They weren't doing anything illegal or improper. No, my dear parents, he thought, if it were me, I'd face Yen's mother directly, no matter the uproar and complications.

Do rubbed his hands together, then said, somewhat guiltily: "Yen and I are going to go down to the river bank for a while and wait for her mother to go back to Hanoi. Why don't you ride around on the bicycle, take a look at the scenery and wait for me?"

"Tan, take this book with you." Yen handed him *The Old Man and the Sea*. As she did so, she glanced quickly into the youth's bright eyes, and then trembled slightly. Those eyes seemed to hold her future in them.

Again the two went back deep inside the sugar cane field, then sat down next to a bush that had pink and yellow vines curling around its branches and leaves. A fishing boat with a brown sail floated slowly by in front of them, leaving in its wake a thin film of smoke from its cooking fire. No one could really know if the life of the couple on the fishing boat was harmonious, but just to look at the scene filled the young couple with aspirations and hope.

"Do, my darling," Yen whispered.

"What, my dear?"

"It's strange. I look at that guy and I think he could be you when you were a student. And I wish..."

Yen didn't say anything more, but Do understood right away. He shared the same wish. They wanted to have a child like him. For a reason they were not sure of, both believed that their son would grow up to be like the youth Do had befriended, lovable and full of confidence, just like him.

*   *   *

Yen's mother waited until two o'clock in the afternoon and then began to worry. Maybe she'd been anxious for no reason. There was no sign of the young man and the things she had prepared herself to say to his face had faded by the hour, become disjointed, dispersed like water lilies scattered in all directions by the winds of a storm. Finally, running out of patience, she decided to walk across the yard to Yen's room. She nodded to the three students inside, then stood, stunned.

"Yen doesn't live in this room anymore, is that it?" she said calmly, regaining her composure.

"Ma'am, Yen still lives here," one of the girls said quickly, "but she went back to Hanoi early this morning."

"Back to Hanoi?" The mother forced a smile. "Since what time, dear?"

"Around nine o'clock," one of the other girls answered smoothly.

The mother tightened her lips slightly, said goodbye to the three students, then carried her basket back across the yard, to the head of the administrative office, who was building his chicken coop. The project was still unfinished, and he was not very satisfied with the work he'd done; he'd been distracted, keeping one ear towards the classy visitor who was sitting in his office, and anxiously awaiting the dramatic event that would probably get the whole school excited. At times, he wished the young man would appear quickly and satisfy his curiosity. At other times, he only wished to be left alone to finish his coop, and secretly hoped the man wouldn't come. When he saw the mother leave Yen's room and walk determinedly towards him, he put down his plane, sat down, crossed his legs, and waited.

"Will the comrade kindly inform me as to where the student Pham Thi Hoang Yen has gone?" the mother said. Her tone was serious, but her choice of words conveyed sarcasm.

The head of the administrative office pointed hesitatingly to Yen's room. "I saw her in her dorm room this morning."

"The duty officer told me the same thing, and I believed him," the mother said, nodding. "But would you please go and check now?"

"You mean she's no longer there?" The head of the administrative office spoke loudly, then stood up. This woman standing in front of him made him feel ineffectual.

Keeping her expression blank, the mother waved her arm, to show her dissatisfaction. When he saw this, the head of administration knew he no longer had to go to the dorm room. Suddenly, his foot caught against a board and knocked it over. It fell on a box of nails which spilled out on the ground. Looking at the mess at his feet, it came to him that being dragged into this tiresome situation was indeed a waste of time.

"It's likely that she's gone to Hanoi," he said, firmly. "Students are allowed to leave on holidays."

The mother's sharp gaze pierced him. "I'm not protesting that. But if your students come and go without anyone knowing, does the comrade consider this school's safety measures adequate?"

It seemed to him that these words were not merely a reproach, but contained an implicit threat that a report about the school's safety measures would be made to some high-ranking official. The head of the administrative office was suddenly tired of all this, to the point where he didn't bother to reply. He stood still for a time, and then said goodbye to Yen's mother. He waited until she was out of the gates and then sat down and returned to his unfinished tasks.

Yen's mother walked her bicycle past the village communal hall, with the old banyan tree in front of it, past a line of white sandalwood trees, past an old pond. Her face was full of the anger she no longer needed to hide or control, since there was no one around now. She hadn't thought that Yen would dare to go against her wishes. Her irresponsible actions now must be the result of that man Do's plans and persuasions. She no longer felt only displeasure towards Do, but now actually hated him. She could not see in him any redeemable or acceptable characteristics.

She had walked almost completely around the pond—it was nearly as large as a small lake—when she was surprised to see a young man sitting and reading by a row of *dien thanh* trees. A Reunification bicycle was leaning next to him. The youth had his back to her and was unaware that anyone was approaching. Her heart was beating fast, but she was unsure who this was, and cleared her throat. The youth turned around. It wasn't Do, even though something about him reminded her of that man. His eyes widened, eyes so clear they would move anyone capable of loving pure beauty.

"Hello, ma'am," the boy said, then stopped. A shock went through him. It was that woman, a woman he had only met once, when he was three years old, outside the State Department Store.

Since then, he had only known his maternal grandmother through the photographs his mother had kept, even though she was still alive and lived on the same street she had always lived in Hanoi. His heart trembling because of this unexpected encounter, Tan stood up awkwardly. The yellow *dien thanh* leaves fell off his clothes.

Even in the midst of her anger, Yen's mother found herself weakening before this youth's sweet manners. "Are you someone from Do's family?" she asked softly.

I'm your grandchild, and you've recognized it, and that's why your have softened your voice, Tan wanted to say. But all he did say, finally, was, "Yes, ma'am."

"Where are they then?" The mother's voice was no longer as bitter as it had been when she left the school.

"They told me to wait here, but I don't know where they went."

Tan's sincerity evoked some sympathy in the mother. She lowered the kick stand and left her bicycle on the side of the road.

"Please tell Do I have no ill will against him," she said, her voice deepening with candor. "But my daughter hasn't even finished school yet, and to be in love right now would have a bad effect on her studies. I can not allow it. If Do had an older or younger sister, he would recognize that what I'm saying is reasonable."

Tan looked into her eyes as she spoke, politely muttering "yes, ma'am," once in a while. It was the first time he had ever spoken to his maternal grandmother and he understood her to a certain degree.

He had first met her on the day he went with his mother to the State Department Store on Trang Tien Street. His mother had left her bicycle on the sidewalk, telling Tan—he was three years old—to watch the vehicle while she went inside to buy a few bars of soap. He had noticed a woman standing next to a display case; she was staring at him with a look of restrained affection in her eyes. It had looked as though she was deciding whether or not she would come over to him. In the end, the blood bond between them overcame the cold, dry voice of reason. She had looked around her furtively, as if afraid someone would catch her, then approached him and took a white swan and a plastic yellow car with red tires from her bag, and handed them tenderly to Tan.

"These are some gifts for you."

"Oh, Ma'am," the boy cried out happily. "Who are you?"

"Just go ahead and take them."

The old woman hastily pushed the toys at the boy's chest, and left immediately, afraid both of showing any weakness by exposing her emotions and that her daughter would see her.

When she heard Tan relate the incident later, his mother was able to guess what had happened. Back at home, she had shown her son the family photo album, and Tan had immediately pointed out the woman who had given him the gifts. Yen had been overcome with joy. She had hoped that having seen her bright grandchild with her own eyes, her mother would soften her attitude towards her and her husband. Yen had suffered for many years because of her mother's stubborn and severe temperament. When her mother had realized she no longer had the power to interfere with her daughter's love affair, she had become very cold and cruel towards the couple. When Do's mother had come to her to plan for the engagement and decide upon a wedding date, Yen's mother hadn't even looked at her. "She is no longer my daughter," she said dryly. "I have no responsibility in the matter."

After Yen had given birth to her son, she had hoped that the arrival of a grandchild would diminish her mother's hostility. She asked her brother to tell her mother about the birth, but the mother neither responded nor came for a visit. Then, as Yen was preparing for the child's first month celebration, she told her mother-in-law that she intended to formally invite her mother. The paternal grandmother thought that merely sending the invitation would not be sufficient, and that it would be proper if she herself, an in-law of the same status, would personally deliver the letter. But when she arrived at the house, Yen's mother claimed to be busy and would not even leave her room. Instead, she let her youngest son receive Do's mother, as one would receive a mere acquaintance rather than a respected family member. She had never forgiven Yen. Her daughter had climbed over the fence and escaped from her control. Surely such defiance was the example that caused her two sons to disobey her as well by refusing to take the entrance exams for the schools of medicine and business administration as she had decided. One studied mechanical engineering, and the other went into apprentice construction training. Her ambitions to be the brilliant mastermind directing her children's every step had been unsuccessful, and she placed all the blame on Yen, and on Do.

But after her mother had quietly offered gifts to Tan, Yen had hoped she was softening. One Sunday morning, she went with Tan to her mother's house, hopeful that the sight of the boy would stir her mother's heart. As she stopped in front of the double grill of the iron gate and started to undo the chain lock, her brother, his face sad, rushed out.

"Mother told me to tell you that she's tired today and does not wish to see you. Please understand and go home. I'll come over later."

Yen and Tan never knew that when they turned away and left, her mother was standing motionless at the window, looking down at them. She felt a pain in her heart. She wanted to throw away all her pride, her hatred, her coldness, and call out to them. But her stubbornness would not allow it. That pain tore at her heart and continued to tear her apart for years.

But that was a story for the future. At this moment, his maternal grandmother was standing in front of Tan, looking at him with such resoluteness that was hard to believe she would ever change. Yet he felt that underneath her steely appearance was fear and perhaps even a sense of insecurity.

"I'll tell Do everything, Ma'am," he said.

"Good. Thank you."

She walked away, pushing her bicycle, resisting the strange compulsion she felt to turn to look at Tan one more time. What link could there be between her and this young man? A gust of wind blew past, swirling the *dien thanh* leaves into the air so that they fell down upon her like golden tears.

Tan felt that his grandmother was not as cold as others judged her to be. If he ever found a way back into the future, he would certainly go by himself to visit her. His presence would mean much to her; he was sure of it. She would be seventy years old then, an age when she would need human warmth more than she would need to hang onto old grudges.

*   *   *

Trinh's mother was in her last moments.

Since early evening, Tan had come to help Trinh, as he had been doing over the past few days. He took her two buckets to the public spigot at the end of the apartment complex and fetched water so Trinh could wash and clean. A moment later, as she was straightening the bunker out, Trinh found a coil of electrical wire in a pile of old junk, and Tan quickly connected it to an outlet and ran the wire from the bunker to the house next door. Now there was light in the bunker. Next, Trinh went into the cupboard and brought out an old record player that her father had bought in the Soviet Union a few years back. She carefully cleaned the surfaces of the records and then the control knobs of the player. Watching her, Tan understood that she had sensed something terrible was about to happen.

As she was preparing the record player, Trinh heard the water begin to boil in the tea kettle on the oil cooker. She went to it quickly and poured the hot water into a tin cup, planning to bring it to the wash basin at the foot of the bed so she would have a little warm water to wash her mother's face. Either because the handle of the enamelled tin cup was hot, or perhaps because Trinh's hand was shaking, some of the water spilled out and splashed onto her mother's feet. Trinh threw the cup down into the basin of water and grabbed a corner of the blanket to wipe the hot water away. As she did, a thin layer of skin peeled off her mother's feet. But her mother lay still, staring blankly at the ceiling, neither moving her feet back, nor uttering a sound.

"Oh, mother!" Trinh cried out, embracing her mother's cold, dry feet.

"Trinh, my child." Her mother struggled to contain the pain burning through her torso. Her body felt as if it were being stabbed and pierced in many places, and her fleshless face creased with the effort. "Bring a chair here and sit next to me."

It was Tan who placed a chair next to her, and guided Trinh into it. Mother and daughter both turned in unison and looked towards the entrance to the bunker. A corner of the sky was held in its rectangular frame. It was deep black, without a hint of stars.

A cold wind blew through it. Trinh trembled and came back to herself.

"Mother, why don't I play the Robertino record, the one we both really like."

She became artificially busy, searching for the record, and finally pulling out an album that had a photograph of a singer who looked like a mild boy. Robertino? Hadn't he heard that name before? But in Tan's time, most of the young people had forgotten the singer, and his records had disappeared, as if by a magician's trick. *Come back to Sorrento*, Robertino sang, in a voice so clear and full of passion it squeezed the heart. Both mother and daughter heard in that song a beckoning call to someone far away. Come back, father, come back, even if only for a few hours this night.

Suddenly the light went out, and Robertino's voice was cut off halfway through a sentence, trailing into the mother and daughter's despairing cry, from a dark corner of the bunker. The sirens had just started to wail when the planes began to tear through the sky. The bunker's entrance became a 30 inch television screen on which played a show of missiles of different sizes flying up from the ground, like fiery birds. The sky filled with a festival of red birds, some flying helter skelter, others on parallel tracks, others crisscrossing, and yet others shooting straight up.

"Trinh," the mother said with difficulty. "Raise my head. I want to see."

Tan went over to the corner of the bunker and relit the oil lamp. It burned bright as a green bean. At the same time, Trinh did what her mother had asked. Although she had been aware of her mother's physical deterioration for a long time now, she couldn't help but shudder when she helped her mother sit up. Her body felt shriveled as a child's.

"Mother, do you remember when I was a kid and lit a match, and the curtain caught fire and nearly burned down the house?" She evoked the story as if to force her mother to reply and prolong the moments of her life.

"It was all my fault—I locked you inside so I could go to work," her mother said, and although her words were full of guilt, her voice was so weak it sounded devoid of emotion. "Then I whipped you," she said. "I beat you just because I was fond of that curtain. I was wrong to do it."

Tan didn't dare look at the mother's face, but he could sense she was speaking through her tears. They were the sparse tears of someone who had led a hard life.

"No, you did the right thing. I was bad."

"You were never bad. I know that now, more than ever. You know how to act in life."

More explosions went off, piercing their ears and making their heads ache. Dust and pieces of dirt fell from the ceiling of the bunker. Through the entrance they could see long, bright bursts of fire, like flames flaring from a dragon's nostrils. Antiaircraft rockets rushed about the sky like fiery ants. In the midst of the blazing rockets, something exploded into a constellation of shooting stars. It burst in a flash of light, shooting out long rays, like the petals of a yellow daisy. The daisy broke into three large segments: one, shaped like an arrow head plunging straight down to the ground. The other two pieces fell more slowly, spinning like pinwheels.

"Mother, they've shot down an American plane!"

Trinh's mother seemed to smile through her pain, as if the shot-down plane harbored the news for which she'd been hoping.

"That means your father will be coming home."

"Yes, of course," Trinh agreed hesitatingly. "Father will come home."

A sharp spasm almost made the mother faint. Her feet had lost all feeling. Death was gradually moving up her body now. Her last minutes were not to be easy ones—as she said goodbye to life, she was still enduring the punishment of her sickness. Trinh seized her mother's stiff, icy hands, wanting to give her some of her own heat.

Soon, her mother struggled to open her eyes. Her eyelids had already become stiff and heavy and difficult to control.

"Trinh, my love." It took all of her strength to get out this one clear sentence without gasping. "When your father comes, you will act on my behalf and make sure he has a family. Your father needs a woman to take care of him."

"No, mother, don't say that," Trinh cried out.

"Listen to me. You'll get married and have your own life. In his old age, your father will not be able to live with you. With old people it's better, my child, if there is a man and a woman who know how to look after each other."

Trinh sobbed. What her mother had said was reasonable, but it would take her some time to accept it. For now, all she felt was a sense of loss. After her mother passed away, she would only have her father in the world. Was she to lose him now, to another woman?

"And please ask your father to forgive me. Once, because he was always gone, I filled out an official application for a divorce. But your father would not sign it..."

A hot wind gusted through the bunker, blowing out the oil lamp. The sky turned red, as if the universe had burst into flame. Pieces of the aircraft flew out in all directions, then drifted towards earth very slowly.

"Mother!" Trinh shrieked in the darkness.

Tan's fingers were trembling so hard it took a moment before he could open the matchbox and take out another match. As soon as the oil lamp flared, he saw Trinh's outstretched fingers, reaching towards her mother's eyes, casting a shadow over her face. The mother's unblinking eyes were closed as the hand moved over them. Tan lowered his head and quietly went over to Trinh, who was sitting still as a corpse.

"Mother," she sobbed, one more time.

She placed her head on her mother's chest and reached for Tan's leg. He bent down quickly to support her. She turned her face into his chest, letting herself cry now for all the days she had held back her tears. Outside, the bombs were still exploding, and the noise drowned out her sobs. The earth shook and the entrance to the bunker revealed a fiery storm.

The counterattack against the sky pirates went on until dawn.

Until that moment, Tan stayed alert. After three months of being constantly aware of her mother's fate, Trinh was exhausted, and her crying had increased her tiredness. She passed out in Tan's arms, her breath faint against his chest. In the dim light of early morning, her face was pale and softly reflected a pure and lonely beauty. Her lips were parted with a slight awkwardness that marked her unawareness of the young man who was admiring her so closely.

He bent to her and carefully kissed those lips.

*   *   *

Trinh sat alone on the same stone bench in the flower garden where she and Tan had once sat to talk to each other. On the other side of the street was a house half-destroyed by a bomb. The columns at its front were cracked and crumbling and looking at it she felt a sense of devastation. By this time, her mother was under the earth, leaving Trinh alone. Her funeral had occurred yesterday. It had been well organized and went fairly quickly. All of her close friends who had not been evacuated from the neighborhood were there. There was Uncle Tuu, Aunt Lam, Aunt Mau, Mrs. Si, and Hong and her husband Ta... Afterward, when Trinh was alone in the house, Mrs. Si helped to set up an altar and organized a prayer service for her mother. Since the night before, there had been a unanimous agreement not to let Trinh be by herself in the bunker. Everyone else in her row of houses had been evacuated and none of the remaining neighbors was at ease, thinking of her there, in her state of mind. Finally, Trinh bowed to their concern and began to spend her nights at Aunt Lam's.

On this morning, Aunt Lam and Do went to work early and only Trinh and Tan stayed home. Uneasy with a situation in which they just sat and looked at each other like two shadows, Trinh left without telling Tan where she was going. In fact, she didn't know herself in what direction she was heading. She only became conscious of her surroundings when a woman grabbed her hand and pulled her under the staircase of a nearby building. The Americans were bombing again. What did they want to do: kill off those who just yesterday had lost their brothers and sisters and other relatives?

The noise from the bombs and the antiaircraft batteries finally stopped. The woman who had taken Trinh's hand was wearing a white funeral turban; now she saw that the young girl was also wearing such a turban, and was slowly losing her confused look. Neither asked a question of the other; they only sat together for a little while, looking at each other in mutual sympathy.

Suddenly they heard a cry from someplace close and both jumped up.

"A sky pirate has parachuted!" someone yelled.

Trinh bolted into the street right behind the woman. The red and white parachute blocked the sky over their heads—the American pilot couldn't be more than three meters from the ground. He hit the street relatively easy, rolled once on the pavement and then stood up, expertly releasing the cords and harness from his body. A corner of his parachute had caught on the *xa cu* tree, and the other was pinned on the roof spire of a refreshment kiosk. The woman behind the counter quickly began throwing glasses at the American. They shattered at his feet, making a breaking sound which scared him.

"*Hans up!*" the woman shouted, her slightly mispronounced English terrifying the American even more, since he didn't know what to do.

A pedicab driver leapt forward and shouted another sentence, then raised his arms up high, pantomiming at the American to follow suit. He understood quickly and raised his hands in surrender just as people began swarming into the crossroads from all four directions. Several militia men raised their rifles and began to escort the American away. He had taken only a few steps when a woman, screaming in a high-pitched voice and wielding a pole, jumped out and tried to hit him. Trinh recognized the woman in the white funeral band who had pulled her under the staircase. She was still screaming, struggling to free herself from the people trying to restrain her. Helpless to do anything, she sobbed into their arms as they led her away.

Trinh sat down on the stone bench and looked at the rapidly emptying flower garden. A few home defense guards were climbing up the *xa cu* tree to remove the parachute, afraid it might become a target if the American planes returned. The woman from the refreshment kiosk had taken out a broom and was sweeping the broken shards of glass off the street, murmuring her regrets at having smashed an entire set of glasses.

Someone sat down next to Trinh. Without turning around, she knew who it was.

"You've been following me, haven't you, Tan?"

Tan just looked at Trinh in a confirming silence.

"Why?" Trinh asked, though she knew right away it was a superfluous question.

"I was worried about you. I was worried about myself too."

"Worried about yourself?"

Yes, about himself. He had no idea where his family was, at this moment. Like Trinh, he was alone.

"Let's go home," he said.

"Which house?"

"Yours. I want to light some incense for your mother."

He had decided that from now on, whenever Trinh went home, he would go with her. He couldn't bear to think of her sitting alone in that cold bunker. When they arrived, he lit three bundles of incense sticks for her mother, then sat down next to Trinh and carefully opened the family photo album she had just handed him. He lingered for a long moment over a photo of a girl of about two years old, holding a doll and crying in fear, her lips askew.

"That's how much I cried the first time I saw a black camera lens pointing at my face," Trinh explained with a faint smile.

The photo had loosened from the page. Tan picked it up.

"Will you let me keep this?"

"I guess." Trinh felt a little embarrassed. "Why not a photo of me as a grown-up instead?"

"I like it."

To drive away her awkwardness, Trinh stood up and placed the Robertino record on the turntable. Although Tan had only heard this singer for the first time the other night, he had grown fond of his voice.

"Tan, listen to this song called *Mama*." Trinh had started the record from the first song, but now she moved the needle to the third groove:

My heart trembled when I heard your voice, Mother
Filled with deep love in the evening
You're happy I am back
And smile at me lovingly...

The two friends didn't understand the Italian lyrics, but that soft and easy melody, heard on a winter morning in a quiet bunker, bruised their emotions. Oh, singer from a faraway place and in a foreign tongue, the love between mother and child would always be understood by anyone who hears your song.

The song held Trinh in her sorrow. And again, she seemed to be turning to stone and needed something to lean against. She placed her head on Tan's shoulder, well aware of what she was doing, of what she needed to do. At this moment, who in the world was closer to her than Tan? At first she didn't even realize that she was swaying with his movements, dancing gently around the bunker. The song had ended and a folk song with a melodious tempo had begun. Tan led her with short steps, trying to move very lightly so that there would be no shock, so that he would not pull her from the soft refuge of her dream.

*   *   *

That evening Trinh went to the market and bought food to prepare the evening meal for all four people in the apartment. As he worked, a man entered the apartment. He looked to be in his forties, and had a bright face and an energetic air. Tan recognized him right away, and shouted his name instead of offering a greeting. "Uncle Tuu!"

The man was startled, and stared at Tan defensively. "How do you know my name?"

Thinking of Mrs. Si's appeal to only tell people things about the future that would make them feel good, Tan said, "You're a Hero of Labor; everybody knows you."

"What did you say?" Mr. Tuu leaned towards Tan, as if he wanted to hear once again this good news. "I know I've just been nominated, but I haven't been officially confirmed yet."

When Tan asked him to sit down at the dining table, he did so immediately, like a man used to following orders. But he sat barely able to maintain his patience as Tan cleaned out the tea pot and brewed some tea. Not until he had poured boiling water into the pot did Tan speak again:

"I can't remember the exact date, but I know for sure you'll be confirmed as a Hero. In all the meetings, you'll be introduced as one."

Mr. Tuu tried to maintain a calm appearance, but in fact he felt submerged in a dreamy state of happiness. He closed his eyes, imagining how all his efforts, all his struggles, would finally bring results. Only 38, he was already deputy manager of the City Construction Company, and had been given a number of important assignments. The neighborhood had even persuaded him to head the security team, to help prepare him to be an official Hero. Even though the Nguyen Van Tuu who accepted all assignments given to him was clearly not someone competent to handle it all, unexpectedly, he accomplished nearly everything with excellence. He solved thousands of problems for the company, while himself directing a project to build new housing units. Evenings, he would be seen back in the neighborhood, stopping by here and there, checking on security and firefighting missions. Wearing a metal helmet, a rifle on his shoulder and a rucksack at his side, he appeared to be a tireless worker. That's Hero Tuu! Uncle Tuu the Hero is here! people would say to each other, pointing to him, accepting as a fact the noble designation for which he was striving. He was always there, telling the young guards in the watchtowers a few riddles to help keep them on their toes, reminding young and old to go to the evacuation areas in order to avoid fatalities. His nomination file grew thick with reports of his accomplishments.

At the time Tan was growing up and had started to judge what he saw around him, he had always been confused when he saw people point to Nguyen Van Tuu and call him a hero. How could that frail old man be a hero? In his immature imagination, a hero had to be a strong, brave-looking, handsome man. But here was an old man whose one distinguishing, down-to-earth habit was sneezing and always cleaning his nose with a handkerchief as he talked to other people. And he wasn't a man of few words either. It seemed he was always complaining to anyone he met about how things had gone downhill nowadays. One afternoon, back in 1987, Tan had come home early to prepare his costume for a role he had in the school play that night. But his grandmother was away at a retirees' meeting, and he found he was locked out of their apartment. He had to go over to Mr. Tuu's apartment in the A2 building, where the elders were having their meeting. Tan didn't want to call out and interrupt everyone in order to have his grandmother come out and give him the keys, so he ended up waiting until the retirees were finished. It appeared to him that they had finished their agenda, and other items such as dues, Party fees, and changes in the pension schedule, and had begun to discuss the current complexities of life. He could not see Mr. Tuu's face, but he could hear his voice:

"There's no morality anywhere these days. Yesterday I saw Ta and Hong attacking each other with knives and scissors, and when I went over to talk to them, the husband cursed me out and said, 'damn all old men with nothing better to do.' All of you know, no one would dare talk like that back in the old days.

Back then, all I'd have to do was say one word, and they'd be kowtowing and saying, 'yes sir,' and would stop right away."

"I don't think we can conclude that everything today has gotten worse," the voice of another old man said.

"Not worse?" The words seemed to drive Mr. Tuu into a frenzy. "Prices are going up, the currency is devalued, people cheat, economic management is a joke, social problems are growing more severe..."

"Doesn't the comrade feel that we may be partly responsible for all that?" another person interjected.

"Why? Why should we be responsible for what people are doing today? We accomplished our tasks, we've retired, we've received our insignias for our long service to the Party..."

Fortunately, at that moment an old woman saw Tan loitering near the door and told Mrs. Lam, who gave him the keys. Otherwise Tan would have had to listen to the rest of Mr. Tuu's tirade, punctuated by his sneezes. It wasn't the first time Tan had heard the man complain: he was ready to do it to anyone, at any time.

Mr. Tuu was always ready to cherish and protect all of the projects he had been associated with in the dozen years before sitting face to face with Tan now, in 1967. Tan seized on this chance to compare the man he had known with this younger version.

"Uncle, aren't you the one that directed the construction project at the Green Meadow Housing Complex?"

Mr. Tuu pressed both his hands around the tea cup, to keep them warm, then answered jovially. "Actually, others built the A2 and A3 buildings. I only directed the A1 project, the initial building of the complex."

Tan was surprised. But then he remembered how once, when a team of workers had been called in to reinforce the foundation of the buildings and repair the cracks in the walls, a few of them had commented sarcastically that the building was the masterpiece of the Hero Nguyen Van Tuu.

"Did you know that the A1 building collapsed, Uncle?"

Tan had lowered his voice, but to Mr. Tuu this was like hearing thunder in the middle of a clear and sunny day.

"Collapsed? What are you babbling about? You and I are sitting right here in the building—how can you say it's collapsed?"

He let out a sigh, but he was trembling inside. When the construction of the A1 building had been nearly complete, it was discovered that the foundation had sunk. But the file proposing to name Nguyen Van Tuu an official Hero had already been sent to high officials, and it specifically mentioned the achievement of erecting the A1 building, initiating a construction project that created a multi-storied housing complex and expanding the housing capacity of the city. Due to his work, the project had been completed on deadline, as planned, and the families living there had happily received their keys and moved in. That had been two years ago, and so far nothing had happened. But in his heart, Mr. Tuu felt uneasy, always expecting to hear of a disaster. More truthfully, he was anxious to receive his official title before any complications occurred.

"It tilted and collapsed because the left side of the foundation had sunk," Tan declared firmly.

"When?"

"In 1987."

Mr. Tuu let out a long sigh, and felt lighter. Such an answer was a joke; it was like saying "It will happen at Tet." But then he at once became irritated. How dare this young man joke with him, a serious cadre working hard to become a Hero?

"Exactly how are you related to Mrs. Lam?" he asked, charging his voice with the authority of his position as head of neighborhood security.

"I call her 'Aunt'," Tan said smoothly, but made an involuntary gesture that showed his tension, and that Mr. Tuu noticed immediately. Mrs. Lam had registered the youth for a temporary residence, making the same claim, and Mr. Tuu was here now to check out the situation. One needed to be vigilant. Spies and special agents from the other side of the border were still being infiltrated into the North to disrupt the revolution. There was nothing wrong with this building, yet here was this boy daring to say it would collapse. Who else but an enemy would want our buildings to fall down, our people to be killed?

I must be vigilant about such elements, Mr. Tuu told himself before he left the room.

*　　　*　　　*

Mrs. Si didn't allow Tan to sit in the living room as she had before. Instead she took him through a rear entrance into a room that had a round window through which one could see into the front room. A curtain made out of a parachute from a flare covered the window. She told Tan that the guest who was about to arrive was easily upset and if she had direct contact with Tan she might not be able to "withstand" Tan's predictions. Actually, Mrs. Si was afraid that Tan would get too excited and spill out damaging details, as he had done with Mrs. Hong the other day. Sitting in the back room, looking out through the curtain, Tan would recognize the guest and be able to tell Mrs. Si what he knew. She would then tell the other woman.

This sort of shadowy arrangement made Tan suspicious. He decided to use the occasion to try to find out what he could about this strange character, Mrs. Si. But as the guest walked into the room, Tan received a shock. It was Trinh. Did she want Mrs. Si to tell her future? He had no way of knowing what it would be—what could he tell Mrs. Si? Besides, he was disturbed and somehow offended at Trinh's appearance in the gloomy room of this suspicious woman. Without hesitation, he slipped through the back door and left the room. But rather than go home, he hid behind a *xa cu* tree and waited for Trinh.

Mrs. Si bantered aimlessly with Trinh, with the intention of allowing Tan, hiding behind the curtain, to get a good look at the young woman. She was sure that this time her credibility as a fortune teller would spread quietly and quickly among the superstitious women who made up her clientele. Mrs. Hong had already given her friends an account of the medium's ability to foretell the future accurately. This time, she wouldn't even have Tan speak directly, so the predictions would flow from her own lips.

Trinh said goodbye after she'd been promised that by the next day she would know everything. After she left, Mrs. Si stepped into the back room, then stood there stupefied. Tan was no longer at the curtain. She looked out at the empty field behind her house, but didn't see any sign of him there either. She felt her plans to take advantage of him disintegrating as she looked.

Trinh, intent and preoccupied, had walked past the *xa cu* tree when she was startled by a question coming from behind her.

"What did Mrs. Si tell you?"

Tan saw sadness and some anxiety in her brown eyes. "You know about this?" she asked.

"That woman asked me to hide in the back room and then predict your future."

Trinh bit her lip and looked down at her hands fumbling at the seam of her shirt, as if she'd been revealed as a liar. But really the person that had been uncovered was Mrs. Si: the two friends had started to understand her real character. Still, Trinh couldn't escape feeling a little embarrassed.

"I don't like you to get involved in such matters," Tan said, a bit harshly, and Trinh nearly broke into tears. At this time, who was closer to her than Tan? All of her remaining relatives were stuck behind the lines in Quang Binh, so that nobody could even come to her mother's funeral. And in such a place, devastated by rainstorms of bombs and fire, who knew if anyone was still alive? Only Tan had stood by her. *I don't like*...How could he dig in and deepen her pain, when she was already full of regret and torturing herself?

The two walked quickly towards the bunker. They played the Italian singer's record again. The soft sounds drifted about the narrow basement, at times present, at times seeming to disappear into a far away place.

In this same room, earlier that day, Trinh had sat still next to a bowl containing three smoking incense sticks. Suddenly she had heard the sounds of someone walking outside, but had thought it was only a home defense militiaman patrolling nearby. The footsteps got further away, stopped, then it seemed whoever it was had turned around and was coming closer, slowly, as if searching for something. Trinh looked through the bunker door and saw a soldier carrying his knapsack on his back, a K54 in a holster at his hip, looking at the locked door of Trinh's apartment. When he turned around, she cried out, "Uncle Dang."

The soldier's eyes brightened and he rushed towards her, just as she emerged. Ecstatic, she grabbed his arm and buried her face into his chest, as if she had just been reunited with her father.

"My little Trinh has grown so much," he said. "When am I going to get to eat my niece's wedding cake?"

Trinh wouldn't let go of her Uncle Dang. Even in these bleak days, she was allowed to have some bit of joy. To see Uncle Dang, her father's close friend, meant she was soon to see her father again.

"Uncle," Trinh closed her eyes on the unexpected joy. "Was Dad so busy he couldn't come back with you?"

Dang's heart jumped in his chest like a bird hit by an arrow. He closed his eyes also, not out of happiness, but because of an overwhelming pain.

"Hey, let me see your bunker," he said, opening his eyes. She led him down to it.

"Is your mother at work?"

Because his eyes had not yet adjusted to the dark, Dang couldn't see anything. First he smelled the scent of the incense, then saw, appearing behind the thin lines of smoke, the portrait of the woman inside a black frame. As he looked more closely, he could make out the face of Trinh's mother. Trinh followed his gaze. This time the metal lance peered through both hearts.

"When did your mother pass away?" Uncle Dang struggled to keep his voice even.

"Yesterday I just completed the prayer ceremony for the third

day after death, uncle." Trinh covered her face with her hands
but could not cry.

The officer removed his knapsack, trying to cover up his
awkwardness. Instead of putting it on the chair, he carefully
placed it on the table, as if it were full of fragile objects. In fact,
there was nothing of his in the knapsack. It contained a notebook
that had belonged to Trinh's father, a few photographs of her
family, some of her father's clothing, and a pillow case on which
her mother had embroidered two white doves. In the few hours
he had in Hanoi, Dang had intended to carry out a task so difficult
he thought he would never be able to do it: tell Trinh and her
mother that their father and husband had sacrificed himself, and
return the belongings to them. He had considered abandoning
his mission, but at the last minute, when his truck had stopped
at the North Gate, he had decided not to avoid dealing with the
truth. Trinh and her mother would be in terrible pain, but they
would survive it, and they would soon be swept up in all the
overwhelming tasks that had to be done in time of war.

But Dang had not expected to find that Trinh's mother had
also died. During the months when he had debated with himself
about whether to bring the sad news to them, he had always
pictured his appearance in their apartment, imagined how both
women would hang onto each other crying, while he remained
silent. Then, just before he left, he would say a few banal words
of consolation. But now the images he had conjured would not
materialize. The two women could have supported each other in
a time of loss. Now, there was only one left, and so young—who
could she rely upon? Through their conversation, he understood
that Trinh still had kind neighbors, who had helped her with the
funeral and the food for the third-day ceremony. But kind
neighbors couldn't replace a mother or a sister.

Uncle Dang lit three incense sticks and placed them in the
joss bowl in front of the photo of the mother. He bowed his head
in deep thought, and murmured to the dead about the losses
gnawing at him. No, I wouldn't tell my niece that her father has
sacrificed himself. I'll leave and take the knapsack with me and
ask my wife to keep it. When peace comes, I'll bring it back and

give it to my niece. I hope you will both forgive me. I can't be here to help my niece any more now, and I will have to trust her neighbors to take care of her.

When he said goodbye, Uncle Dang again caressed the head of the girl who was clinging to him, not wishing to let him go. It was time and he didn't want to prolong these moments of weakness. He removed her arms and started towards the bunker's entrance.

"Uncle, your knapsack," Trinh reminded him.

It was cold, but Dang felt drops of sweat at his temples. One moment of forgetfulness, and after he had gone, the girl would have opened it and he would have never forgiven himself.

Uncle and niece came out of the bunker, walked past the thatched huts, and crossed the empty field in front of the Green Meadow Housing Complex.

"Uncle," Trinh said, "my father doesn't have malaria, does he? They say it's easy to get malaria in the jungle."

"No, your father is fine," Uncle Dang answered, without looking at her. The objects in the knapsack seemed to push hard into his back, tearing through the cloth of the knapsack to demand the truth.

"I just regret that when mother died, father couldn't come back."

"Couldn't come back," Uncle Dang echoed, the words full of a pain he couldn't conceal. They had reached the platform, and the tram was approaching, its bell ringing. Uncle Dang suddenly grabbed Trinh by the arms and spoke hurriedly. "Trinh, study hard, wait for peace. After the war, your skills will be needed for reconstruction. I'll be back."

This was the kind of advice a father gave a daughter. But to Trinh, his promises had sounded incomplete. She called out to him, as he jumped onto the tram:

"You mean you'll be back with my father, right?"

There was no reply. Uncle Dang did not have the heart for one more lie. And Trinh only thought that the noisy train had drowned his answer as it sped away, rocking along the tracks.

But once alone, she had begun to realize there had been

something unusual about her conversation with Uncle Dang. How could a strong man like him be so awkward and lacking in confidence? Her heart had begun to pound, as if it were hitting against something hard in her chest. How was her father? Why hadn't Uncle Dang talked to her about her father's life? Extremely agitated, she had thought suddenly of Mrs. Si. All this time she had never believed in the stuff people whispered about her. But in her state of shock, unable to be sure of anything, the only thing she could think to do was go to Mrs. Si. How was she to know that Mrs. Si was a con artist? Trinh's saints and spirits had turned out to be this young man standing in front of her now.

"Do you know anything about my father, Tan?" she asked, though she no longer believed there was anyone who could help her.

Tan shook his head. "Unfortunately, no," he said bitterly. "I know that twenty years from now, these thatched huts will no longer be here. But I don't know anything about your fate."

"It's hard for any of us to know our future," Trinh whispered.

Robertino was singing about Santa Lucia and a bright moon and a boat and a calm sea. It was the dream of humankind: a peaceful life, without war, without bombs and rockets, without killing and dying. It was the future the two young friends were hoping for, even though outside it was a cold winter day and there was a somber mood on the streets.

"Tan," Trinh said, destroying the dream that had blended into the song, her voice unnaturally serious, "I'm going away. Yesterday I asked Mr. Tuu to let me be a Vanguard Youth. He didn't agree, because my mother is dead, my father is on active duty and I'm the only child in the family. But I'm going anyway."

"Where will you go?" Tan jumped up, horrified.

"To the fighting zone. Maybe all the way to the Truong Son trails. Maybe I'll meet up with my father and Uncle Dang."

"No, don't," Tan cried out. "Don't go, Trinh."

He remembered the stories he had read about the girls in the Truong Son mountains. Under the bombs, their lives were still full of desires, and they would look up at the distant stars to dream of a life after the war. But their loneliness, desires, and losses could not be relieved. Even worse, many never would live until victory day. If Trinh were to leave, that would be her future, a future Tan could clearly see now.

Trinh was staring at him dumbfounded, unable to believe he had said such words. "Is that the advice you're offering me?"

Tan sobered. He realized that if indeed she thought that was his advice, then its cowardly nature would not be forgiven. His reaction had been one that came from the time of twenty years from now. His generation had come to understand the price of war through the memories and stories of older people; they knew how many had died and had come to hate war in general, did not want to think about it or be connected to it. Never would they spontaneously decide to enlist and join the fighting the way Trinh had. And now he had expressed that attitude in front of her.

"No—it's not advice. You should act according to your decision." He hesitated, bowing his head slightly. How would Trinh know where to find her father and uncle? And he, wandering blindly, totally unsure of where he would go, in what direction would he go? if Trinh were to leave, Tan would lose a friend, a companion who could understand him, however slightly.

*   *   *

During dinner, Mrs. Lam said to Tan and Trinh: "This Sunday, I won't be busy with extra work at the factory. We can have a fresh meal at home. Whatever you want to eat, I'll cook for you."

Do pretended to be a hungry glutton. "Spring rolls, Mom. But definitely, we need cured meat rolls, with ground pork and fried eggs."

Do wasn't deciding on a menu for himself. He remembered that Yen had once said that she really liked spring rolls. This Sunday, he wanted to bring her home and introduce her to his mother. His father had died ten years before; he had fallen ill while with a group of settlers that had gone to the western region. Since then, his mother had had only him. She loved every one of his friends as if they were her own children, and she was always happy to have guests in her home. Do understood this very well and he was sure she would warmly welcome Yen. The young couple was being chased away by Yen's mother and were hoping to find support and refuge with Do's.

"What about you?" Mrs. Lam was particularly kind to Trinh. She had always wished for a girl. Besides, the fresh meal she had suggested was particularly because of Trinh; she wanted to get the girl involved in cooking to help alleviate the tension from her recent loss.

"Me?" Trinh replied, perplexed, as if she thought Mrs. Lam already knew she was going to leave before Sunday. To avoid admitting her intentions, she pretended to add to the menu. "I'm the same as brother Do; I like spring rolls," she murmured.

"Me too," Tan added quickly, before the mother could ask.

He forced himself to finish his bowl of rice, then put down his chop sticks and stood up. Without stopping to reply to Mrs. Lam's look of surprise and her question, he walked out. It was hard for him to think about a Sunday with his grandmother and parents, just as his family would be twenty years from now— but without Trinh. For the first time he realized that his family was not complete. He didn't just need his grandmother and his parents. He needed a girlfriend. A real one, not a temporary, dancing-lesson girlfriend.

He walked through the empty field and sat down next to the hedge that surrounded a house whose owners had left for the refuge areas. The lamp cover on the nearby lamppost was vibrating, causing the light shining towards him to tremble as well. The shadows of the trees jumped back and forth, from the road to the grass. Planes were coming.

He saw that Trinh had followed him outside. She sat down silently next to him. She had understood his reactions to the conversation about the Sunday meal.

"Trinh," Tan said, without looking at her, his voice choking. "If I told you sincerely that I am a person from twenty years in the future, would you laugh at me?"

Trinh shook her head. "Why would I? If you told me the truth, then I would believe you."

He didn't dare question such a resolute reply. He knew Trinh did believe him, even if she didn't believe the details of his stories about the future.

"Is there any way you can help me get to that place?"

"Just live, Tan. Live for today, and we will get to that day."

He had thought about that. But he wanted to return right at this moment. This was his home. His parents, his grandmother also lived there; where else could he go?

A shadow fell on them. It was cast by a man wearing a red armband and carrying a rifle. He recognized Trinh right away, but stared at Tan.

"Who are you?"

The young couple immediately stood up. Trinh said, "He's Do's cousin."

"Where are your papers?"

"Papers?" Tan asked, his voice still full of despair. Earlier that day, two militiamen had already asked him for his papers, and he had shaken his head, the gesture full of bitterness. They had read the pain of a youth who no longer had a home or relatives in that movement, and they had let him go.

The same thing happened now. The militiaman looked directly into Tan's dull eyes for a few seconds, then waved his arm to signal the two to go home; this was an unsafe area if any airplanes came. Even though no one had offended him, Tan was irritated because it seemed he was being followed. He thought that perhaps after his conversation with Mr. Tuu, he had been classified as an element that needed to be under constant observation by the neighborhood home defense forces. He was now a stranger in his own home.

The jet planes didn't fly towards Hanoi. Instead they swerved to the southeast of the city and destroyed a small town along the railroad running south. The distant explosions from the bombs shook the ground lightly under their feet.

"I'll go with you, Trinh," Tan said. The decision had just burst into flame in his mind.

"It will be very tough," Trinh said seriously. "Do you think you can take it?"

How strange; it should have been him asking her that question. He felt embarrassed. Even though he was a man, he had never suggested such a course of action—it had come from a woman. In the summer of 1987, Tan and all his male friends had been very fearful of being drafted before entering college. Tan had been lucky enough to pass the entrance exam for the Foreign Languages University, while several of his friends had had to go into the army and were sent as far as the border region in Lang Son. But during this time, things were different. Napalm bombs were burning a town near Hanoi, and a girl was preparing to go away.

*   *   *

Their departure plans were quite simple. Trinh found an old knapsack belonging to her father, and put a few sets of her most beautiful clothes into it (she knew it was ridiculous—going to the war, bringing nice clothes so she could look beautiful in the jungle—but she couldn't abandon them). There were also a comb and a mirror, a notebook to use for a journal and to copy love poems and song lyrics into...not too much of anything. Tan, for his part, didn't have much to begin with, and he felt he should leave behind the clothes he had been wearing that belonged to Do. Trinh looked through her closet, found one of her father's uniforms, and gave it to him to try on. It was both a little too large and a little too short. In the end it didn't matter, for what appeared in front of Trinh's eyes now was a newly recruited soldier, a trace of bluish stubble where a moustache should have been, bewildered as a chicken. After Tan had changed clothing again, Trinh packed the uniform into the knapsack and took the knapsack to hide in a hole in a ruined house not too far from the public complex. When the time came, they would stop by the ruin, Tan would change, and they would go to the train station together.

That morning they had both gone to the station to look at the train schedule. Tonight, only a military train and a passenger train would be going south. Trinh immediately ruled out the military train. It would be closely monitored and as a girl Trinh would be discovered right away—she couldn't be sure if the train would carry female soldiers or Vanguard Youth she could blend in with. To be safer, they should board the passenger train and get off at some station in the central region, then hitch a ride south on a transport truck, pretending to be two soldiers separated from their units. Once they had gone that far, no one would want to send them back, and even if they did, it would be difficult because of the lack of transportation and the heavy bombing.

Tan couldn't believe how clearly and precisely Trinh could plan and calculate. She seemed no longer the young innocent girl, but a sharp and pragmatic mind thinking for both for them. But still, she took pen and paper and wrote a short letter to leave behind in the bunker, thanking Mrs. Lam, Do, and the others in the housing complex for all their help. "However I couldn't sit and do nothing while our fathers and uncles are fighting at the front, and while our enemies are killing our people every day, every hour." The words seemed strong and harsh, but what else could Trinh write to express her resolution?

Watching Trinh write, Tan decided he should leave a letter also for his grandmother and father. He sat across the table from Trinh, toying with the pen in his hand for a long time, unsure how to begin.

Hanoi...

Dear Grandmother and Father,
Before going away, I want to confess something I
have not been able to tell you all this time: I am in
fact...

Tan shivered. To suddenly disappear and leave behind such a weird letter would only create a terrible shock for everyone. Even his own grandmother and father would not believe him. They might, by instinct or because of their deep affection for him, sense the truth in what he said, but in the end they would conclude that he was afflicted with some mental illness, or that they had been dragged into some dark and fantastic situation. He needed to just leave his relatives in peace and go away. Whatever would happen, he would be born in three years and continue to live with his family until 1987. Once he had made this decision though, Tan was still disturbed, and felt regretful and bitter that no one in the year 1967 would understand him. He crumpled up the paper and threw it outside, where it was picked up by the wind and tumbled away over the grass,

Still, he couldn't leave without any acknowledgment. He thought of a way he could say goodbye to Do without him knowing. Only by the next morning, when Do thought about it, would he understand.

The evening meal was ready early, but Do was absent. He had duty that evening with the antiaircraft unit at his company. Tan ate quickly and asked Mrs. Lam if he could go visit Do at his post. Although their conversation was only a matter of a few sentences, his voice choked, as if he had a cold.

"It's chilly outside," his grandmother warned. "Put on your wool cap so you can keep your ears covered."

"Yes, aunt."

God, his last words before he left, and he was still forced to call her "aunt." Unable to bear her teasing words, and fearing he might soften, Tan grabbed the wool cap and walked quickly out of the house. Because of his love for his grandmother, he allowed himself to take this hat—which she had knitted herself—as a souvenir. Besides, he would certainly need it during the long trip.

Do's antiaircraft unit was set up on the terrace of a three-story house whose owners had all evacuated to a refuge area. Tan walked up a steep and narrow staircase, just wide enough for two people to pass each other. On the terrace, a small rocket launcher had been wedged against the sandbags arranged into a circle like a bird's nest. Next to the launcher were cases of rockets. The unit had stacked some of the cases on top of each other to serve as chairs. In their attempt to avoid missiles and flak, American planes often carried out surprise attacks on Hanoi at low altitudes. It was at these times that such antiaircraft teams would go into action. Many planes had been shot down by their low-altitude rockets.

At first, Tan didn't understand what the men on the terrace were doing in the dark. Their shadowy figures rocked back and forth and there were sounds of rhythmic handclapping and a male voice trying to sing softly. He stood silently, and it took him a long moment to understand that the guys in the antiaircraft unit—their postures and movements all wrong—were attempting to dance a waltz.

"Who's there?" Someone shouted. He had spotted Tan's shadow near the door to the terrace. The men jumped towards the rocket launcher and then each quickly sat down in his position, as if pretending there had been no dancing. Tan hadn't even had a chance to be surprised and ask them why, when they started singing loudly and in unison:

> We stretch a net of fire in the sky
> We stretch a net of bullets in the sea
> Our hands firm on our rifles,
> soldiers and militiamen at the ready
> We will not let them escape...

The singing was starting to kick into high gear when Do interrupted it with a big laugh. "Don't worry, guys; it's just my little brother."

The song died. Everyone stood up. There was laughter all around.

"My God, I thought Mr. Toan had come to inspect us."

"Come on in, young man. Come dance with us."

Tan joyfully squeezed through an opening into the circle of sandbags.

"Look," he said to Do, "your movements are all off." He pulled Do towards him so they were facing each other as dancing partners and began to demonstrate. "Your right hand must be placed lightly on my hip, your left hand touching mine at shoulder level. Let's begin."

He guided Do through a few elegant steps. The delighted antiaircraft team broke into applause, and then the men formed into a circle of pairs around Tan and Do, earnestly following Tan's every step and movement. Their bodies grew warm with the exercise and the excitement. They forgot the coldness of the winter night. They forgot to assign someone to watch for the company cadres who might come to inspect them and catch them in a "degenerate dance." They forgot that in perhaps just a few minutes American planes might be roaring overhead.

"You guys go ahead," Tan said, signalling Do to follow him. "I have to go now."

"OK—but come back tomorrow."

"Tomorrow, teach us the tango. You know how to do the tango, don't you?"

The loud voices followed them and gradually faded behind them. Tan and Do came to the bottom of the narrow, winding staircase and stepped out into the street. Most of the people had been evacuated from here, the night was cold, and now, at just past eight o'clock, the streets were deserted.

"Brother Do," Tan said, "I've forgotten where we stopped and smelled the scent of the *sua* flowers."

Do shook his head. "It's all gone. I went back there yesterday, but there was no scent there at all."

But Tan's regret now was not for the scent of a flower. This might be his final farewell to the past, or more accurately, to his grandmother and father as they were. But the past, like the sunken boat in the river, did not have the right to sleep quietly in the river bed. One day, it would be dug up, some of its parts replaced, and it would be repaired and refurbished. Then that boat would sound its foghorn and glide again on the Red River, reminding everyone of its presence in the future.

"Brother Do, Yen is a very good woman. I'm sure you and she will have a happy life together."

Only because he knew he was about to leave could Tan speak like this: he knew that any other time such a statement, coming from the mouth of a youth of seventeen, would sound contrived.

"Thank you, Tan. I believe so also."

Tan stopped, unable to suppress the emotions boiling inside him, on the verge of bursting out. He raised his arms to embrace Do.

"And you—do you know how much I love and value you? I'm truly grateful to you and aunt..."

Do laughed loudly, to calm him down. "I understand very well."

Do's ringing laughter helped Tan control himself. "No, you don't understand it all," he said flatly. "Go ahead back. I have to go."

He turned and left immediately, afraid of his overflowing emotions.

Do stood stunned. Had something snapped inside that young man again? He felt badly that in the last few days he'd been too consumed with his work, with the antiaircraft team, with his concerns about Yen's mother, and had had little time to be with Tan.

Do felt a wave of pity for him.

"Tan, hey Tan!" He ran after the boy, who had already walked some distance away. "Wait for me at home tomorrow; we'll all go see a movie."

He said "we'll all" to indicate Trinh was included.

But Tan had regained his composure. He shook Do's hand firmly and calmly walked away. By the time the movie was beginning the next evening, he and Trinh would be on a train, already far from Hanoi.

*   *   *

Tan should have gone directly to the meeting point he'd arranged with Trinh. But he decided to take one more walk around the Green Meadow Housing Complex. Twenty years from now there would be eighteen blocks of five-story buildings here. Right now, there were only three buildings sitting quietly in the otherwise empty field. Most of the inhabitants had locked their doors and gone to the refuge areas: only a few windows had their lights on. Right over there was his window. His grandmother would be reading the newspaper or mending Do's work shirt that had been torn at the shoulder seam.

Trinh was sitting behind the wall of the collapsed house, waiting for Tan, pressing the knapsack to her stomach against the cold. As soon as she saw his shadow, she opened the knapsack and pulled out the uniform. Tan went behind another wall that only reached up to his neck and changed his clothing quickly. When he had finished, he slung the knapsack over his shoulder. Their plan now was to head across the field of bombing debris to the train station.

Suddenly they heard noise coming right from the other side of the wall. Two militia men walked by, holding their rifles ready, examining the area.

"I just saw him walk in front of the complex, and then he disappeared," one said.

"He was suspicious looking. Come on—let's look down that street."

The two friends became frightened, as if they had just committed a crime and were being pursued. It would be possible for Trinh to explain herself. But Tan, without papers and with a dubious identity, would have a tough time defending himself if he were caught in a soldier's uniform while "running away." They waited until the two militiamen had gone a good distance, then Tan took Trinh by the hand and they started running. After a few seconds she found it difficult to maneuver through the piles of debris and pulled away from him. Sneaking away after dark, unable to walk openly through the streets, made what they were doing feel like a retreat. And both of them were frightened and worried that something would keep them from making the 11:15 train.

But once they were among the crowd at the train station, the two friends became a little calmer. They would look simply like a pair of lovers saying goodbye to one another, the boy on his way to the fighting, his girlfriend staying behind. Trinh had no difficulty buying their tickets with the money she had brought wrapped in her handkerchief. But they didn't really feel free until they'd gotten on the train and it began to roll out of the station.

Tan looked at the houses and streets sailing by his window. Goodbye, Hanoi of the past. Goodbye to a place of golden hearts, to a people ready to take in and care for lost children, a people suffering from losses and tortured by war. Goodbye also to a place where he was a stranger, doubted and hunted. He was sad he had to leave, yet relieved as well.

"Where are you going, soldier?" The man who asked appeared to be a village cadre. He had a *Xuong Mao* radio at his hip and spoke with an accent from the central region.

"I was separated from my unit; I'm going back to find them." Tan spoke calmly, but his heart was trembling slightly. If the man asked him for the number of his unit or which station he was supposed to get off, he would have no idea what to say. But apparently the guy had asked just to make conversation. He began to yawn repeatedly and then fell asleep.

The train rocked steadily. Trinh was still holding her knapsack against her stomach to keep warm. Hours passed, and Tan and Trinh started to drift off.

Suddenly a terrible explosion shook the train. It tilted so far it seemed it would roll over, and then jerked to an abrupt stop. The passengers began to shove each other, trying to get to the main door, or jump from the windows. In the flashes of red light, Tan saw Trinh, carrying the knapsack, jump down to the ground. He jumped after her, stumbled, and rolled over. As he did, he caught a glimpse of Trinh's worried face turning to look for him, her eyes opened wide, shining from a face tinted red by the fire. A stream of people rushed by, dragging her along with them towards some mounds of dirt.

Tan got up and lunged in the direction he had seen Trinh. The myrtle bushes and wild grass around him burst into flame. Another gust of fire exploded near him. Tan plunged to the ground, the hot wind blasting over him, tearing his shirt open, searing the skin on his back. The explosions seemed to raise the level of the ground, push it back down, then throw it up again, like someone trying to submerge a board in water. Fire and explosions. The hot wind. Over and over...

When he came to, the flames were still blazing on the mounds of dirt, going off into the distance along the tracks, but the train could no longer be seen. It had disappeared as though it had never been there. He sat up. His right foot pulsed with pain and one side of his face felt numb, as if it were frozen.

"Trinh!" he screamed. The scream flew into the seared, immense landscape and was lost, without an echo.

He stumbled along the tracks, following the direction the train would have travelled. But it was nowhere in sight and he could not hear its whistle. There was nothing at all in the deep darkness of that night, except for the fires still burning like ghosts, stretching as far as he could see on both sides of the tracks.

"Trinh!" Tan called out again, crying and hopeless now, his voice hoarse. The bombs had torn them apart and he was left alone in a deserted wasteland that stank from the fires the bombs had left behind. He gasped, completely exhausted after running so much on his wounded foot. Abruptly, he stumbled and fell down. But it wasn't like his fall before. This time, in the blink of an eye, Tan felt as if he had been thrown into a deep abyss. Very deep. He thrashed around in a puddle of hot water, his limbs jerking. Finally, his body relaxed and he surrendered to unconsciousness...

*   *   *

Something magic is happening again. Tan feels himself being lifted up, feels very light. The sole of his foot and one side of his head ache, but it is a soft, even pleasant, pain. He hears the faint echoes of voices.

"Doctor, aren't you the author of that theory claiming memories from one generation can be passed on to another?"

"Yes. We're working on it now. But we don't expect any results in the near future."

"I read your article. Would you please give me more concrete details about your hypothesis?"

"As you know, uncle, man is capable of imagination, to one degree or another. For example, one day your descendents may read your diary and they'll be able to imagine what your life was like, in the distant past. Those who have stronger imaginations will have the more accurate and lively mental images."

"That's natural, doctor."

"True. But what I want to talk about is a different matter. Suppose one doesn't write anything down for future generations, and there's no one left to fill us in about life in such times. That's why, for example, there have been so many arguments about Mozart's music, and the circumstances surrounding Shakespeare...tons of ink and paper have been spent on such speculations, but we really can not get to the truth in these matters."

"So what can be done?"

"Our hypothesis can be summed up in a few sentences: perhaps man has the ability to biologically pass on his memory to future generations. For example, we don't know precisely whether the beautiful and popular version of *The Lament of a Warrior's Wife* is in fact by Doan thi Diem or not. Could it have been written by somebody else? The answer to that question has actually been passed genetically on to the descendents of the poet. If there existed a certain kind of stimulant we could apply to that particular part of their brain, reviving those ancestral memories, then they might very well be able to write down the exact words of the woman poet, even those she wrote down, crossed out and replaced..."

"As if they themselves had written the poem," the other person finishes, "so—if I might add, doctor—today I talk to you but I don't write down anything in my diary about our conversation. But a few hundred years from now, my offspring, if their brains are stimulated where their memories are stored, can 'imagine' and repeat this conversation exactly. How wonderful!"

"Yet some people say that if this hypothesis ever became a reality then it would be an immoral discovery. They say it would be terrible if descendents, through the ability to store such memories, were able to see and feel their ancestors' actions and emotions even in their bedrooms....Oh! Look—my patient has woken up!"

The doctor cries out the last sentence happily and runs over to Tan's bed.

Tan opens his eyes. Everything is white. The ceiling, the three blade ceiling fan, the curtains, the clothing of the people around him. As his eyes begin to focus, he can see clearly the deep wrinkles on his grandmother's happy face. She has aged greatly since the time he had carried her out of the collapsing building.

"Do you recognize me?" she asks, her voice choking.

Why shouldn't he? But he is in a hospital. Why did he need to be in a hospital? He smiles weakly at his grandmother and at the strangers around him, busily trying to help him revive. Seeing Tan move his lips, trying to speak, the doctor gestures at him. "Lay still. You're alive and will have many chances to talk."

Tan remains silent. So silent he can hear each drop of blood falling into the transfusion container.

After everyone else goes, leaving only his grandmother by his bed, Tan tries again to open his cracked lips and ask a question. He isn't sure if his grandmother understands him, or if she is simply saying the things he wants most to know.

"Your parents and I have been taking turns here. They're both at work right now."

Tan moves his eyes again; then his lips.

"You've been here nearly two months," the grandmother says, accurately reading his "question."

Nearly two months. But he'd been lost in 1967 for only two weeks. It is like the story of Tu Thuc getting lost in paradise and then returning to his village. Again, he smiles wearily at the thoughts unfolding slowly in his mind. An article in the newspaper his grandmother is holding to her chest catches his eye. He signals with his fingers that he wants to see the paper.

"You're too weak to hold it. If you want to read, I'll turn the pages for you."

She pulls her chair close to the head of his bed and turns the pages of *New Hanoi* near his face. The headline that had drawn his attention reads: *A Bitter Lesson for Superstitious People*. Tan tries to indicate by nodding that he wants to read the article. He has just recognized the woman in the photograph.

"Oh, that's an article about Mrs. Si, who used to live in our complex. You wouldn't know her."

He can't tell her that he does. The article pulls him in. One Nguyen Thi Si, aka "Si the Medium," had manipulated a Ms. Nguyen Thi Kieu Khanh, a lovesick engineer who had lost her balance. Si the Medium had conned Ms. Khanh out of much of her property and then, telling her it was the will of the spirits, pressured her into a fast that would allow her to reach nirvana, and which allowed Si to get rid of a witness. The writer of the article hadn't been content to only report what had happened, but adds an opinion: "While we respect each citizen's right to worship, we are still determined to punish those who take advantage of religion by 'selling' the spirits." He then asked rhetorically: "Why has the problem of superstition, which we had thought wiped out for decades now in the North, been reemerging over the past several years?"

Tan closes his eyes, tired of focusing on the columns of words. His grandmother withdraws the newspaper, certain that Tan will fall back into a peaceful sleep.

But he doesn't. Instead he plunges again into a windy tunnel and is whirling around forever without reaching the bottom. His body feels weightless, like an astronaut floating in space.

Then begins a new sensation. He is shaken lightly, hears tinkling sounds in his ears. Someone sits down next to him. He opens his eyes wearily. The deserted tram is lunging ahead in the darkening afternoon light. Only he and the person who had just sat down are in the compartment. The other—Tan feels somehow he is a friend—pays the conductor. The conductor gives him back his change and then gestures impatiently to Tan, looking annoyed.

Tan, confused, searches through his pockets with difficulty. He is ashamed because unlike the other youth he has no money. Yet he also feels too tired to care and only wants to lie back against the seat. His companion immediately understands the situation and gives a coin to the conductor.

"You look like you're ill," the other says to him, apparently trying to elicit sympathy from the conductor. But the man just takes the fare and moves away.

When the train stops and his companion gets up to leave, Tan drags himself after him. They stand on the platform directly under the light from a lamppost, facing each other, and are both shocked. They look exactly alike, as if they are twins. Tan understands immediately.

"Is your name Do?"

"You know my name?" The young man smiles awkwardly. "You're right. I've just come to the university to finish registering. What about you?"

"My name is Tan. But you wouldn't know me."

But Do isn't paying much attention to Tan's response. He's happily thinking about his future at school, and is about to turn and walk away when he remembers Tan's tired look.

"Do you need any help getting home?"

"No, thanks."

Do walks away as Tan remains leaning against the lamppost at the tram station. He had thought he'd returned to 1987, and can't believe he has gotten lost even further back in time. He calculates that his father must be about seventeen, his own age, and this would be 1961. *Greetings to nineteen sixty one, the highest of summits*, he remembers: a line of poetry he had heard in a classroom echoing now in his head. He is going further back into the past, day by day, and the road back is becoming more remote.

The tinkling sound grows louder. A tram has come to a stop at the platform. But this is definitely a different tram, for on the side of the first car, painted in red letters, is the inscription: THE FUTURE. This is it, Tan whispers. Not even thinking about his empty pockets, he jumps on the tram. Some moments later, it seems as if the wheels jump off the tracks as the tram lurches forward.

*   *   *

He is sitting on the exact stone bench where he had sat with Trinh. He remembers that before Trinh had arrived, an old man had carefully laid out the treasures he had rescued from the half-standing remains of a bombed building. But that half a building is no longer on the other side of the street. The debris has all been cleared away. Surrounding the area are rows of newly erected thatched homes, temporary dwellings for the families that have returned from the refuge areas.

The scene has changed in other ways as well. The wooden refreshment kiosk is still here, but the attendant isn't standing inside it. Instead she has taken out a chair to sit by some beer cartons scattered in a disorderly way next to the flower park. She is drawing beer into cups with a plastic tube. She looks older and thinner, marked with the kind of changes that come to a woman who has started a family of her own.

"Tan? Is that you, Tan?" A man riding past calls out, and brakes his bicycle.

Tan stands and the man stares at him, as if he can't believe what he is seeing. He turns the bicycle around and pushes it onto the sidewalk. He looks harried.

"Brother Do!" Tan grabs his shoulders excitedly.

Do looks no less happy. He pushes his kickstand down with his foot and lets his bicycle lean near the stone bench. He invites Tan to sit back down.

"My God, you left so suddenly back then; you made my mother and I worry so much. Did you ever find your family?"

Tan avoids Do's eyes. He lowers his head and says, shortly, "Yes, brother."

He can see Do understands that the answer is "not yet." The atmosphere grows tense.

Then he sees the woven basket hanging from the handle bars of the bicycle. A hot water bottle protrudes from the basket, along with the edges of some diapers, and a few cans of milk. Do follows his gaze to the basket. "My wife gave birth yesterday," he announces. "A boy weighing three and a half kilos. I'm actually on my way to bring them some things they need."

He has the embarrassed air of someone who has just become a father, and looks unsure what to do with his arms and legs. His eyes are red from lack of sleep, his chin darkened with the shadow of a beard as if he has forgotten to shave.

"The entire family was unanimous about naming the baby Tan," Do says suddenly. "Now I understand why. We all thought about you, and wished our boy would grow up to be like you."

Almost forgetting that Do is standing next to him, Tan calculates in his head. If he was born yesterday, that meant today is the fifteenth of September, 1970. If the train has taken him here already, it means he's heading in the right direction.

"Hey, Tan!" Do shakes his shoulder enthusiastically. "Come to the hospital with me. My mother is there, and I'm sure the whole family would be happy to see you again."

Tan returns to reality. He knows he has to show he is sharing Do's joy and not sit pensively. He forces a smile, but feels depressed. He has lost the moment of farewell when Do ran quickly after him and made plans to see a movie together the next night. His father's mind is now at the hospital, where a little red faced boy has just been born.

"Was the half of the museum that remained after the bomb attack destroyed, brother?" he asks, to chase away the feeling he is losing a friend.

His thoughts elsewhere, Do is taken back for a moment.

"No; it wasn't destroyed. There was a time-delay bomb in it. People searched for it a long time, but when they couldn't find it, they decided that the militia unit counting the falling bombs had made an error. Three years went by, and the Americans temporarily halted their bombing of the North. Then one Sunday, when the street was full of traffic, the bomb exploded. Nearly fifty people died; four cars were destroyed and many nearby houses were damaged."

How horrible. The day the time-delay bomb had fallen, Tan

had been here, watching the sappers searching for it. But just because of a mistake, just because people were not alert enough or were irresponsible, they had allowed it to sleep, only to explode three years later during a time without bombing, so that the casualty count was higher than it would have been.

Tan bows his head, in a moment of remembrance. But there is something he has wanted to ask from the beginning, and he decides to let it out, casually, now:

"Do you have any news of Trinh?"

"Which Trinh?" Do seems lost for a moment, then remembers. "Oh, it wasn't until the beginning of the year that I got a letter from her, describing the way she's detonating bombs and repairing the Truong Son trails. She wrote also that she had been separated from you halfway, and that she was still looking for you in passing units, but hadn't been able to find you..."

The honey-colored autumn sunshine spreads through the flower park, glistening on each *xa cu* leaf. The breeze tousles Do's sunlit hair, making it shine. My dear Trinh, I am warmed to hear of you, but still worried. Life at the front is fragile, threatened every second. When will we ever see each other again?

"Let's go, Tan. My wife doesn't have milk and the baby has to be bottle-fed. Everyone is waiting for me to bring the milk," Do said, standing.

Tan stands as well. But he holds out his hand to Do. "I'm waiting for a relative and have to do something urgent.

He sees Do has believed his lie.

"I'll be back," he says, this time speaking the truth. A firm promise.

He keeps his gaze on Do's awkward figure, getting smaller and smaller as the bicycle rides away. He wants very much to go and see the baby boy who had just left his mother's womb, wants to face him, wants to understand more about his own first minutes. At the same time, he finds himself a touch jealous of that boy waiting to get his milk. He has just been born, which means Do's heart has changed, and perhaps it is the same in grandmother's heart. How can he go to hospital to see everyone gathered around the baby boy, kissing and caressing him, praising the way he eats and sleeps, and even how loud he cries? Even as Tan told himself not to be petty, he can't help feeling abandoned.

The FUTURE train has once again stopped at the station on the other side of the street. Tan walks quickly to it, just in time to jump aboard as the train begins to move. A red mist covers the sky, dulling all the bright colors of the fall season. Behind that mist, there are again images of people moving about on the sandy beach, putting up tents and beginning to dig.

*   *   *

"Do, Mother, our son has woken up!" His mother's voice rang out.

The curtain of red mist faded away. The figures of the people digging came closer. But these were his father's and his grandmother's faces, rushing towards him. And sitting behind them was his mother. He was back in the white room, without a hint of the red mist anywhere. He moved his fingers slightly, trying to signal to them.

"Just tell us whatever you want," his father said. "You're allowed to speak now."

But what could he want now, when all he had wanted for so long was to return here? For a moment, his eyesight dulled, and again a thin veil of mist began to creep over his vision. A lonely young man runs in front of him, stumbling, calling out in despair: Trinh! The cry hits a wall of rocks and echoes back. Trinh! And then it echoes from all around him: Trinh! Trinh!

A single tear formed in the corner of his eye. It wasn't so much to shed. He was alive again and had returned to his family.

"Father..." he called out, and was startled to hear his own voice. He couldn't ask his father about Trinh in this shaky and abnormal voice. But then, terribly, it came to him that he could not ask at all. Where would Trinh be now? Twenty years had gone by. Surely she had become a woman, someone who might be living a life full of the usual worries, and with a bunch of children. He couldn't stand thinking about that bitter reality. Let me keep that last image of Trinh, her stunned face, her searching eyes, stained red by the fire. Let me bury my feelings deep inside my heart and keep them only for myself.

His father moved to one side, leaving Tan's view of the door to the room clear. "Look who's come to visit you."

The silhouette of a girl appeared; she hesitated, seemed unwilling to come closer. He wished for a red flame to see her face more clearly. But there were no flames and the mist was slowly disappearing as well. Tan recognized her.

It was his classmate, the girl who had paired up with him for dancing lessons. She came closer, her back to the window that was bright with autumn sunlight, and because of this, because her face was in the shadows, she didn't seem nearly as unattractive to him as she once had.

June, 1989
Translated by Nguyen Qui Duc and Wayne Karlin

HO ANH THAI, who was born in 1960, was evacuated from Hanoi when he was a child because of the U.S. bombing, and lived in refuge areas in the countryside between 1966 and 1973. He graduated from high school in 1977, and then studied at the College of Diplomacy, earning his B.A. in 1983. He was drafted into the People's Army and served in the 47th Battalion until 1987, after which he entered the service of the Foreign Ministry. Ho Anh Thai is presently an editor for *World Affairs Weekly (Tuan Bao Quoc Te)*, and a member of the Executive Committee of the Hanoi Writers Association. He defines himself mainly as a writer of fiction: a contention supported by the eleven novels and short story collections he has published, and by work published in the most prestigious magazines and newspapers of Vietnam. He was married to Nguyen Bich Lan, a teacher at the Foreign Trade University, in 1996, and has one son.

THE TRANSLATORS:

Chief translator, NGUYEN QUI DUC, was born in Dalat and came to the United States in 1975. He has been a radio producer and writer since 1979, working for the British Broadcasting Corporation and National Public Radio. His work has appeared in *The Asian Wall Street Journal Weekly, The New York Times Magazine, The San Francisco Examiner,* and *The San Jose Mercury News.* He has published essays in *Zyzzyva, City Lights Review, Salamander*, and has published fiction in *The Vietnam Review.* He was a co-editor, translator and contributor to *Vietnam: A Literary Traveler's Companion*, and one of the translators for *The Other Side of Heaven: Postwar Fiction by Vietnamese and American Writers.* He is also the author of a memoir: *Where the Ashes Are: The Odyssey of a Vietnamese Family.*

REGINA ABRAMI is a Ph.D candidate at the University of California-Berkeley, doing sociological research in Vietnam and China. She speaks Vietnamese fluently and is planning to write a book about her impressions of Vietnam during the last decade of the century.

BAC HOAI TRAN came to the United States in 1991, and is the instructor of Vietnamese at the University of California-Berkeley. He was educated in Ho Chi Minh City and Dalat University. An Associate Editor of *The Tenderloin Times*, he wrote the textbook *Anh Ngu Bao Chi: Introductory Vietnamese; Intermediate Vietnamese*, and served as a consultant on the film *Which Way is East*. He was a contributing translator to *The Other Side of Heaven : Postwar Fiction by Vietnamese and American Writers*, and co-translator of *The Stars, The Earth, The River*, short fiction by Le Minh Khue.

PHAN THANH HAO lives in Hanoi. She is the Assistant Editor-in-Chief of *Education and Times*, published by the Ministry of Education and Communication, and Communication Advisor for the Scanconsult Company. She has translated *The Class* by Eric Segal and *Evening News* by Arthur Hailey into Vietnamese, and is first translator for Bao Ninh's novel *The Sorrow of War*, published in England in 1991. She has also translated *The Virgin Fairy, The Land of Many Ghosts and Many People*, and *The Cattle Station*. Her poetry appears in the anthology *Visions of War/Dreams of Peace*, and her short fiction has been published in Australia.

DANA SACHS is a journalist specializing in topics relating to Vietnam. Her work has appeared in *The Far Eastern Economic Review, Mother Jones, Sierra*, and *The San Francisco Examiner*. In collaboration with her sister, Lynne Sachs, she made the award-winning documentary film about contemporary Vietnam, *Which Way Is East*. She was one of the translators for *The Other Side of Heaven: Postwar Fiction by Vietnamese and American Writers*, and co-translator of *The Stars, The Earth, The River*, short fiction by Le Minh Khue.

THE EDITOR:

WAYNE KARLIN served in the Marine Corps in Vietnam. He is the author of five novels: *Crossover, Lost Armies, The Extras, Us*, and *Prisoners*, and a novel/memoir: *Rumors and Stones*. In 1973, he contributed to and coedited, with Basil T. Paquet and Larry Rottman, the first Vietnam veterans' anthology, *Free Fire Zone: Short Stories by Vietnam Veterans*. In 1995 he co-edited, with Le Minh Khue and Truong Vu, and contributed to *The Other Side of Heaven: Postwar Fiction by Vietnamese and American Writers*. He has received a fellowship from the National Endowment for the Arts and four individual artist awards in fiction from the State of Maryland.

ABOUT THE SERIES:

VOICES FROM VIETNAM, a series of contemporary fiction from Vietnam, is a long-term project of Curbstone Press. Over the next decade, Curbstone will publish some of the best contemporary writers of Vietnam, including (as of press time) Ma Van Khang, Ngo Thi Kim Cuc, Nguyen Minh Chau, Nguyen Khai, Nguyen Khac Truong, Nguyen Manh Tuan, Nguyen Thi Minh Ngoc and Vu Bao. The series will also publish *To the West of the Eastern Sea: Folk Tales of Vietnam*, compiled by Nguyen Nguyet Cam, Dana Sachs and the artist Bui Hoai Mai.

BOOKS BY HO ANH THAI

Chang trai o ben doi xe: Tap truyen ngan, N.x.b. Tac Pham Moi, Ha Noi, 1983. (*The Young Man at the Bus Stop:* short stories, New Works Publishing House, Hanoi, 1983).

Phia sau vom troi, N.x.b. Quan Doi Nhan Dan, Ha Noi, 1986. (*Behind the Sky:* a novel, Army Publishing House, Hanoi, 1986).

Van chua toi mua dong, N.x.b. Thanh Nien, Ha Noi, 1987. (*Winter Hasn't Come:* a novel, Youth Publishing House, Hanoi, 1987).

Nguoi va xe chay duoi anh trang, N.x.b. Tac Pham Moi, Ha Noi, 1983. (*Men and a Vehicle Run in the Moonlight*: a novel (New Works Publishing House, Hanoi, 1987).

Nhung cuoc kiem tim, N.x.b. Hai Phong, Hai Phong, 1988. (*Searches*: short stories, Haiphong Publishing House, 1988).

Nguoi dan ba tren dao, N.x.b. Lao Dong, Ha Noi, 1988. (*The Women on the Island*: a novel, Labor Publishing House, Hanoi, 1988).

Mai phuc trong dem he, N.x.b. Tre, Ho Chi Minh City, 1989. (*A Trap in a Summer Night*: a novel, Youth Publishing House, Ho Chi Minh City, 1989).

Trong suong hong hien ra, N.x.b. Tac Pham Moi, Ha Noi, 1990. (*Behind the Red Mist*: a novel, New Works Publishing House, Hanoi, 1990).

Manh vo cua dan ong, N.x.b. Hoi Nha Van, Ha Noi, 1993. (*Fragment of a Man*: short stories, Writers' Publishing House, Hanoi, 1993).

Nguoi dung mot chan, N.x.b. Tre, Ho Chi Minh City, 1995. (T*he Man Who Stood on One Leg*: short stories, Youth Publishing House, Ho Chi Minh City, 1995).

Lu con hoang, N.x.b. Ha Noi, Ha Noi, 1995. (*A Bunch of Bastards*: short stories, Hanoi Publishing House, Hanoi, 1995).

TRANSLATIONS FROM ENGLISH TO VIETNAMESE:

Truyen ngan my duong dai, nha x vat ban Van hoc, 1997. *Contemporary American Short Stories*, edited by Ho Anh Thai and Wayne Karlin, Literature Publishing House, 1997.

Legend of the Phoenix, National Book Trust, India, 1995, (editor and contributor).

CURBSTONE PRESS, INC.

is a non-profit publishing house dedicated to literature from many cultures that reflects a commitment to social change, with an emphasis on contemporary writing from Latin America and Latino communities in the United States. Curbstone presents writers who give voice to the unheard in a language that goes beyond denunciation to celebrate, honor and teach. Curbstone builds bridges between its writers and the public – from inner-city to rural areas, colleges to community centers, children to adults. Curbstone seeks out the highest aesthetic expression of the dedication to human rights and intercultural understanding: poetry, testimonies, novels, stories, children's books.

This mission requires more than just producing books. It requires ensuring that as many people as possible know about these books and read them. To achieve this, a large portion of Curbstone's resources are dedicated to arranging tours and programs for its authors, working with public school and university teachers to enrich curricula, reaching out to underserved audiences by donating books and conducting readings and community programs, and promoting discussion in the media. It is only through these combined efforts that literature can truly make a difference.

Curbstone Press, like all non-profit presses, depends on the support of individuals, foundations, and government agencies to bring you, the reader, works of literary merit and social significance which might not find a place in profit-driven publishing channels, and to bring the authors and their books into communities across the country. Our sincere thanks to the many individuals who support this endeavor and to the following organizations, foundations and government agencies: Josef and Anni Albers Foundation, Connecticut Commission on the Arts, Connecticut Arts Endowment Fund, Connecticut Humanities Council, Lawson Valentine Foundation, Lila Wallace-Reader's Digest Fund, Andrew W. Mellon Foundation, National Endowment for the Arts, the Soros Foundation's Open Society Institute, and the Puffin Foundation.

Please support Curbstone's efforts to present the diverse voices and views that make our culture richer. Tax-deductible donations can be made by check or credit card to Curbstone Press, 321 Jackson Street, Willimantic, CT 06226, ph: (860) 423-5110, fax: (860) 423-9242.